THE **ROAD** TO **EMPIRE**

JOHN WEMLINGER

Published by Mission Point Press
2554 Chandler Rd.
Traverse City, MI 49696
(231) 421-9513
www.MissionPointPress.com

Design by Sarah Meiers

ISBN 978-1-961302-04-4
Library of Congress Control Number 2023912025

Printed in the United States of America

THE ROAD TO EMPIRE

*September 11, 2001, changes things forever for
18-year-old Jack Rigley and everyone he loves.*

JOHN WEMLINGER

MISSION POINT PRESS

This story is dedicated to our three grandkids, Marissa, Anthony, and Peter, as each of them approach their graduation from high school over the next several years. My love for you gets in the way of my eloquence; there are so many things I wish for each of you. So, I borrow from a fellow writer. Here's what I wish for you and all who read this novel:

That you may:
> "...look back at your life as a spectator
> and smile at God's Plan as you see the dots connect.
> . . . thank not just God but all those beautiful souls
> that served Him to meet His grand plans for you.
> . . . be proud that you did not give up when all seemed to be falling
> apart.
> . . . be humble because you realize that you would have never been
> able to stand up
> without people who loved you,
> believed in you, and brought you up even higher.
> . . . be happy and content because you have everything you should at
> this moment
> and will have all that accrues to you
> at the right time."

—Drishti Bablani

FOREWORD

I served in the US Army for twenty-seven years. I am not a hero in the common understanding of the word. As a junior officer, I was a helicopter maintenance officer and served a 12-month tour of duty in Vietnam. If I was ever shot at, I wasn't aware of it. My job was to test fly helicopters coming out of maintenance. Those test flights almost always were in a relatively secure area. Later in my career, as a more senior officer, I commanded military seaports around the world. None of this was particularly dangerous—there was seldom any excitement—just routine but necessary work.

A lot of history has happened in my seventy-seven trips around the sun. I have witnessed the end of ten long years of war in Vietnam. I saw the military transition from a mostly conscripted force to all volunteers. I witnessed the change in America's attitude toward military service away from one of disdain and disrespect to near reverence. I watched our troops return triumphant from incursions into Panama, Grenada, Haiti, and the First Gulf War. Though I am not a proponent of either of the wars in Afghanistan or Iraq, I am proud of how our troops did the incredibly hard job asked of them by administrations and Congresses whose inept foreign policies seemed to refuse to look at recent history and learn from it. Why didn't we learn from the harsh lessons of Vietnam? Why did we ever think we could succeed in Afghanistan after watching Russia's dismal failure there? Why did we ever believe an American-style democracy was possible in either Afghanistan or Iraq, two countries where religion and government commingle to the point they are indistinguishable from one another?

After Afghanistan and Iraq, I can understand why some argue we spend too much on defense. Instead, we should be spending tax dollars on our country's aging infrastructure. But this argument fails to realize the true reality of what it takes to protect our way of life in this post-Cold-War era. Our enemies emerge out of nowhere, wear no identifying uniform, and have no moral compass, especially when it comes to valuing human life. Cutting spending on defense fails to realize the reality of what it takes to wage war in the twenty-first century.

The fact of the matter is there are many more behind-the-scenes jobs in today's military than ever before, and every one of them is absolutely necessary. In the army, the service I am most familiar with, there is a thing called *the tooth to tail ratio*. The *tail* represents the number of soldiers it takes to supply and support the *tooth,* or one soldier engaged in combat. In Iraq, for example, the tooth to tail ratio was 8:1, meaning it took eight soldiers to supply and support just one soldier whose job it was to actually face the enemy in combat. *Supply and support* involves such things as training, maintenance, transportation, construction, housing, food, water, ammo, fuel, and today, the ubiquitous computer requires technicians of many varieties. We have the best military in the world because we know the importance of these things and pay attention to them.

What is it today that makes a young man or woman want to join our military? There is no pat answer to that question. Because America's military is all volunteer, the reason a person signs up is far less important than the fact that we do, in fact, have people joining. And, sadly, every year we have competent, well-qualified people leaving because military service is not easy. You are about to meet Jack and Annie, the book's main characters. They are fictional, but their story is real. It's repeated in some form or another hundreds, maybe even thousands of times each year. The needs of the service will take precedence over everything—until they don't. This book is my attempt to provide an insightful look into what life in the military is like in the twenty-first century. For those who are serving, or if you are a veteran who has served, my story is meant to be a mirror in which you may see your reflection and the honor of your service. If you, on the other hand, are curious and want to get a glimpse of what the military way of life is like, I intend this book to be a window through which you may look and learn.

May God bless our country's truest heroes and may God bless America. I hope you enjoy the read.

John Wemlinger
Summer 2023

PART I

A CALL TO ARMS

SEPTEMBER 11, 2001–JULY 10, 2006

ONE

Where were you when ...?

My name is Jack Rigley. This time next year I will be in my freshman year of college, although at this particular point I have no idea where that might be. I'm a pretty good athlete, but a better student; so good, in fact, my guidance counselors here at Glen Lake High School have encouraged me to apply to the United States Military Academy at West Point. I've done that, but I'm not really convinced that is right for me. To be honest, I'm not at all sure I could cope with all the regimentation and discipline required to flourish there. I like working on mechanical things, a trait I developed in my early teen years hanging around boats—big ones, the more engines the better—at my father's marina in Miami. He's an international yacht broker. And, while he makes a lot of money, he's not a very good role model. For that matter, neither is my mother, who I live with. She's a drunk. Most of my friends think I'm pretty lucky. I'm well liked, live in a big house overlooking Lake Michigan, drive a late model BMW, and my father supplies me with the latest model cell phone. But today something evil is about to happen that respects neither money, status, intellect, or physical ability.

Morning, September 11, 2001

I'm sitting in Advanced Placement American Lit. It's my second class of the day having already survived AP Trigonometry. I have reached the long-anticipated and highly regarded status of "senior" and, though I like school, I find myself staring out the window into an azure blue sky, ignoring all the chatter going on around me, the beauty of the day making me wish I was back at my summer job at On-the-Narrows Marina in Glen Lake. Our teacher, Mr. Calderone, is oddly late this morning.

Charley Kimball, a football teammate, sits two rows away from me talking up Missy Banks, a cheerleader. Charley and I already know Mr. Calderone pretty well. He's an assistant football coach, coaching quarterbacks and running backs. After two years on second string, I'm the starting QB this year. Charley is a great running back and not a bad receiver. Coach calls the two of us "his protégés."

I like Mr. Calderone. He's a man of letters. I mean, this is an English class he's teaching. But he's also an athlete, having played NCAA Division III football as a QB himself. He's also pretty unflappable, having coached us this season in a couple of close games, never losing his cool, offering good advice and telling us, "OK, I know you guys can do this. Now go out there and execute!"

This morning, however, as he enters the classroom, I am struck by a rather vacant look in his eyes. There's no hint of his usual smile. He steps behind his desk, turns to face us and somberly asks, "Have any of you heard what's going on in New York?"

The class grows quiet. Though cell phones exist, they aren't commonplace, even in this well-heeled community; those of us who had them didn't bring them to class. We all collectively shake our heads and give him our undivided attention.

"There's been a terrible accident. A passenger plane has collided with one of the World Trade Center towers." A few students gasp, but then the room falls eerily silent. "No one on the plane could have survived," he says. "Don't know how many people in the tower might have been killed. It'll probably be a few days before anyone can figure that out. Terrible pictures coming in on television."

In that brief moment, my brain suddenly became a jumble of synapses wanting to fire a dozen questions. I could tell I wasn't the only one in the room feeling the same thing, yet we all sat there silently mired in our utter confusion over how something this horrible could have happened.

Mr. Calderone moves on in an attempt to get back to some type of normality. "OK, sorry to be the bearer of such bad news, but let's continue our look at Thoreau."

We barely get our books open to the passage in *Walden* he wants to discuss when the room's public-address speaker crackles. For some reason, I glance at my watch: *9:10 a.m.* Mr. Counts, the principal, informs us that a second plane has inexplicably flown into the second World Trade Center tower. This time there are more gasps among my classmates, and I see Mr. Calderone span his right forefinger and thumb across his forehead. He lowers his head and shakes it as if he is in even more disbelief than we are. I think, *What the hell is going on?* But my thoughts are interrupted by Mr. Counts' directions, "Teachers, for now, I am going to ask that you keep your students in your classrooms until I direct otherwise. Ignore the bells. I will keep you informed as I learn more." We hear the click as the PA system goes quiet. We all look to Calderone for direction, but all we get is a shake of his head, his eyes averted from ours. He doesn't know any more than we do.

Thoreau and *Walden* fall far to the wayside. For an agonizing hour we sit and talk, not the same idle chatter that preceded our teacher's late arrival to class this morning, but a more subdued speculation about what is happening. We have a TV in our classroom, but it's not hooked up to cable, though there are rumors that is coming soon. We try to get a signal, any signal at all. Traverse City isn't that far away and there are several television stations broadcasting from there, but our school is nestled down between large, heavily forested dunes. We get nothing.

Then, at 10:10, Mr. Counts' voice comes over the PA again. "Ladies and gentlemen." That was the way he always spoke to us collectively. Individually, it was always Mr. or Ms., like we were adults. And I guess that was very appropriate on his part, for in the next few minutes, hours, days, months, and years, we were all about to come of age. "I have just sent an all-call to your parents cancelling school for the remainder of today and alerting them that there may be similar cancellations over the next few days. In addition to the accidents at the World Trade Center, a third plane has struck the Pentagon in Washington, DC, and a fourth has crashed in western Pennsylvania. For those of you who ride busses, they are waiting outside in their usual places to take you home. If your parents are your usual ride home, please report to the gymnasium and wait for their arrival. If you require other assistance with transportation, please come to the office and we will make arrangements for you."

The public-address system has no sooner gone silent when Mr. Calderone's cell phone rings and he answers—teachers are allowed more latitude with cell phones than are students. He listens, nods his head, and says, "I understand," and then ends the call. No one moves for a minute which seems longer to me. Mr. Calderone tells us to go meet our transportation, and as the first students begin to trickle out of the classroom, he says, "Mr. Rigley, Mr. Kimball, may I see you before you leave?" Charley and I glance at one another and step to the front of his desk. "No practice today. We'll get word to you when the next one will be. Not sure yet about the game on Friday, but depending on what exactly is happening, it might be cancelled."

Charley pipes up, "Cancelled or postponed, Coach? We can't cancel *that* game . . . not the Frankfort game!"

Mr. Calderone holds up a hand. Charley backs down. I just stand there for a moment before asking, "Do you think there's going to be more, Coach?" He gives me a puzzled look and I clarify, "More planes, I mean."

Calderone shrugs, his face still etched with solemnity. He tells me, "Dunno, Jack. But here's what I do know: neither of you—" He points back and forth between Charley and me, and then waves his hand around the room, "None of us here this morning will ever forget where we were when we got this news. This must be what it felt like when the Japanese attacked Pearl Harbor."

10:25 a.m., September 11, 2001

The parking lot at the school is a mess. We are a consolidated school district and our facility is a new one. Glen Lake/Maple City Elementary, Middle and High Schools are clustered on one campus. From the looks of it, there won't be many students riding the school bus home. The parents I observed on the way to my car were all scurrying after their kids and had a near-panicked look in their eyes. Annie is waiting at my car, and as soon as she sees me, she bolts toward me, wraps me in an embrace, and whispers into my ear the question everyone is asking, "What's happening, Jack?" We've been girlfriend/boyfriend now for several months. She's a year younger than me, a junior. I squeeze her tighter and say, "I don't know, Annie," thinking somehow using my pet name for her will provide a little comfort.

We hold onto each other for a long time until we are rudely interrupted by her younger brother, an elementary school student. "C'mon you two. Break it up. Can I have a ride home?"

"Sure," I say. Annie rolls her eyes at him and we all get in the car. I take my cell phone out of the glove box and hand it to her. "Best call your parents. Let them know you're OK and I'm bringing you and Pete home. I'm sure they're worried. I'll see if I can find a news station."

The normally uneventful trip back home to Empire today was filled with terrible news of people jumping off the upper floors of the twin towers and of mounting deaths at the Pentagon. We listened to the reports of United Flight 93 that had crashed into a field in western Pennsylvania. Some of the passengers apparently had the presence of mind in their final minutes to call their loved ones on their cell phones, to say their final goodbyes, knowing their deaths were imminent. Later stories would emerge as a result of these frantic phone calls; the passengers of Flight 93 weren't going to go meekly to their deaths. And then came the horrible news that the twin towers had collapsed. All of us are stunned into silence by this barrage of horror, even Pete who is normally an endless stream of questions about this or that.

I pull to a stop in the driveway of the Miller's modest ranch-style home. Annie asks, "What are you going to do, Jack?"

I just shake my head. I hadn't given that any thought. It was only 11:30 in the morning, yet it seemed so much later to me. "I dunno," was my very honest answer. There wasn't any reason to go home. It was entirely possible my mother wasn't even awake to have heard the news. Even if she had, her solution would be to have a drink and then another and another.

As if she were reading my mind, Annie reaches across the Beamer's console, takes my hand and says, "Stay here with me. We'll watch the news together."

From the backseat, Annie's brother says, "Yeah, Jack. Stay with us. We can play some video games." Annie again rolls her eyes.

Danny and Rebecca Miller are in the family room glued to the television. Annie says with some surprise in her voice, "You're both home. Who's minding the store?" Empire Feed and Grain is truly a mom-and-pop operation; the two of them, Danny and Rebecca, are its only full-time employees.

Mr. Miller says, "Closed the store. Put a sign on the front door to call if it's an emergency. Nobody's called; doubt anyone will. Everyone's home tryin' to figure out what the hell is going on." The scene on the TV screen was of dust-covered people, some running, some walking like dazed zombies on the streets of lower Manhattan, the blue sky of earlier that morning obscured by the smoke and dust of the burning heap that was once the World Trade Center. He adds, "Thanks for bringing Anne and Pete home. We appreciate it." Then he directs Pete to go to his room. He tells him he can play some video games.

Pete looks at me, "C'mon, Jack. Wanna play?" I decline.

When the boy is gone, her father looks at Annie's mother, Rebecca, and then to Annie and me and says, "He doesn't need to see this."

Annie and I take up a position on the floor, sitting cross-legged in front of the TV; she's holding my hand. It still makes me a little uncomfortable showing our affection for one another in front of her parents like this, but Annie isn't bashful about it, and neither of them seem to mind. Being here with her and her parents is comforting. With the radio, we couldn't see what was happening. Now, in front of the TV, we could see the horror. The first distant pictures of the plane crash in someplace called Shanksville, Pennsylvania, are starting to show up. These are from the ground. In the background we can see emergency vehicles, their red and blue lights flashing around the accident scene. Understandably, reporters are kept back away from the point of impact. Though their cameras try to zoom in, all we can see is rising smoke. No debris is visible at this distance. A reporter speculates no part of the doomed airliner can be seen because it lies at the bottom of the huge crater created by its impact. He apologizes for the lack of aerial coverage. News helicopters are banned from flying. In fact, everything that can fly has been grounded except for a few air force fighters allowed aloft as protective measures against . . . against what? Who could know?

At some point a tray of sandwiches appears on the coffee table. I take my first bite of one of them and hear the reporter say that someone named Osama Bin Laden and another equally foreign sounding organization, Al Qaeda, are taking credit for the attacks. For the next few hours, more foreign sounding Arabic-based words begin popping up; there are words like *Sunni, Shia, Jihad, Jihadists,* etc. I bookmark them in my brain, wondering how these people will impact our lives as I recall Mr. Calderone's comment earlier this morning, *"None of us here this morning will ever forget where we were when we got this news."*

An all-call comes into the Miller's home phone at about 7:00 p.m. School tomorrow is cancelled for Pete, Annie, and me.

Annie asks her dad if he plans on opening the store tomorrow, and still glued to the TV, he distractedly shakes his head, and says, "I doubt it."

Annie asks if I'd like to take a walk. Despite the day's events, it's a beautiful evening outside and we leave holding hands. Samantha, the Miller's border collie whom everyone simply calls *Sam*, comes along with us and as we walk, I ask Annie, "Your dad's pretty locked in on what's going on. You think he's worried there might be more attacks?"

She screws up her face and says, "Maybe." There's a pause. We continue to walk and then Annie adds, "He hates war, Jack."

Flippantly, I respond, "Yeah, don't we all."

With a hint of anger, Annie comes back at me, "No, Jack, I mean he *really* hates it. He had an older brother . . . quite a bit older than him actually—ten years—who was killed in Vietnam." I immediately regret my flippancy, but it's too late. I'd triggered memories in her. "Obviously, I never knew my Uncle Max, but I feel like I do. Dad worshipped the ground he walked on. He was a carpenter before he got drafted. He took some kind of test when he first went in. Dad says he was the only one that passed it. They asked him if he wanted to fly helicopters. He was shot down in 1971 . . . killed. He was flying something called . . . oh, what was the name? Oh, yeah, I remember now. It was some kind of helicopter my dad called a *gunship*."

"Annie, I'm sorry, I didn't mean to—"

She waves her hand dismissively. "It's OK, Jack. My dad feels like Vietnam robbed him of someone he dearly loved. Maybe he thinks this is the start of a war or something like that. I don't know. All I know is that he was relieved when that last war . . . the one in Kuwait . . . what was it called?"

I say, "Desert Storm."

"Yeah, that's it. It only lasted a few days. Dad was absolutely convinced we were going to get dragged into another long war when that happened. He's always paid attention to what we get ourselves into in other countries. You should ask him about it sometime. He'll quote George Washington to you. I can't remember the quote exactly but the gist of it is, we shouldn't butt in in foreign countries, period. . . . 'no entangling treaties' is how Washington put it. Dad just doesn't want to see American lives wasted like he thinks his brother's was." She squeezes my hand harder and adds, "And I agree with him."

"But Annie," I respond, "this Osama-guy attacked us, just like the Japanese did at Pearl Harbor. We can't just sit back and let that kind of thing happen, can we?"

She repeats the day's most commonly used catchphrase. "I don't know, Jack. I just don't know."

I bend down and give Sam a pat on the head and then kiss Annie goodbye in the driveway after returning from our walk. Dark is settling in on one of the darkest days in modern American history. I should go home and check on my mother, but my mind's eye sees that scene, and I decide against it. I think to myself, *Not tonight, not after a day like this one.* I drive to the Lake Michigan public beach in Empire. I walk toward the water's edge, take a seat in the sand, and pull my knees up to my chin. The beach is oddly empty, I assume because everyone else is home still reeling from the terrible events of the day. The sun has already set, but its red remnants rim the horizon. The lake is calm with only a gentle breeze coming in from the west. In front of me are the gray outlines of rippling waves breaking at the water's edge. I am alone with my thoughts. Gazing upward, the sky over Empire is dotted with thousands of stars splotched in an ever-darkening sky. I am suddenly dwarfed by the universe's vastness just as I have been dwarfed all day by the huge tragedy that has befallen America. Before today, I was a kid whose biggest worries in life centered around the next test that needed passing, how effective my passing might be during Friday night's football game, where would I go to school next year, or if I would be good enough to play the game at the next level. Now sitting here in the sand, in the quiet solitude of a place I had come to love, I realize how inconsequential those things are in light of what has happened this day. I can't comprehend exactly how any of it might impact my life; I simply know there will be an impact. I recall Annie's comments about her father hating war. *Will we go to war over this?* I've studied enough history to know that in both world wars, in Korea, in Vietnam, the lives lost were predominantly among the young: men and women my age or just a few years older. A chill runs down my spine, but I chalk it up to the cool night air.

TWO

It's Personal Now

The last two and a half years have flown by. Annie and I are still together despite the geographic distance that separates us eight months out of the year. I did not accept the appointment to the United States Military Academy I was offered. Instead, I am attending Western Michigan University in Kalamazoo, Michigan, studying aviation science. Annie is about to finish up her associate's degree in accounting from Northwestern Michigan College.

My father, I think, is still upset with me for declining West Point. The terms of my parents' divorce decree requires him to pay for my school, and my degree is one of the most expensive anywhere because of all the flying I must do to qualify for the diploma. West Point would have let him off that hook. There my college education would have been free. My mom? Well, initially she was upset, but vodka continues to be her cure for everything.

Annie and I have discussed marriage, but both of us know that's not a real possibility until I graduate. Generally, I would describe my life as *good*, but the US is at war. Our country's efforts in Afghanistan have not yet yielded Osama Bin Laden, our stated purpose for being there. We've invaded Iraq because we wouldn't believe the reports of United Nations investigators that its dictator isn't harboring weapons of mass destruction. Thus far, all I know about war is what I've studied in school. But now it's about to get very personal.

WMU's W.K. Kellogg Airport's classroom building, 3:55 p.m., March 23, 2004

I walk into the classroom a few minutes early. I'm tired after flying all morning and then having to hang around waiting for this navigation class to begin. Just as I am about to sit down, my cell phone vibrates. "Hey, Annie."

"Jack . . . " There was something about the way she said my name I could tell something was up. She continues, "I'm so sorry . . . "

"Annie, what is it? What's the matter?" My first thought is something has happened to my mother.

"It's Charley Kimball and Zeke Hatch . . . "

I was aware three of my high school football teammates, Charley Kimball, Zeke Hatch, and Jeff Barlow, had enlisted together in the marine corps. I'd had dinner with them two summers ago when they were home in Empire on leave after finishing their basic training. Her pause makes me queasy. Americans are dying every day in places we'd never heard of before 9/11. I try to remain calm, even though I'm now prepared for some bad news. "What's happened, Annie?"

"They just announced it on the news up here. I didn't want you to hear this like I just did . . . out of nowhere."

"What's happened?" As I repeat the question, my voice's urgency ratchets up.

"Charley and Zeke were killed in Iraq. The news report says it was an improvised explosive device. It killed them and six other marines riding in a truck."

"Jeff . . . Jeff Barlow . . . was he . . . ?"

"No, his name wasn't mentioned." I am stunned into silence, sick to my stomach. Two of my teammates, good friends, were dead. "Jack, are you still there? Are you OK?" Stupidly, as if she can see me, I nod. Annie repeats, "Jack?"

I come back to reality. "Uh . . . yeah . . . Annie . . . I can't believe—"

"I'm so sorry, Jack."

April 9, 2004

Annie and I wait hand-in-hand just outside Grace Episcopal Church on Washington Street in Traverse City. A bright sun rides high in a cloudless blue sky. I find it ironic that such a beautiful day is the occasion for such a solemn event. For two or three blocks on either side of the church, the sidewalks are filled with people two or three deep. Many of them are holding American flags in a variety of sizes, the largest of which wave in the light breeze blowing through town off nearby Grand Traverse Bay. The church's sanctuary has long ago filled up. Surrounding the church are those who were too late to gain entry. These are the undaunted onlookers who still want to pay their respects. Some of them are wearing American Legion or Veterans of Foreign Wars hats, some wear articles of military uniforms like a field jacket, or camouflage fatigue shirts, a few are in full uniform. In front of me and Annie are Charley Kimball's mother, Marie, and next to her are Zeke Hatch's mother and father, Alice and Bill. We are waiting to follow the fallen into the church.

As two hearses approach from the north escorted by police on gleaming white motorcycles with lights flashing, a hush precedes them and lingers behind each hearse as they pass the onlookers. All of us, Annie, me, the parents, and those who are here to pay their respects, are trapped in this mournful silence. I observe a ripple of hands and hats being placed over hearts; some salute, others just bow their heads as the hearses convey their honored cargo along the street. Marie, Alice, and Bill hold onto one another, and all three cry the tears of loving parents that have lost their sons to a war so very, very far away.

The hearses pull to a stop in front of us. Just behind them are two vans. A dozen marines spill out and assume their positions behind each hearse. They are clad in their dress uniforms like the ones Charley, Zeke, and Jeff wore that night we had dinner together, an eon ago—or was it just yesterday? I can't recall. Time, in moments like this, is unimportant. Once the marines are in place behind each hearse, a man dressed in a black suit gets out of each hearse and moves to the rear of it. Each man opens the rear door of his assigned hearse at exactly the same time, revealing flag-draped silver caskets. Solemnly and with the utmost precision, the marines slide the coffins out on whisper-quiet rollers, their every move a carefully choreographed, slow, sad dance. They move past us. Inside the church we hear the organ begin to play and the church's choir sings the old hymn, "Amazing Grace," its sad, mournful words perfectly befitting this occasion.

Annie and I follow Charley and Zeke's parents into the church and take seats in the front pew next to them. Annie still grasps my hand and lays her head on my shoulder. For the first time, I glance at the memorial card handed to me by the usher as we entered the church. There's a picture of Charley and Zeke at the top of each card. They are in their dress uniforms with an American flag as the portrait's backdrop. Neither of them is smiling; their eyes piercing, straight forward; their expressions serious and resolute; their jaws square. Under the picture are their names: LANCE CORPORAL CHARLES ALOYSIUS KIMBALL and LANCE CORPORAL EZEKIEL ABRAHAM HATCH. I think, *Why didn't I ever know them like that?* Zeke's unabbreviated name sounded so biblical—*Ezekiel Abraham.* Charley's so formal—*Charles Aloysius.* In this most serious of moments, I can't help myself. A smile creeps across my face. *Aloysius! If only I'd known that when he was alive. What kind of hell I could have given him! Nice run there, Aloysius! Or Nice catch there you little leprechaun!* The smile fades as a priest welcomes the mourners and prays over the caskets. Another hymn is sung and now, all too suddenly, it's my turn.

I'd been asked to eulogize my friends. My knees are weak, I feel adrenaline roll in the pit of my stomach. As I make my way to the pulpit, I reach in my inside coat pocket and remove my eulogy, carefully worked out over the last few days. I suddenly become aware of the tears rolling down my cheeks. I somehow know my voice is lost to me, even though I have not even begun. I put my prepared remarks back in my pocket, dismissing them as inadequate, wipe my tears away with a handkerchief, clear my throat, and begin to speak with a very heavy heart but with words flowing straight from it. "Charley Kimball and Zeke Hatch are two of my closest friends. We were teammates together playing football in high school. Charley was the guy that, if two yards were needed for a first down, I knew I could give him the ball and he would get it. Zeke was the guy that blocked for Charley and me. In the years since then, I don't think the three of us ever thought we'd be on a team as good as that one. But today, I think, if I were able to ask either of them—and how I wish I could do that very thing—I'd ask, 'What's the greatest team you've ever played for?' Neither of them would say it was our Glen Lake team. No, they'd say it was the marine corps." The lump in my throat returns. So do the tears. I pause to wipe them away and recompose myself. "Just like they did at Glen Lake, they gave everything they had to their team—the marine corps—and, now, they've given everything they have to this country. None of us here today, no one calling themselves an American, should ever forget how well they played or how much they gave for us." I can't look at their parents as I return to my seat. I feel so lacking, so inadequate in the face of such terrible loss.

We go to the graveside service. The two are buried next to one another, a choice made by Marie, Alice, and Bill. It was Marie Kimball who told Annie and me, "If they could tell us, we know this is what they would want." It is the same contingent of marines at the graveside as were at the church. I watch them as they perform their solemn duties in absolute synchronization, including the folding of the American flags and the presenta-tion to Marie, and then, Alice and Bill. Annie and I both flinch as the honor guard fires off the first of two three-gun salutes; one for Charley, one for Zeke. As the ringing of the shots fade, a bugler sounds "Taps." It's turned cooler now as the sun has moved lower in the western sky. The huddled mass of mourn-ers listens to the sorrowful notes of the somber song ring out over the surrounding gravestones. Then, it's over—this terrible day—and I see him, a lone marine standing off to the side, his dress uniform immaculate, the brass buttons gleaming in the lowering sun of early evening. Annie and I walk over and hug a sobbing Jeff Barlow.

7:00 p.m., April 9, 2004
We sit on the screened-in porch at the rear of Jeff Barlow's par-ents' house. Jeff has a beer in his hand. Annie and I have Cokes.

Jeff's father has supplied the beer to his underage son. He said to us, "Shit, if you're old enough to die in Iraq, then you're old enough to have a beer in the privacy of your own home." After today, no one here is going to object to that logic.

Jeff is home for a week. He apologizes for not being at the church. "I just couldn't bear it. I shoulda . . . " He stops short there and tells Annie and me, "My commanding officer in Iraq knew how close the three of us were, so he appointed me to escort them home."

I don't know what to say, but ask, "What happened, Jeff?"

It takes him a while to answer. I assume it isn't easy for him to talk about it, but I know him well enough. If he didn't want to talk, he'd tell me and Annie. Instead, I detect a sense of relief as he begins, "I was supposed to be with them."

Annie says, "Oh no, Jeff!"

"Last minute change. Charley and Zeke went off with the rest of our squad to scout a small village, a suspected Al Qaeda stronghold." He pauses here for a moment and shakes his head and then continues, "The damn place wasn't even a fly-speck on the map. The road into it had been swept the day before, but the bad guys must have come in after the sweep and planted an IED expecting a bunch of marines to show up at the village at some point. They drove right into the trap." There was a pause and then, "Bastards," he swears, followed up by an apology to Annie who reassures him none is necessary. "The lieutenant pulled me out of the truck just before we left base camp, said he needed an RTO." He must see our puzzled looks, so he clarifies, "Radio Telephone Operator." He pauses again. "Can you freakin' believe that?" Jeff sits shaking his head.

Annie and I keep our eyes on him and our mouths shut. What could we possibly have said to comfort his sorrow anyway?

He continues, "When Charley and Zeke were getting fired up, I was at some damn ammo dump, just hanging around while the lieutenant finished some paperwork. I got the call on the radio about what had happened." Annie and I remain at a complete loss for words. Jeff, in tears, stammers, "I shoulda been there. I shoulda been with Charley and Zeke."

All Annie and I can do is look at one another and then I manage a muffled, "No, Jeff, you can't think that way." But the truth is I didn't know how I'd think in his situation.

THREE

It's Complicated

The loss of Charley Kimball and Zeke Hatch changed me forever. War was as ugly to me as it ever was, but it was a reality and I'd lost two really good friends to it. Their loss made me feel inadequate, overly privileged, and vengeful all at the same time. Annie and I had talked about it. The decision was mine to make and two years ago I'd joined the Army Reserve Officers' Training Program. I'd also applied for and received a two-year Army ROTC scholarship. My father was thrilled.

Danny Miller, Annie's father, however, was not, and when I told him I was going to fly helicopters in the army, the exact duty that led to his brother's death in Vietnam, I became *persona non grata* at the Miller house.

Early evening, May 19, 2006
The crowd is beginning to gather inside the Shaw Theater, part of the more extensive Gilmore Theater complex here at Western Michigan University in Kalamazoo, Michigan. I pull Annie—who is now my fiancé—aside from our two mothers so I can talk with her before having to rush off to do a few things before the

commissioning ceremony begins. "Listen, I'm sorry I have to leave her with you like this."

"Jack Rigley, stop it," she said, giving me a playful thump on my chest. "We'll be fine."

"You're used to it, but your mother—well, she isn't. That wine at lunch is all she's had today, I'm pretty sure." But I can't really know for sure. She did slip into the ladies' room at one point. Annie and I both suspected she keeps a bottle stashed in her handbag, an oversized thing easily capable of hiding a 750ml bottle of booze. Even though I'd secured a promise of sobriety from her for the next several days, her alcoholism doesn't allow me to trust her.

"Well, she's not going to pull it out here, and she can have a couple of drinks at dinner tonight after the ceremony. How long do you think it will last?"

"An hour . . . maybe an hour fifteen."

"We'll be OK. Don't worry about us. Is your dad coming?"

I shrug, "I dunno. Last text I had from him yesterday he said he'd try and make it, but I'm not counting on him."

Annie lays a comforting hand on my arm, "It's his loss if he misses this, Jack."

Annie's my rock. We come from completely different backgrounds. Her family is bolted together like an armored vehicle. Mine? Well, if you were to look in the dictionary for a definition of *dysfunctional* you'd see my family photo. I would truly be shocked if my father were to make it tonight to see me be commissioned an army officer, or tomorrow for graduation. But if he should, I only hope he leaves his latest squeeze at home. She is the fourth one I know about since my parents divorced. The common thread among all four is their big tits and lack of brains. I'd met this latest one a year ago when I visited Dad in Miami. All of us would be better off if she just stayed there with one of his limitless credit cards. Here she would create sparks that might well set the booze in my mother's purse ablaze.

As the commissioning ceremony is about to begin, I turn around in my seat and quickly scan the audience to see if my father is here. Relief washes over me as I see no sign of him or his girlfriend. Just making sure my mother stays sufficiently sober for today and tomorrow is pressure enough.

Our guest speaker this evening, who will administer our oaths ushering us into the ranks of the army's officer corps, is a two-star general, Major General William Standish. He's the adjutant general for the State of Michigan, a political appointee of Michigan's governor, who, as coincidence, or perhaps planning, would have it—I suspect coincidence—will be the speaker at tomorrow's graduation ceremony. I had met the general just an hour or so earlier as he'd arrived. Lieutenant Colonel Roberts, the Professor of Military Science here at WMU, made introductions. "General Standish, welcome to Western Michigan University. Allow me to introduce this year's top cadet, soon-to-be-Second Lieutenant Jack Rigley. He is a two-year Army ROTC scholarship recipient, a Distinguished Military Graduate, a *summa-cum-laude* graduate of our aviation college, and will be commissioned tonight in the regular army as an aviation officer." Standish, whose bio I'd read, came from an infantry background in the Michigan National Guard.

He shakes my hand and offers, "Hmmm, a flyboy, huh. Well we need those helicopters." I'm struck there's not the slightest congratulatory hint as he immediately turns his attention to Roberts. "All right, Colonel, fill me in on this evening's plan," followed by a quick glance at his watch. It was my impression the general couldn't get this evening behind him fast enough.

Wondering if my mother was continuing to behave herself, I realize the general and I are of the same mind.

Right on time, the preliminaries of the evening begin with a musical military tradition. "Ruffles and two flourishes," via recording, is played to recognize the presence of a two-star general. The twenty-five of us to be commissioned come to attention as this plays, and Standish and Roberts enter, take the stage, and stand in front of their seats. From behind we can hear the rustle of seats as the audience takes its cue from us and rises to their feet as well. Then the ROTC detachment's sergeant major steps to the podium and directs, "Would everyone please remain standing for the National Anthem and the invocation given by Pastor Amos Tillis from Allen Chapel African Methodist Episcopal Church." Pastor Tillis's son stands just a few seats away from me in the theater's first row, waiting, like me, to be commissioned as one of the army's newest officers.

Annie believes I sometimes judge people too quickly, too sternly. Tonight proves her point. After Lieutenant Colonel Roberts introduces General Standish who begins with, "Your future lies in front of you," I allow my first impression of him to take over and think, *If he'd rather be somewhere else, then so would I!* I dismiss him with the thought that I will hear this very same rhetoric tomorrow from the governor at graduation. I'll listen to it then.

By 10:00 p.m. I'm lying in bed in my room in the Candlewood Suites in Kalamazoo. My uniform, the gold bar of a second lieutenant sparkling on each epaulet, hangs in the closet. It's official now. I'm in the army. The four of us had gone to dinner following the commissioning ceremony. I watched the look on Rebecca Miller's face when my mother ordered her second, third, and fourth vodka and tonics during the course of the meal. She was fully aware of my mother's alcoholism. Annie and I had long ago disclosed it to her and Annie's father, Danny. Seated across the table from Mrs. Miller, I could read the look on her face, pleading for me to say something. If she only knew how often I'd tried. *Mom, maybe you should take it easy. Mom, don't you think you've had enough.* But I didn't say anything to her because it would not have done any good and it would have risked the possibility of riling her up sufficiently to cause a scene. All day she'd denied herself the clear liquid she depended upon. At least this way she's watering it down with tonic, something she never did at home when drinking alone. As I'm deep in thought convincing myself my actions, or inaction, this evening was the right thing to have done, the ringing phone on the bedside table startles me.

"Jack, I didn't wake you did I?"

Annie and her mother are sharing a room down the hall from mine. My mother's room is further yet down the hall. "No, I'm awake."

"Mom's in the shower, so I can't talk long. Do you think you should check on your mother? She was really pounding them down at dinner. If she gets into the bottle in her purse—"

I break in, "Thought about that but decided there's no point. I'm not her nurse. I'm not going to camp out in her room like I'm some kind of security guard trying to protect her from herself. Even if I were, she'd still find a way."

"I suppose you're right. I wish I was there beside you in bed right now."

Two years ago Annie and I had foregone the celibacy of our first three years together. "Me, too," I say. A smile crosses my face as I remember that first time. We were driving back home to Empire from Fort Knox, Kentucky, where I'd gone through a six-week-long ROTC summer camp. She'd flown in to watch the closing parade and ceremony. I still chuckle to myself every time I remember how, in our amateurish haste to get the damned thing on, we absolutely shredded the first condom, or French letter, as Annie prefers to call them, because she hates the word *condom* or *rubber*.

In the background I hear Rebecca Miller say, "Anne," (I'm the only one who calls her Annie) "could you get me the shampoo from the counter? I forgot to get it."

"Gotta go."

"I heard. I love you, Annie. Breakfast about nine in the morning?"

"Love you, Jack. Sounds good."

I hang up the phone and lay my head back on the pillow. I'm not sleepy, so my mind begins to work. Only Annie knows how much I've been affected by 9/11 and then, again, by the loss of my two friends. She says she understands. I believe her. But I have not shared my motivation to serve with either my parents or hers. I honestly believe mine don't care about my decision to serve in the army, my mother because of her disease, my father because he's too busy making money. Rebecca Miller might understand. Annie says she would, but I've never tested that. Her father, Danny—well, let's just say, "that's complicated."

A text comes in from Jeff Barlow. "Sir (that's what I have to call you now 😊) Congratulations on your commissioning. My commanding officer approved my June leave. See you at the wedding. I think you should make it a military affair." Jeff will be my best man, but the wedding will most certainly not be a military affair. At some point I manage to fall asleep thinking about Annie and the life we will shortly begin to forge together.

The next morning, May 20, 2006

I decide I'd better make a call to my mother's room. The plan is to get some breakfast and then head to the Miller Auditorium on campus, and get there early so everyone can find a good seat for today's graduation. My first sign that today might not work out as I'd hoped comes when my mother doesn't answer the phone.

"Mom," I say in a normal tone of voice after knocking several times on her room door. Nothing. I knock again, this time more rapidly, a little harder and raise my voice, "Mom." I try three more times to rouse her, but failing, I return to my room and try again to reach her by phone. No response. I call Annie's room hoping she, not Rebecca, will answer. When I hear Annie's voice, I say, "My mother's not answering her phone or my knocks on her door."

"You think she's gotten—"

While something like this might be a real cause of concern among normal people, my mother is anything but *normal*. Before Annie can complete her thought, I say, "Yeah, that's exactly what I think!"

"I'm sorry, Jack."

To me it seemed Annie had spent all of our years together apologizing for my mother. I'd stopped doing that a long time ago. "Not your fault. I'll meet you and your mom in the lobby at nine just like we planned. I'll try and raise her a few more times, but we aren't waiting around on her. She isn't going to spoil today."

"OK."

1:00 p.m., May 20, 2006

Graduation was exactly how it should have been, peppered with pomp and circumstance and great words of encouragement by

Governor Jennifer Granholm. In her second term, she's been identified as a rising star in the Democratic Party. I found her to be much more motivating than the previous evening's speaker, General Standish. The only thing missing was my mother. The loose plan at this point is to return to Candlewood Suites, pick her up, stop for lunch and then get on the road back home to Empire. Although, I have no idea what to expect once we get to the hotel.

1:15 p.m., May 20, 2006
The room door opens slowly; my mother appears disheveled in a white slip, her hair a mess, her eyes barely able to focus. "Jack, where have you been? I called your room . . ."

I think, *Oh, pllleeaase!* But, I've long learned there is little point in getting angry at her. I step into the room. "We were at graduation, Mom. You missed it." On the bedside table I see an empty bottle of vodka confirming the stash Annie and I suspected she'd carried with her. "Get dressed, we have to head back to Empire."

"But . . ."

"But what, Mom! You missed it. Graduation's over. I've checked you out of the room. You have to hurry. You've already missed your checkout time, but they aren't going to charge you for another night. Just get it together." Her dress from the evening before is thrown over a chair back, shoes and stockings haphazardly lay around it. The dress she was going to wear today is still folded in her suitcase. I close it after throwing in a few bathroom items she has scattered around the sink. I step in front of her and make sure she focuses on me. "We'll be waiting in the car. I'm parked in front of the lobby door. Hurry up."

While I may not be angry, her utter lack of responsibility

disgusts me. I should have known something like this would happen. Her alcoholism is so bad, she cannot be relied upon for anything. It's why right after I'd left home for college I'd nagged my father to hire someone to come into the house, clean it, and check on her general well-being. This is what I'd been doing, it seemed to me, ever since their divorce. He didn't want to put out the money, but when I described the mess I found when I came home for Christmas in 2002, I sold him on the idea of protecting his investment. The house is in Storm Hill, a pricey Empire neighborhood filled with expansive homes, most with breathtaking views of Lake Michigan. I told him, "If she keeps living like this, rats, mice, and other animals might move in, but no human being will." That's when I found Liz Oxford, and Dad added her to his weekly payroll.

On the three-hour trip home, I asked Annie if she'd prefer to drive while I sat in the back with my mother, but she'd demurred. I could tell by the look on Rebecca's face when my mother came out of the hotel lobby and walked to the car, that she'd like to distance herself as much as possible from this drunk. So, Rebecca sits up front with me. We stop at McDonald's in Rockford on our way home, not exactly the nice lunch I'd had in mind when the day began. My mother sleeps as we go through the drive-thru. Annie asks if she should wake her up. I shake my head. "Let her sleep."

Our first stop in Empire is at Annie's. I am not happy to see Mr. Miller in the front yard cleaning out an accumulation of leaves, twigs, and dead flower remnants from a flower bed in front of their house. He stops what he's doing as he sees us pull in the driveway and walks toward the car. He greets his wife and daughter with a smile and a hug. His acknowledgement of me is a quick wave of his hand in my direction. Our relationship—Mr.

Miller's and mine—well, I have to keep coming back to, "It's complicated."

For a while, a few years ago, he and I were OK. I'd turned down that nomination to West Point for a couple of reasons. First, I didn't really care for the regimentation required at any of the service academies. Second, and most importantly, I had decided that a career in aviation—especially in aviation maintenance—is what I wanted to pursue, and WMU, which was a lot closer to home than West Point, had an excellent college of aviation. At that point I think he thought if Annie and I were to wind up marrying, his son-in-law would be a commercial pilot working for one of the big airlines. And, while that might mean she'd be moving out of Empire, if I were working for an airline, then that meant she'd at least be able to come home often.

Then Charley Kimball and Zeke Hatch are killed in Iraq, and I grow a conscience, along with the realization that I might be able to advance my aviation career aspirations by flying in the army for a few years. *Why not?* I thought. *Get some flight experience, get into the maintenance field. Then get out and parlay your experience into a career in commercial aviation.*

For the last several years, since I'd enrolled in Army ROTC and took that scholarship, my relationship with my soon-to-be father-in-law had soured. If I were at the Miller's house, even if just to pick up Annie for a date, he would disappear. When I asked his permission to marry his daughter, something I felt obligated to do because I knew Annie loved and respected both of her parents so much, I never really got an answer. "Anne loves you. I won't hurt her. I won't stand in the way." He'd been invited to join us for this past weekend's ceremonies but told Annie he needed to stay and keep the store, Empire Feed and Grain, open. I knew that was bullshit. He had several part-time clerks who would have been happy for the extra hours and were more than capable of opening and closing. Danny Miller wanted no part of me because I was going to go in the army, and then, as if to rub salt into that wound, I was going to do the very same thing in the army that had killed his brother, Max, all those years ago in Vietnam—fly helicopters.

I'd driven a wedge between father and daughter. Annie was forced to walk a very thin line between her love for me and her love for the man who'd raised her. So, while Annie had no reason to apologize to me for my mother's behavior, I, on the other hand, owed her every apology as the cause of her fractured relationship with her dad. I was the sole cause of this rift in their family. I hope Mr. Miller will be sufficiently forgiving of me and walk his daughter down the aisle, because I am hopelessly in love with Annie Miller and I am going to marry her, no matter what.

I don't linger in the Miller's driveway. My mother—who's awake now, but still disheveled, and would likely be wobbly if she were to get out of the car—gives him a thin smile and a tentative wave through a backseat window. I offer my goodbyes and tell Annie I'll see her tomorrow. As I back the car out of the driveway I see Rebecca and Danny talking seriously with one another. *Probably wondering if they should allow their daughter to marry me.*

When we arrive at the house on Storm Hill, my mother, still in the backseat, finds a burst of energy, emerges from the car without my help, and heads straight into the house. I know all too well why that is. Lingering behind, I see I have a recent text from my father. "*Jackson—*" I hate it when he calls me that—my name is Jack "—sorry to have missed this weekend's events, but congratulations anyway. I am in Bahrain finishing up a big mega yacht deal. Count on us for the wedding. Love you." Besides the name-thing, I found two other things distressing about this text. First, he used the word "us" as in "count on us," which means he's bringing good ol' boobalicious Lindy with him, a presence that will surely prove incendiary. And second, he closes with *Love you,* words I haven't heard or seen from my father in—well, I can't remember the last time.

FOUR

Starting a New Life Together

1:30 p.m., June 17, 2006

The room where the groom prepares for the wedding at Traverse City's Grace Episcopal Church is small compared to the spacious room dedicated to the bride and her attendants. I am standing in front of a floor-length mirror adjusting my bow tie. In the mirror, I can see the reflection of Jeff Barlow, my best man. He asked if it would be all right if he wore his marine corps dress uniform even though the wedding was not going to be a military one. I had agreed, even though I knew I was running the risk of pissing off my soon-to-be father-in-law. While I don't yet know the meaning of all the ribbons above Jeff's left breast pocket, I have newfound and immense respect for each of the dozen or more he wears. He reaches over and smooths the shoulders of my tuxedo jacket. "Well, this is a lot happier occasion than the last time we were in this church. You look great, man."

Before I can even acknowledge the truth in that statement and thank him, the door opens and my father steps in. The last I heard, he was in Dubai closing the deal on a several-hundred-million-dollar mega yacht with some oil-rich Arab. I am in complete shock, and maybe that's why I don't offer a handshake or a hug. We simply aren't that close. I manage to stammer, "Dad . . . uh . . . I wasn't expecting . . ."

He pulls me up short, steps toward me and wraps me in a hug. I'm caught completely off guard. "Rita told me to get my act together and get the hell back here. She made it clear that I only had one son and he was getting married, so I'd better get my ass to the wedding."

I look at Jeff, who has a bewildered look on his face. I make introductions and the two shake hands. I have no idea who *Rita* is. All I can think to ask is, "How long are you in town?"

He shakes his head. "Not long. We'll be leaving this evening, but we wanted to give you this." He reaches in his inside coat pocket and produces a piece of paper. "This is a NetJets open-ended reservation. Rita and I want you and Anne to come to Florida—"

Now it's my turn to interrupt. "Who's Rita?"

A broad smile breaks over his face. "Someone I really want you and Anne to meet."

I think, *He's done it again. Broken up with one brainless babe and found another.*

But, as if he's reading my mind, he says "Jack, she's not like the others. I really want you and Anne to spend some time with us."

I glance at Jeff, who's looking at his watch. It's getting near time for us to head to the chapel. "Listen, Dad, I don't know."

My father's a salesman and always refuses to accept the first "no." "When do you have to be at Fort Rucker?"

"Thirty days from now."

"That soon? I was kind of hoping you'd have longer. We really want you to come to Miami."

All of this was out of character for my father. I couldn't ever recall him wanting me to meet his girlfriends, and frankly, I'd been equally as uninterested in that prospect. But somehow this one, this Rita-person, had convinced him to get to my wedding. He sticks the NetJets reservation out further. I take it from him.

Confirming Jeff's concern, one of my groomsmen sticks his head in the door and says, "Pastor says to give you the 10-minute warning, Jack."

Dad says, "I'd better get back to Rita. She's with your mother. Everything seems to be OK, but, well, you know. I'd just better get back." I think, *Wow! He left her with Mom. That's gutsy!*

As I stand on the steps to the altar waiting for the ceremony to begin, I catch my first glimpse of Rita. She is chatting up my mother, who appears as normal as I've ever seen her in the last five or six years. My mom is smiling at my dad and this new woman in his life. *Geez, what is going on? Unbelievable.* Rita takes me by complete surprise. She is nothing like the others. She's seated, so I can't tell how tall she is, but she is attractive, and older than his past lovers. I quickly estimate if there is any difference in age between my father and Rita, it can't be by more than five years. She's wearing a stylish cream-colored dress accented by a modest necklace and bracelet. Her hair is moderately long, well styled. If it's colored, it isn't obvious and looks very natural to me. Makeup, if she's wearing any at all, compliments her tanned complexion.

There are about two hundred guests and the sanctuary is nearly full. I am able to recognize some, but many of them are friends of the Millers whom I don't know. On each side of the aisle, on the end of each pew, is a magnificent bouquet of pale blue irises surrounded by generous clumps of delicate, white baby's breath. Blue is Annie's favorite color. The Episcopal priest who will marry us stands on the altar's top step flanked on each side by much larger arrangements of the same flowers. Annie's maid of honor and four bridesmaids precede her down the aisle. All of them are longtime friends of hers, three of them are high school volleyball teammates.

The service is a traditional one; our rings are simple gold bands. When the priest says, "You may kiss the bride," I just happen to catch Rebecca Miller, a broad smile across her face, as she wipes away a tear or two. Danny Miller, however, sits head down, eyes averted away from us.

The photo shoot after the ceremony goes well enough. Somehow, my mother and Rita have struck a truce, maybe just for the evening; it really doesn't matter to me, I'm just happy for it. Dad is his equanimous self, moving from person to person, shaking hands, smiling—as if he's trying to sell sand to a sheik. Just after Annie and I cut the wedding cake, the two of them excuse themselves; their private jet is waiting at Cherry Capital Airport. But just before they leave, Dad says to Annie, "We really want the two of you to visit us in Miami. Jack's got the tickets. Come see us, Anne."

We have reserved the honeymoon suite at the Park Place Hotel in Traverse City. It's after midnight before we get into our room. We're both tired, but it's that kind of tired which requires one to stay awake just a bit longer as if trying to relish the day's events because you know they are once-in-a-lifetime things. The hotel has given us a bottle of champagne, and as I pop the cork, Annie says, "You know, Jack, your dad is nothing like the man you've described to me."

Honestly, if I based my opinion of my father solely upon what I saw tonight, I would have to agree, but I've known him a lot longer than just tonight. "Ummm, well—"

"Can we go?"

"To Miami?"

"No, Jack, to Timbucktoo!"

"Listen, Annie, the man you and I saw today—the woman, Rita, we met—I honestly don't know what to make of them. My dad actually gave me a hug today before the wedding. He hasn't done that in years. I can't remember the last time. Rita, well, it looked today like she'd won my mother over and I have absolutely no explanation for that."

"So these are reasons why we should absolutely go."

"Why's that?" My skepticism still makes me—well, skeptical about it all.

"So we can get to know them better. So *I* can get to know them better. Please, Jack, let's go."

"We need to spend some time with your parents before heading to Fort Rucker. I don't know when we will get back to Empire once we leave for the army and—"

"And, what?"

"You know as well as I do, your dad isn't looking forward to your leaving."

"Look, Jack. My father doesn't like that you're in the army, and I'll admit that makes it hard for him to show his approval of anything we do. But that's my father's problem to deal with. Until today, I knew nothing about your father except what you've told me, and you must admit, based on today, you're wrong about him. Let's go to Miami and find out for ourselves. We've got no real honeymoon planned, and it sounds like this might be the perfect chance to get away. We can go to Miami tomorrow or the next day, spend some time there, and then come back here before we head to Fort Rucker. What do you say?"

June 19, 2006

Two days after our wedding, Rebecca Miller pulls the Jeep Cherokee to a stop in front of the general aviation gate at Cherry Capital Airport in Traverse City. Danny Miller has, again, chosen not to come along under the guise of having to keep Empire Feed and Grain open. Annie, Jeff Barlow, and I get out. The two of them, Annie and Jeff, have been talking about this flight the entire forty-minute drive from Empire to the airport. In her entire life, Annie has only flown a couple of times, the last time being her visit to Fort Knox to watch the closing parade for ROTC summer camp. Jeff, on the other hand, has flown quite a bit, but all of it in military aircraft sitting in what he refers to as "red seats." "They are," he opines, "the most uncomfortable seats ever invented. So bad, in fact, even a box of cargo would complain." Annie laughs at this. I'm rather quiet. I honestly don't know whether to look forward to this trip to Miami or run headlong in the opposite direction.

A few hours later, the Gulfstream 550 business jet touches down at Beaufort Executive Airport on the outskirts of Beaufort, North Carolina. We taxi to a VIP spot near the terminal's entrance and stop a few yards short of a waiting SUV. My dad has arranged for a car to meet Jeff and take him to his apartment. "Well, I'll say this for you Rigley, your old man sure knows how to travel in comfort. I never in a million years thought I'd have a trip like this one; not sure I can ever ride in one of those red seats after this." He smooches Annie on the cheek and he and I collapse from a handshake into a bear hug. I tell him to be careful. He replies, "Always, man. You, too, flyin' those whoopdecopters." We wave goodbye as the SUV pulls away. Five minutes later we are airborne again, heading for an executive airport somewhere in the Miami area where Dad has said he and Rita will be waiting.

We touch down at Miami Executive Airport. I've watched Annie since we left Traverse City this morning and can tell she is bursting with excitement. My father had managed to captivate her at our wedding in that brief first meeting. And, if I'm totally honest, it wasn't hard for me to see how. My father seemed different, more down-to-earth—even though I thought he could have spent more time at the wedding. And Rita . . . well, Rita was a complete surprise. Annie and I had speculated over her. Was she the reason my father was so different from the man I knew, from the man I'd described to her? Annie, who'd reminded me once again of my tendency to judge too quickly, had chastised me for being too hard on my father. But I'd known him a lot longer than her. So, I was not so inclined to jump to that conclusion. My father could definitely be charming. It took a lot of that to close the big-time yacht deals he was so good at snagging. As for Rita, I decided to take a wait-and-see approach despite Annie's insistence that I was being too cynical.

As the plane comes to a full stop and the pilot turns off the seat belt sign, I see my father hop out from behind the wheel of a black Mercedes-Benz SUV. He's dressed casually in a pair of white slacks, a flowered-print shirt worn untucked, silk I suspect, and tan leather deck shoes with white soles. Around his neck is a thick gold-link necklace with a matching bracelet on his right wrist. If one were to look in the dictionary for a definition of *nouveau riche*, my father's picture would appear there. On the other side of the car, Rita steps down. Her long reddish hair ruffles in the breeze, as does the cream-colored dress, which I again guess to be silk just from the way it moves in the gentle wind. As they step to the front of their car, they are holding hands and smiling and waving at us as we deplane. At the bottom of the plane's steps, Rita hugs Annie and welcomes us to Miami while Dad smiles, shakes my hand, and then pulls me into an embrace. "Jackson, so good to have you here." That name, *Jackson,* continues to grate on my nerves, but, as I always have done, I let it go.

Though I am not familiar with all of Miami, I have spent enough time here visiting that I know my way around somewhat. We are no more than five minutes out of the airport when I realize we are neither heading for the marina nor to my dad's house. Rita and Annie are talking about Rita's dress, so I lean forward from behind the driver's seat and ask my father, "Where we headed?"

"It's a surprise."

We drive south through Little Havana and into Coral Gables before turning east, entering a posh gated community fronted by a magnificently landscaped sign identifying Gables Estates. I say, "You've moved since I was here last."

My father turns his head over his shoulder, momentarily taking his eyes off the road, and says, "A lot of things have changed since you were here last, Jack." Returning his attention to the road in front of him, he swings the SUV into a semi-circular driveway of a home whose magnificence defies description. Even I was overcome by its obvious opulence. I look at Annie, whose eyes are as big as saucers.

"Oh, Rita . . . Ben . . . this is . . ." She turns to me as if asking me to help her find the right words. "I-I've never seen anything like this. It's just . . ." Annie reaches out and grabs my hand.

"This is the surprise?" I ask.

"Yep. Rita's a realtor . . . high-end properties here in Miami. She found this place. We moved in right after we got married . . ."

I nearly choke. "Wait! You-you're married?"

A sheepish look crosses both of their faces. Annie sits back in her seat, smiling, trying to take all of this in. I look at her and ask, "Did you know they were . . ."

Annie answers before I can finish, "No, Jack. No. How would I know if you didn't?" She was right, of course.

Rita begins to explain. "I know this is a lot for the both of you to wrap your heads around. Believe me, sometimes I don't even understand it myself. But we met about six months ago. One of my clients bought a huge house on Star Island. It came with a forty-foot boat, which my client had no interest in. He asked me to get rid of it."

"Get rid of it," I stammer in amazement. "You don't just *get rid* of something like that!"

Rita nodded. "That's what I told my client, but he didn't want to be bothered and offered me a twenty-five percent commission on whatever I could get for it."

"This is where I come in," Dad pipes up. "Rita calls me and says she has a boat for sale. She sure did. It was a Tiara, only a couple of years old. She had twin diesel engines, all the communications and navigation equipment was factory installed. I bought it from the guy at a good price. Rita got her commission, and on resale, I made a boatload of money—pardon the pun." Annie laughs, I roll my eyes. Dad reaches over and takes Rita's hand, "But best of all, I got Rita. Life's changed a lot for me—for us—since we married, Jack. Don't get me wrong. Both of us still work hard, me at the marina, Rita at real estate. But we're both taking more time to smell the flowers. Know what I mean?"

This was so unlike the Ben Rigley I knew.

Rita says, "That's why we're so glad you and Anne could make this trip. We want to get to know both of you and we want you to get to know us. So, these next ten days, we've promised each other that we are going to unplug from our businesses. We are going to show both of you the time of your life before you head off to Fort Rucker and the army."

Out of the corner of my eye I catch a see-I-told-you-so look from Annie, but I have too many years of difficult memories to be so easily dissuaded. The SUV rolls to a stop, and from the apex of a semi-circular drive, the four of us walk down a wide, arbor-covered walkway. On each side are neatly trimmed rows of schefflera. Wisteria twines over the arbor, creating a green tunnel with bunches of sweet-smelling flowers dangling from the dense vines surrounding us. Annie gently cradles one of the bunches in her hand. "Oh, it's so sweet smelling . . . everything is so beautiful." She was right. My father's former house, located near the trendy South Beach area of Miami, was big, with lots of windows and a pool, but nothing like this place. I turn to my father and ask, "So when were you married and when did you move here?"

"Married four months ago. Moved in two months ago. This was our wedding gift to each other. Really, it was Rita's idea. She had the listing and loved the house. Her client knew a good deal when he saw it. We made an offer and the rest is history."

Wow! I have to admit I am blown away by all of this. As we move into the home, Dad and I move to the pool area, Annie and Rita to the kitchen. Dinner is the topic of their conversation. Rita claims to have a special touch with shrimp creole. Annie says she's never had it. Rita says, "Well, then, we'll make it together, and if you like it, it's a great dish for entertaining anytime, anyplace." Another difference between Rita and Dad's past girlfriends; I never knew any of them to cook. But this one . . . his wife . . . an apparent real estate mogul, is going to teach Annie how to fix shrimp creole. Perhaps there is a slight chink starting to appear in the armor of skepticism that surrounds me and my relationship with my father.

A week later, June 26, 2006

Annie and I have been in Miami for a full week. I am the first to admit that what I anticipated as being a potentially miserable visit, has turned out to be nothing short of spectacular. Annie and Rita have become close, and if I am honest, I can say I have seen a sea change in my father. He's gone from the money-matters-above-all-else businessman to a loving husband and dang near-doting father trying to reacquaint himself with a son from whom he distanced himself. For example, a few days ago, he'd called me *Jackson*. When I told him I hated that name and that, "My name is *Jack*, Dad, not *Jackson!*" He'd apologized, telling me he was sorry, but what he was intending to imply is that I am *Jack*, his *son*. I had to admit, that was a twist I'd not ever considered—it made more sense to me now. I have tried to account for the source of my ever-improving opinion of him, but every time I arrive at the same conclusion. Rita has somehow crafted this change in him, every bit of it for the good.

In the last week, we've eaten out just once; the second night here. It was with their neighbor, a high-powered Miami lawyer and his wife. The evening had started out pleasantly enough until the lawyer asked what I did for a living. When I told him we were on our way to Fort Rucker where I was to learn to fly helicopters, he looked at my dad and said, "Geez, Ben, all the money you and Rita make, you'd think he could come down here and work for you."

If he was trying to be funny, he wasn't. The look on his wife's face was a plea to be anywhere besides this suddenly cramped and stuffy restaurant. He had hit a big nerve with all four of us, but my dad was the one who took up the gauntlet. The tense hush that had fallen around the table was broken by the sound of Dad laying down his knife and fork on the edge of his plate. "Roger," he said, steeling his gaze at the lawyer, "I'm not sure you meant to be as crude as that remark sounded, but if you say one more thing about Jack's decision to serve, I will punch you in the face, right here." There . . . *bang!* That was my ol' Dad; the one who once impounded a sheik's yacht in his marina when the sheik told him he'd have to wait for the final payment on the boat. The sheik then headed out with his entourage on a Miami shopping trip. When he returned he found his yacht impounded by the Miami-Dade sheriff's department. An hour later my father had his money and was bidding the sheik a less-than-fond farewell. My father was the master of "scrappy!"

I watched Roger, the lawyer, squirm in his seat for a second. I could feel Annie's hand on my knee signaling me not to do anything rash. I looked at her and nodded before saying, "I don't know why you might object to anyone wanting to serve in the armed forces, but the great thing about this country is you are surely entitled to hold that opinion."

Dad picked up his knife and fork, cut a piece of his steak and said, "So, let's start over, shall we. Roger, Sylvia, this is our son, Jack, and his new bride, Anne. They are on their way to Fort Rucker, Alabama, where Jack will learn to fly helicopters. We have them for ten glorious days and intend to show them a good time."

The lawyer and his wife nodded. She managed to force a smile. Roger looked at the mashed potatoes on his plate as if he wished he could crawl inside of them. The rest of the evening remained awkward. It was good they had driven separately. Any doubts that Dad and Rita would ever dine publicly or privately with these two again were shattered as Rita announced in the car, "Jack, Anne, I . . . we are so sorry. We had no idea he was such . . ." Rita paused, searching for the most socially acceptable word. She smiled demurely at Annie and I, "He's a putz."

The rest of our meals, except for a few light lunches, were taken in the calm, peaceful surroundings of their new home. One night, Dad and Rita cooked; one night, Annie and I made dinner; another, Rita and Annie cooked again and made an exquisite sesame-encrusted tuna every bit as good as the shrimp creole the two of them had made our first night here. Last night, Dad and I made a marinated pork roast, slow cooked over the grill in their outdoor kitchen next to the pool. We would spend time each day trying to find the exact wine to pair with the evening meal along with the perfect bread. We avoided shopping centers, chain stores, and the big grocery chains, instead roaming the back streets of Miami neighborhoods looking for small businesses that often held the biggest surprises. True to their words, if they worked at all while we've been here, neither Annie nor I have seen it. It seems they are with us all the time, and when one of them would wander off—which didn't happen often—we would notice their absence.

At night, in the privacy of our room, Annie and I would talk, mostly about them, about how happy they seemed together, about how different Ben was from the man I'd described to her.

9:00 a.m., June 29, 2006
But now it is time to go. Dad pulls the Mercedes SUV to a stop a few yards from the plane's wingtip. Rita and Annie are teary eyed. Dad and I hug and pat one another on the back, something we've done more of in the last week or so than we had done in the previous decade. Annie and I trade places and I say goodbye

to Rita, and Annie tells Dad what a great time we've had with the two of them. He hugs her and tells her he wants us to promise we will come back— the sooner, the better. He's still dressed like Al Pacino in the movie *Scarface*, but the cold businessman in him seems to have warmed considerably. I am thankful to Rita for the changes she's managed to make in my father.

It is easy to adapt to this kind of elaborate luxury. Annie and I have talked about this quite a bit while we've been down here with them. Early in the visit, Annie felt a pang of conscience. She told me she felt like she was "enjoying this a little too much." On the other hand, I knew full well the things money could provide. I'd benefitted from it my entire life. Over time and through further discussion, we managed to reach the mutual conclusion that while we have enjoyed our time with the two of them tremendously, neither of us envy their lifestyle. One of the things that brought this around to us were the walks we would take around their gated neighborhood, Gables Estates. Beautiful as it may be, what it lacked was humanity. Rarely did we ever see anyone out, except for the variety of laborers who kept things up; carpenters, electricians, painters, gardeners, pool maintenance people, etc. We never saw any of the residents out and about, working in their yards, swimming in their pools, enjoying the beauty of the place they worked so hard to afford. Annie was the one who asked, "What's the point of having all of this, if you don't have the time to enjoy it?"

In reply, I commented, "Dad and Rita seem to enjoy it."

Annie, whose glass is always half full, suddenly became a bit pessimistic. "While we're here. But we don't know what it's like for them when we're not around. You saw what an ass their neighbor is." She was right. I knew full well the kinds of people my dad dealt with when he was making mega-yacht deals. I could only assume Rita's high-end real estate clients were cut from the same overindulged, overentitled swath of America's uppermost socioeconomic strata.

11:30 a.m., June 29, 2006
Danny and Rebecca Miller are waiting for us at Cherry Capital Airport. Pete, Annie's brother, isn't with them. He is at Glen Lake High School participating in a summer conditioning program in order to get ready for freshman football tryouts. He wants to play quarterback.

As we approach the car, Samantha, the Miller's border collie, sees us coming and begins barking. Annie drops my hand, runs to the ancient Jeep Cherokee, and reaches in through the open window to love on her dog.

These next few days are going to be hard on everyone. We . . . Annie and I . . . will be leaving Empire on July 2, and at this point, neither of us know what to say if we are asked the question, "When do you think you'll be able to come home?" It's that word *home* that strikes such a deep chord with both of us. This is where Annie was born and raised. If a town could have DNA, Empire's would run through her. The same is true of me to a certain extent. I've lived here since I was eight.

But more important than the place are the people; and in a few days, we will be leaving them all behind, as if closing the cover of a book we have enjoyed so much but have gotten from it all that we can. Annie will leave behind her brother, who is no longer the pain in her ass he once had been. She will leave behind Sam, her faithful dog. And, she will leave behind her mother and father, who were sometimes uncompromisingly strict; but I know if I were to ask her, she would bear no resentment. She would say she had always felt loved by them.

Then there's the matter of my mother. Thinner, frailer, drinking as much as ever, I have refused to allow her sickness to dictate my existence. But, in the next few days, Annie and I have decided we must carve time out for her, probably in the mid-morning to early afternoon, when she is at her best—after she's had a chance to wake up but before she starts overindulging in the alcohol that will eventually sedate her once again. There will be no shopping excursions or well-thought-out meals prepared together because she rarely leaves the house. What little strength she has, she will reserve for drinking. For the few days we are home, I've given Liz Oxford, her housekeeper, time off. She certainly deserves it, and now that Annie and I are leaving, Liz's responsibilities will become even more important to my mother's tenuous grasp on survival. For these few days, however, Annie and I will keep house for her. In her more sober moments, my mother likes to stand at the wall of windows overlooking the bluff and Lake Michigan below and watch for an eagle—*her eagle,* she calls it—so, we will help her keep watch. We will endeavor to give her comfort as best we can.

My reporting date to Fort Rucker, Alabama, is Monday, July 10. Annie and I will take that first full week of July to find a place to live in one of the towns surrounding the post. A quick map reconnaissance of the area reveals Daleville and Enterprise seem to be the closest. Dothan, Alabama, is a third, but more geographically distant possibility, and we are looking forward to finding our way around as we search for a place to live. And, yes, I am somewhat nervous about July 10. The army is a big institution, impersonal, and from everything I'd come to know about it at this very early stage, it is an institution with very high expectations of its membership, especially its commissioned officer leadership.

In the meantime, we have to walk the fine line between being excited about starting our married life together in the army, and reassuring the Millers that their daughter is in good hands. Empire is still a place we will always call home, a place we know we can always come back to.

PART II

COMPANY-GRADE

Military rank applying to army officers below major as second lieutenant, first lieutenant and captain

10 JULY, 2006–30 OCTOBER, 2012

FIVE

A Warm Southern Reception

12:00 p.m., July 2, 2006

The NetJet's Learjet 60, courtesy of Ben and Rita Rigley, touches down at Dothan Regional Airport and taxis to a parking spot near the terminal. I am fully aware of how extravagant such a luxury as a private jet must appear to folks like Annie's mother and father. But Ben and Rita's gift has allowed Annie and I to enjoy this first month of our marriage in a way we will always remember, lingering in Empire for as long as possible before setting out for Fort Rucker.

Annie and our flight attendant make small talk until we feel the plane rock to a full stop and the pilot turns off the seatbelt sign. We are standing in front of the door as it opens, and as the folding steps deploy, a blast of hot, humid air brings back unpleasant memories of the heat I'd experienced at Fort Knox the previous summer during ROTC summer camp. I thank the two pilots for a pleasant trip. The captain says, "Our operations office sent us a note. You're here for flight training."

"That's right. Rotary wing flight training."

He smiles back at me, "Good luck. They are amazing machines, but a lot different than flying one of these."

I ask, "Are you rotary-wing rated?"

"Naw. Cost me an arm and a leg just to learn how to fly one of these."

I nod knowingly and then follow Annie down the steps to the tarmac.

In front of us, about twenty yards away sits a brand-new, gleaming white Chevy Tahoe. Leaning against the grill is a rather rotund man in a pair of tan gabardine trousers, a white short-sleeve dress shirt with an out-of-date, narrow, red-and-white polka dotted tie pulled down from his bulging neck and over to one side. He's fanning himself with what looks like a folded newspaper until he sees us descend from the airplane, at which point he stops fanning, shoves himself away from the automobile, and waves at us. This is yet another gift from Ben and Rita, one we have not told Danny and Rebecca Miller about. Annie and I wanted to avoid the perception we were rubbing the Millers' noses in the extravagance of Ben and Rita's gifts to us. The Millers paid for our wedding. Their wedding gift was an exquisite, old bird's eye maple dining table and chairs that belonged to Rebecca's parents, a true family heirloom, that had been relegated to the basement of their modest home in Empire. The comparative dollar value weighs heavily in Ben and Rita's favor, but the heartfelt value of the Millers' gifts can't be measured.

Chester Dunwiddy has a deep southern drawl and introduces himself as the owner of Dunwiddy Chevrolet, telling us to just call him *Chet*, how much he appreciates our business, and then adds, "Your Daddy told me I should help you out anyway I can. Tells me you're here for flight school." He extends his hand and I notice a drop of perspiration fall from his elbow. It is hotter than hell. Dunwiddy hands me the keys and says, "Let's get out of this heat. You drive, I'll navigate. We can go back to the dealership. I got one of these on the air-conditioned showroom floor and I can show you all the features under more comfortable conditions than this."

I climb behind the wheel after opening the door on the passenger side for Annie. Dunwiddy gets in the backseat behind me. The car is running, and the air-conditioner is blowing cold air. Annie exclaims, "Oh that feels so good!" She looks over her shoulder at Chet and asks, "Is it always this hot?"

"It is this time of year, ma'am. Welcome to southern Alabama. Likely it's gonna be this way 'til 'bout late September, early October, then it'll cool off a bit. Mr. Rigley tells me y'all from northern Michigan. Bad news is, it'll take you a bit to adjust to this heat and humidity. Good news is, y'all gonna love the winters down here, 'cause there really ain't none . . . least not like the ones y'all are used to." He snorts a laugh.

3:00 p.m., July 2, 2006
Chet Dunwiddy has done exactly what my father asked him to do. The Tahoe is beautiful, but he's also very helpful in guiding two Yankees around. His daughter, Naomi, a sophomore at the University of Alabama who works in the summer months at her "daddy's dealership," has made Annie and I a two-night reservation at the Hilton Garden Inn here in Dothan. Her southern drawl, even deeper than her father's, takes a bit of getting used to.

In chatting Annie up, Chet found out she has an accounting background. "Well, now, Miss Annie, I sell a lot of cars to service people and a lot of those cars are financed with The Army Aviation Center Federal Credit Union. I know they are always lookin' for good people. If you're interested, just let me know.

I'd be happy to put you in contact with the people there." Also, very helpfully, he's given us a list of apartments in the surrounding area that rent to military personnel, and offered some sage advice. "Now listen to me, check your lease over to make sure it's got a military-orders clause in it. Most of these places know if you're here to learn how to fly that you gonna be here for a year and then you're off to who knows where." He waves his arms around for emphasis. "So they's all gonna require a year's lease. If you ain't got that 'military orders clause' in that lease and then you don't," he pauses here ominously, "I mean if you don't succeed at the training, then the army gonna ship you out before that year's lease is up and you'll get stuck with losin' your security deposit. Don't like it that they do a soldier that way, but some of 'em that's what they do. Just make sure that clause is in there. OK?"

I thank him and nod, but Chet's advice makes me consider for the first time the question, *what if I don't make it through the training?* The answer is discomforting! I wouldn't be an aviator. The army could assign me to anything, anywhere. Such a thing would mean I owe the army four years of service and I would not get out of it what I was looking for: aviation maintenance experience. Chet brings me back into reality when he says, "OK, Jack. Let's step over to this new Tahoe right here. It's got exactly the same trim package as yours do. Let me show you how it all works."

About an hour or so later, Annie and I both thank Chet and Naomi profusely. As we head out of the dealership in our new car, we realize neither of us has had a thing to eat since early this morning. I look over at Annie and ask, "Hungry?"

She looks over at me. "Gettin' there." She lets that linger for a minute and then says, her eyes bright, a lilt to her voice, "This is all so exciting, Jack. Let's go check in first. Then maybe we can try that Thai place Naomi suggested." At the Hilton, we aren't in the room more than a couple of minutes before we are in bed. After we make love, we put on our suits and go take a plunge in the pool. It's late afternoon, the heat is abating a little, but the humidity continues to make everything sticky. We lounge in a couple of cheap chaise lounge chairs and soak in the early evening rays of the slowly setting sun before we return to the room and get ready for The Thai House. Annie's right; this feels like the beginning of a great adventure.

SIX

Settling In

6:00 a.m., July 10, 2006

My orders, published by the Department of the Army, were quite specific. Yesterday, I had to sign in at Building 2709 on Fort Rucker. Annie went with me for this. Since it was Sunday, I was prepared for the building to be locked up tight, but it wasn't, and we were greeted by a duty officer who knew exactly why I was there. The entire thing took about five minutes, if that. He gave me a rather thick package and told me to look at the first sheet, The Schedule for Officers Reporting for Aviation Officer Basic Course, 14-2006. Like my experience at Fort Knox, everything seemed to be highly organized. But Fort Knox was more like a boot camp with surly directions, people yelling at you to do this and do that. So far, Fort Rucker was much friendlier.

Annie and I had found a two-bedroom, one bath apartment in Enterprise, Alabama, just a short ride to Fort Rucker's Enterprise entrance. While the extra bedroom is non-essential and makes our monthly rent more expensive, we could not find a one-bedroom place that we liked any better. Our lease agreement contained the appropriate "military orders clause," just as

Chester Dunwiddy had insisted it should. So, if I couldn't pass muster as a helicopter pilot, our thousand-dollar security deposit was fully refundable upon proof of my failure, a prospect that still made me queasy. The bathroom's double-sink vanity is proving to be very utilitarian, as this morning Annie is interviewing for an accounting position with The Army Aviation Center Federal Credit Union. I am a scant two hours away from the official launch of my first day in the army. As I pull the razor across my face, Annie, who is applying eye makeup at the sink next to me, asks, "Nervous?"

I nod and say, "A little. You?"

In her mirror I see her flash that great smile of hers. "Not gonna lie. I think it's only natural. But, you'll do great, Jack. You always do."

I reassure her, "You will too, Annie."

We'd worked the day's transportation arrangements out. It looked like I was going to be all day, so Annie would drop me off at the building designated on the schedule and then pick me up at the same place at five this afternoon. Neither of us had any idea what our routines were going to look like, so we decided we would have to make transportation plans day-by-day until things began to take shape.

7:45 a.m., July 10, 2006

As Annie pulls to a stop in front of Building 315, there is a lot of foot traffic heading inside. She leans over toward me and says, "There's your people, Jack. Go, get 'em."

I give her a smooch on the cheek and say, "See you this evening. Good luck, today." A jolt of adrenaline rolls through me as I open the door and head toward the others. Inside the building, in the spacious lobby, I quickly estimate there are about fifty or sixty of us, a mix of newly minted warrant officer 1s and equally new second lieutenants. I'm so green, I don't even know how to correctly refer to the warrant officers' rank. We are shepherded into an auditorium where we are given courteous, but firm instructions to fill in the center section from the front to the back; don't leave any seat between you and the next person unfilled. I wind up in the center of the fifth row back. As I sit down, I offer a nod and a smile to the person next to me, a female, the only one I've seen up to this point. I'm barely seated before a male takes the seat on the other side of me. I can tell, I am not the only one in the room feeling a bit nervous.

Just as I am thinking, *this is silly. Relax, Jack, you've got this*, the woman extends her hand and says, "I'm Paula, Paula Schlafferty." She has a firm grip.

"Jack Rigley." As I say this, I happen to notice the guy on my left looking our way. So, I take Paula's lead and turn to him and offer, "Hi, I'm Jack, this is Paula."

"Will, Will Offerman."

Will and I shake hands and then Paula reaches across and says, "Nice to meet you both." She follows up with, "First day?"

The question takes me aback a bit and I think, *Like it's not yours, too?* I am not disappointed to hear Will say, "Yep."

To which I quickly add, "Me, too. I don't even know what to call the warrant officers."

Paula leans back in her seat and says, "*Mister*. Most of them have some enlisted time under their belts, but when it comes to flying, they are as new to this stuff as we are. So, sit back and relax, you've got a real treat coming." Her voice is rife with sarcasm.

Will and I look at each other and then I ask, "So, this isn't your first day?"

"Nope. Got here about sixty days ago. I've already been through this crap once. I was supposed to be well into my training by now but had a little hiccup on an EKG. They were ready to send me packin' but I got the CG involved. He saved my ass."

"CG?" Will asks before I have a chance to.

"Commanding General," Paula clarifies and laughs. "Boy, you are new."

If Will is offended, it isn't obvious. He asks, "What'd he do for you?" I'm equally interested in her answer. I may be the new kid on the block here, but I know a bad EKG is a knockout punch most times on a flight physical.

"I had to go all the way to Walter Reed in DC. They did an echocardiogram on me. Ever heard of it?" Both Will and I shake our heads. "Specialized . . . not a part of the regular flight physical. My echo showed a left axis deviation but everything else was OK. Flight surgeon at Walter Reed explained to me that my heart sits at a slightly different angle in my chest than most. It'll show up every time on a routine EKG as out of the normal range, but the fact is, I'm OK. Had to get a waiver from DA to stay in the flight program." Since she'd been a little condescending about Will not knowing what "CG" stood for, I wasn't going to ask what a DA was. Will didn't ask either. Learning to navigate the army's river of acronyms is obviously something that is going to take some time. It wasn't until later that day that I would find out it stood for Department of the Army.

Will asks, "So, if you didn't know anything about this until you went to Walter Reed, how did you convince the CG to go to bat for you?"

"That was easy. I showed him my summa cum laude degree from MIT in mechanical engineering and told him I didn't want to be anything else but an army helicopter pilot. He convinced the chief flight surgeon here to take the extra step." She paused for a moment. "Besides, take a look around. How many females you see here?"

Will and I look around. I comment, "You are definitely in the minority."

Paula responds, "Exactly. So, the CG didn't want to let a precious checkmark on his diversity worksheet get erased."

I'm thinking, *Well, you're pretty jaded for only sixty days in.* It was my distinct impression she'd rather be anywhere else than here right now. So, I ask, "So, you've been through all of this before?"

"Yep, but the student company commander told me I had to be here today, so here I am . . . again."

Will laughs and offers, "Well, welcome back, Paula." She shoots him a snarky smile.

I ask Will, "Where's home for you?"

"Scranton, PA, but I went to school at Cornell. Started out in pre-med but switched to electrical engineering after my freshman year. Didn't have the patience for all that post-grad work. So, I did the two-year ROTC-thing. Asked to be commissioned in aviation, thinking it probably wouldn't ever happen—but look at me now. How 'bout you, Jack?"

"Western Michigan University in Kalamazoo." I could tell immediately this had zero impact on these two ivy leaguers. "Aviation Science." I didn't feel the necessity to add Paula's *summa cum laude* to my abbreviated resume, but I could have.

"You're a rated pilot?" Paula asked.

"Yes, but only in fixed wing . . ." This time I decide to flesh things out a little bit, "multi-engine and instruments."

"By the FAA?" Will asks, some incredulity apparent in his voice.

I nod and add, "Those two ratings are a degree requirement." Somehow, I feel like I have achieved equal footing with these two academic snobs. I begin looking around at the mass that has now pretty much assembled around me. It is then, in the front row, center, I see Ross Haverman. *It can't be . . . not possible.*

Ross Haverman and I aren't archenemies—that would be overstating the facts. We were, however, two very competitive individuals, and I had come out on top of a competition at Fort Knox during ROTC summer training camp. I was the number one cadet in our company. Haverman finished second. There were several things I didn't like about him then and I had little reason to believe anything had changed in the year since I'd seen him last. I found him too loud, too big of a know-it-all, and I could give a good goddam about his father being a retired four-star general. My father was a millionaire, maybe even a billionaire, but that doesn't define me. Genealogy doesn't define anyone—or at least that is what I thought.

I am still thinking, *here we go again, the game is back on,* when we are jolted out of our seats by a booming voice from the back of the auditorium, "ATTEN-SHUN." All of us spring straight up out of our seats, head and eyes pointing straight ahead. Shortly, in my peripheral vision, I see a major general and two colonels walk down the aisle to my left and step onto the stage. The two-star and one of the colonels take seats in chairs prepositioned in front of an array of flags. The other colonel approaches the podium and commands, "AT EASE," and then "take your seats." We spend the next ninety minutes being welcomed to Fort Rucker and initial entry rotary wing flight training. The general is the first to speak. About ten minutes into his remarks, I catch Paula's eyes fluttering open and shut; she is clearly bored out of her gourd.

The general completes his welcoming and congratulatory remarks and excuses himself, explaining he has a busy day ahead and must leave. He assures us we are in "the capable hands of these two gentlemen seated behind me." No command is necessary. We all automatically come to the position of attention as he departs. The same colonel who'd introduced the general returns to the podium and introduces himself as the Garrison Commander. As he talks, I notice Paula's eyes are remaining shut for longer and longer periods of time. By the time the second colonel, who tells us he is the commander of the 145th Aviation Student Brigade, is into his remarks, she has given in to sleep until, from somewhere behind us, a cell phone rings. At this point, Paula's eyes fly open and she leans slightly toward me and says, "Oh, shit. Watch this!"

Cell phones are beginning to proliferate in bigger numbers now. The cost of not only the phones, but also their monthly charges, has started to become much more affordable. My father was still paying for mine, but Annie and I are going to go shopping for one for her in the next few days. They are a miraculous convenience. But this morning they are a curse for one unfortunate person in this room.

The colonel stops mid-sentence as the phone rings yet again. Shaking his head, he looks out over us. I observe a few heads looking from side-to-side. Sternly the colonel commands, "Would the owner of that ringing cell phone, stand up." We'd been warned to mute or turn them off when we arrived. I can't be sure, but I estimate the ring came from two or three rows behind me. Back there I can hear some hushed tones, but I am not going to turn around. The colonel says, "If anyone else isn't sure that you've turned your phone to mute or, better yet, off, check it now." And then he asks the offending phone-owner who is now standing per the colonel's direction, "What's your name Lieutenant?" Paula leans slightly in my direction again and under her breath repeats, "Oh, shit!"

"Lieutenant Wolf. I apologize, sir. I . . . I thought I had . . ."

"You and I should have a conversation about the difference between thinking we did something and being sure we did it. Now, with your permission, may I continue, unless, of course, you think that phone call is more important than anything I might have to say." This brings a modicum of uneasy laughter, none of us fully sure if we should attempt to make light of Lieutenant Wolf's predicament, but all of us glad it's him and not us who have stepped into this unfortunate spotlight. "When I'm finished, we'll have a talk. For now, sit down, Lieutenant Wolf." The room quickly comes back to order as the colonel picks up where he left off.

When the School Brigade Commander completes his remarks, we are brought back to the position of attention. As he's leaving, he stops momentarily at the seventh or eighth row behind me and says, "Lieutenant Wolf, come with me." No one moves their eyes from the straight-ahead position, and I can hear Wolf begin walking to whatever monumental ass chewing he might be facing. When the two of them are gone, a woman in civilian clothes goes to the podium and tells us we have earned a 30-minute break and to please be back in our seats at 10:30 a.m. sharp, adding a final warning, "When you return please ensure your cell phones are on mute or off."

Will, Paula, and I make our way to the lobby and then outside into the bright, sunny, but stultifying humidity and heat of a summer Alabama morning. I had already made up my mind I was not going to seek out Ross Haverman. I figured he would find me and, sure enough, as the three of us stand talking, I hear behind me, "Rigley . . . is that you?"

As many times as I've cringed at my father's schmoozing, I revert to it. "Ross, how are you?"

He rolls up on us and extends his hand. I introduce him to Will and Paula. The three of us notice it at the same time: on his left sleeve just below the shoulder is an olive-green tab with black lettering, RANGER. Will blurts out, "You're a ranger?"

For the next five minutes he regales us with how that very difficult qualification was earned just a week earlier. I am struck by how every sentence begins with *I*, as in *I did this* and *I did that*. He concludes by looking at me and saying, "You should give it a try, Jack. Every regular army officer should go to ranger training."

I am familiar with what it took for him to earn that tab and the first to admit to some surprise. Slots to ranger training are scarce, usually reserved for infantry officers. I jump to the conclusion his father pulled some strings to get him in. At Western, one of our instructors was a ranger. Unlike what I'd just heard from Haverman, Sergeant First Class Krasnowski spoke objectively about the difficulty of the three phases of training. By contrast, there was no poorly disguised braggadocio from Sergeant Krasnowski. In fact, I distinctly recall him emphasizing "getting through the entire nine weeks is as much of a team effort as an individual one." He believed it made him a better soldier and that was all he ever wanted to be. I look at Haverman, shake my head and say, "Yeah, I don't think so, Ross. Let me fly the helicopter. You rangers can jump out of them." He moved on.

5:00 p.m., July 10, 2006
Annie waves as she pulls the Tahoe to a stop in nearly the exact

spot she'd dropped me off earlier this morning. I am loaded down with books, and an olive-green helmet bag that, in addition to the helmet, is so chock full of other equipment that I can't close the bag's zipper. I know what all of it is and how it is used, unlike many of my classmates. I open the rear door on the passenger side and set everything on the backseat and ask, "How was your day?"

"You are looking at one of the newest employees of Fort Rucker Aviation Center Federal Credit Union." She raises her hand and offers me a high five, which I reflexively return. "They hired me as an account manager in receivables. How was your day?"

"You're not going to believe . . ." I cut myself off as I close the door, walk to the front and then slide into the passenger seat. "You remember me telling you about Ross Haverman, the guy I beat out last summer at Fort Knox."

She nods and, as if she were reading my mind, "Don't tell me . . ."

"Yep. He's in my class . . . again . . . and, my first impression from a year ago hasn't changed. He's as obnoxious as ever."

SEVEN

Every Day Is a Test

Initial entry rotary wing flight training in the army is divided into four phases. The first phase, ground school, is the shortest by far at only two weeks. The class has been split into two sections, with about thirty students in each, each section a mix of second lieutenants and warrant officer 1s or, as I've heard them called by more senior warrant officers over the last several weeks, *Wobbly-1s*. There's no flying during ground school. Most of the time we meet in our smaller sections, but sometimes we are thrown together in one large classroom. I am thankful Ross Haverman and I are not in the same section. In fact, I haven't spoken to him since that first day.

In order to move on to Phase Two, you have to pass every exam, all of which are comprehensive and frequent, about two a week. If you fail a ground school exam, you are offered the opportunity to retake it one time and that has to be done before the next exam. A few of my classmates required this "extra opportunity to excel," as our instructors called the retest. All of us made it through, though. For me, it was mostly a rehash of everything I'd studied so diligently as an undergrad at Western Michigan University.

By a stroke of pure coincidence, Will Offerman, Paula Schlafferty, and I are in the same section. We've become close friends along with a few others, and Annie and I socialize with them after school and on weekends. However, while Annie likes the accounting end of her work at the credit union, she has a woman supervisor she does not like. Teasing her when she originally brought this to my attention, I had said, "Remember what you are always telling me, 'don't judge people so quickly.'"

"It's been two weeks, Jack. I'm not the only one who notices it. Two of my co-workers whose husbands are also student pilots have said she doesn't like us because we're only here for a year and then she has to find someone else and train them. She can be downright nasty."

I suggest, "So, report her."

"To who? She's been there over twenty years. She's smart enough to be careful about who's around when she says things to us. They aren't going to let her go. The manager loves her. The other girls and I've talked about it. The money's too good. I'll just ride it out. It's just a damn year!" Annie never swears. "And we'll be gone."

July 24, 2006

Ground school finished last Friday. Now we get down to the nitty-gritty—flying! Phase Two begins today, and with that so does the process of separating the wheat from the chaff. It's ten weeks long. We fly five days out of every seven. It has now become clear why we have been split into two thirty-person sections: half of us fly in the morning and go to class in the afternoon, the other half go to class in the morning and fly in the afternoon. The schedule flip-flops each week. This week, I'm flying in the mornings.

We are at a stage field that's about a twenty-minute flight from Hanchey Army Airfield, Fort Rucker's main heliport. Everyone launches from Hanchey and returns there at the end of each day of flying. But the early part of this initial phase of training takes place at stage fields like this one. Each one is like a mini-airfield with landing pads, control towers, fuel trucks, fire trucks, etc. This has been my first flight in a helicopter. The instructor pilot, or IP, did all of the flying. I am sitting in the right seat. He is in the left seat across the center console from me. In the jump seat immediately behind the console is my stick buddy. Today, I will fly the first session, we will refuel, and he will fly the second session. Both of us have already been trained in the preflight inspection and startup procedures. Today is our first crack at the three controls that actually make the helicopter fly: the cyclic, the collective, and the anti-torque pedals. The goal today is to learn how to hover, defined as holding the helicopter over a spot on the ground for an extended period of time. I've watched the IP do this several times as he's explained to both of us what he's doing. He picks the helicopter up off the ground smoothly and establishes it in a hover. Then he says, "OK, Lieutenant Rigley, I want you to put your right hand on the cyclic." As I move my hand toward the control in front of me that sticks up between my legs from the floor of the helicopter, he cautions, "The cyclic is very sensitive. Handle it very gently. Small movements." Within ten seconds of him handing me that one single control, the helicopter has moved fifty feet to my right, and we are increasing speed with every foot we move. I try to bring the cyclic left but input too much correction. At this point, I'm gripping the control as if it were a chicken I'm trying to choke to death. The instructor pilot calmly says, "I've got the controls."

I acknowledge, "You've got the controls," and within a matter of a second or two we are at a stable hover over one spot on the ground.

Patiently he says, "OK, see what I mean about sensitivity? Look at me and notice how very little the cyclic needs to move." Almost imperceptibly he moves the cyclic to the left and the helicopter responds by moving to the left. Then, again imperceptibly, he moves it back to the right and brings us to a hover over the original spot. "Let's try it again. You've got the cyclic." This time I manage to go approximately twenty seconds before he says, "I've got the controls," as we careen from left to right.

There's no getting past my disappointment in myself. I'm sitting at the kitchen table holding my head in my hands when Annie arrives home from work. She gives me a kiss and then asks, "So, how was it today?"

I tell her, "I spent two hours today just trying to hover."

Looking for more, she asks, "And?"

"It's hard, Annie . . . completely different from anything I've ever flown. The controls are super-sensitive. Just the slightest move of one necessitates a correction in the other."

"How many controls are we talking about here?" she asks.

"Three. There's a cyclic that controls forward, aft, left, and right movement. A collective that provides lift. And then there's the pedals controlling the tail rotor. If you raise the collective even a little bit, there's a pedal correction you have to make, and while you're doing that the cyclic wants to drift one way or the other."

"Sounds like a lot." All I can do is nod. Sensing my frustration, she says, "C'mon, Jack. It's your first day . . . how'd everyone else do?"

Truth of the matter is, no one got up to a three-foot hover and held the helicopter over a spot on the ground for more than a few seconds. So, while Annie doesn't know it, she's helped me put everything in perspective. I get up, give her a hug and say, "We all pretty much sucked today."

August 4, 2006
Phase Two is all about the fundamentals of flying a helicopter, a TH-67 to be exact. We were told we should solo somewhere around sixteen hours of flight time. I have completed a full twelve hours of flying in the TH-67. I am at the controls as we land at the stage field and taxi off the Maltese cross to a parking area. From there we will drop off my stick buddy and the IP and I will continue our flight session. As the other student pilot is getting out of the aircraft, the IP tells me, "OK, Lieutenant, the aircraft is yours. You're going to solo today. I'd like for you to take off, and then perform three takeoffs and landings before bringing the aircraft back here and shut it down."

The adrenaline bolts through me. "Yes, Chief," I manage to say as he unbuckles his seat belt and climbs out of the aircraft. When he's clear of the spinning rotor blades, he stops, turns to me and gives me a thumbs up. I think to myself, *OK, Rigley, don't fuck this up!* Our stage field is named Stage Field Stanley after a warrant officer helicopter pilot killed in Vietnam and awarded the Congressional Medal of Honor. I key the UHF radio and say, "Stanley Tower, Army Three Niner Six at Parking 5, request clearance for taxi to take off."

"Army Three Niner Six, Stanley Tower, cleared to taxi to the Maltese. Call for takeoff clearance."

"Three Niner Six, Roger." I pick the aircraft up to a hover and taxi as directed. "Three Niner Six on the Maltese for takeoff."

"Three Niner Six, Roger. Winds two-seven-zero at ten, altimeter two-niner-niner-eight. Cleared for takeoff and three laps around the traffic pattern. Congratulations, you're the first to solo in your section. Call base to final."

"Three Niner Six, Roger, altimeter two-niner-niner-eight, cleared for takeoff and thank you." I check to ensure my altimeter is set correctly, ease the cyclic forward, and within a few seconds feel the blades bite into the wind; the nose dips slightly and then comes up as the helicopter transitions smoothly through translational lift into full flight. I had felt a sense of accomplishment when I first soloed in a fixed wing, but today there's a greater sense of that. These machines are so much more complicated than anything I'd ever flown. TGIF!

Schlafferty would manage to solo the next Tuesday, Offerman on Wednesday.

August 10, 2006
We are flying in the afternoons this week, which means we have classroom instruction in the morning. We are about midway through the class on how the bleed-air system on the TH-67 helicopter works, when a captain none of us have ever seen before comes in the classroom and announces he is from the student brigade headquarters. He wants to see two of our classmates in the hallway. The instructor drops his head as if he knows what this interruption purports. The rest of us are clueless, except that all of us know these two underwent what is called a "proficiency check ride" earlier this week. The scuttlebutt on these proficiency rides is that they rarely end in a satisfactory performance. Two minutes later, the two return to the classroom, their glum

expressions telegraphing to all of us what is happening. They each pick up their notebooks, books, pens, pencils, etc., and leave. Once they are gone, our instructor says, "I wish the school would figure out a better way to handle these things. It's almost like a perp walk." We never saw either of our classmates again.

I get home around six-thirty in the evening when we are flying the afternoon schedule. Typically Annie has something she is preparing for dinner. But not this evening. "Jack let's go out to eat. I'm in no mood to cook. Sorry."

"I take it you didn't have a good day."

"Today was my turn in the barrel with the bitch." Annie is rarely profane, and when she is, it is usually of a humorous nature. But I know who "the bitch" is and I know there is absolutely no humor associated with her. "The bitch" is Annie's supervisor at the credit union.

"Tell me about it, and then I've got some news as well."

"I have a client that is two days overdue on a loan payment. Our policy manual says I have no action required until the payment is two weeks past due. Then I call and ask if we can expect payment or make some other arrangement. But the bitch insists I call him today. I've learned not to argue with her. So, I call, and the gentleman says the check is in the mail. I record this in the notes section of his computerized loan file, and it doesn't take her but a minute to stand in front of my desk directing me to immediately file a late payment notification in his credit report."

"Wow, remind me never to be late on a loan payment," I say.

"Well, it doesn't need to happen that way, but the bitch says, 'look at his file, Anne. He was late six months ago. You've got to learn to stay on top of these farmers around here or they'll take advantage of us every time.' You know what's so ironic about that statement, Jack?" I shake my head. "Her husband's a farmer.

They own a big chicken farm just out of town. Can you believe that!"

I shake my head and tell her I can't, and that I'm sorry she had a bad day, then I proceed to tell her about the two classmates who were dismissed from training today—permanently.

We both quickly agree that Thai food sounds good to both of us, so we head to the Thai place in Dothan we'd found on our first night here. As our dinner arrives, I look up to see Ross Haverman and a woman enter. Just as I am about to look away, he spots us and beats a path toward our table. *Shit! And now a bad day gets worse.*

"Jack, how's it goin' man?"

I shake his outstretched hand and introduce him to Anne. I don't want him calling her *Annie*. He, in turn, introduces me to his wife, Elizabeth. "May we join you?" he asks.

I know what I want to say. *No, Ross. We've both had a bad day and you'll only make it worse.* Instead, Annie says, "Sure."

Liz, as Ross calls her, has a distinct southern drawl. She asks Annie, "So, what do you think of Alabama?" It's the way she says *Alabama* that tells Annie and me she sees a distinction between it and whatever part of the south she might be from.

Annie buries the events of the day and simply responds, "No complaints so far."

Liz curls her lip. "Well, I'm from Atlanta. Whatever do you find to do with yourself all day, in this godforsaken part of the country?"

"I work at Fort Rucker Federal Credit Union . . ."

A stricken look on her face, Liz interrupts, "Oh, you're working. I'm so glad I don't have to do that."

I smile at Annie as if to say, *So, what do you think? Have I been too critical of Ross? How 'bout his wife?*

Annie keeps her composure, but asks, "What do you do with yourself all day then while these guys are out flying?"

"Oh, there's a group of us women, some of them permanent party here at Rucker . . ."

Annie, who's never been afraid to admit her lack of experience with the military, breaks in, "Permanent party?"

A patronizing look breaks over Liz's face, "They are assigned here, rather than TDY." I was glad Annie knew that TDY meant Temporary Duty. Liz continues, "But there's a few student wives in this little group, too. We play tennis, golf, bridge . . . just socialize. It's good for Ross's career. Some of the wives are married to majors, lieutenant colonels, colonels—you know, the kind of connections that might be helpful in the future."

As the evening wears on, we learn Liz is the daughter of a retired air force colonel who flew fighters. She and Haverman met during Ross's senior year at The Citadel when Liz was a senior at Furman. Her major was theater arts, but from her comments, it seems what she'd really studied was How to Land a "Citadel-man"—her words, not mine.

Of personal interest, I was able to learn Haverman didn't solo until sixteen hours of flight time. *Pretty average for a Citadel-man,* I thought, my disdain for these two growing by the minute.

There was no lingering after dinner to engage in conversation. I couldn't wait to get away from these two, and I was pretty sure Annie felt the same. We'd no sooner gotten in the car for the trip back to our apartment when Annie piped up, her anger apparent, "Can you believe her?" I only nodded. "They are perfect for one another."

I looked over at Annie with a smile, "You think so?"

"Hell yes. She's more into his career than he is." Annie shakes her head, "Golf, tennis, bridge, contacts, connections, helpful in the future. Geez, I thought I was going to gag! If I never see either one of them again, it will be too soon."

With my hands at ten and two on the steering wheel, my eyes glued to the road ahead, I sarcastically ask, "So, would you like to play golf tomorrow?" Annie, who's never played a single hole of golf in her life, who leaves the room if I allow the television to linger for even a moment on golf, erupts into laughter. I give her a sideways glance, "What's so funny?" She laughs even harder.

September 11, 2006
My classmates and I have all become proficient in handling the helicopter in the basic maneuvers required for operation under visual flight rules—in other words, when the weather is normal, one can see the horizon, it isn't rainy, cloudy, etc. Now we have to learn how to manage flight under less than optimal conditions. Phase Three, instrument flight training, begins today. My instructor pilot, IP, is Chief Warrant Officer Five Lathrop. My initial assessment of him: *crusty*. This phase I am paired up with Gerald Bosterman, a student pilot in my section. I know who he is, but we aren't friends per se, and I've never flown with him. But, I expect by the time we have completed this next eight weeks, we will be well acquainted.

We are about to begin our preflight briefing when Lathrop directs, "Lieutenant Bosterman, take a break. I'll start with you Lieutenant Rigley." Bosterman wanders off toward the break area and I sit down at the table opposite Lathrop. "Lieutenant Rigley, I see you're already fixed wing and instrument qualified."

I almost interject, "and multi-engine qualified, too," but catch myself, realizing that means absolutely nothing here in rotary wing flight training. So, I nod and respond, "That's right, Mr. Lathrop."

He holds up a hand and says, "Call me, *Chief.*"

Ummm . . . maybe not as crusty as I thought. I respond, "OK, Chief."

"I don't think I have to tell you, you're one of the better students in this class." It's flattering, but I suspect he isn't having this conversation to flatter me.

I don't respond with anything more than a shrug and, "There's still a lot to learn, Chief."

He gives me a hard stare. "You're right. This is the phase of training where we lose the most students." Chief Lathrop just confirmed the rumors all of us students have heard. This is the toughest part of our training. He continues, "Flying a helicopter under instrument conditions isn't anything like flying a fixed wing under instruments. There's no such thing as an autopilot in a TH-67, or any other helicopter for that matter. It's all about control touch, getting the radio procedures down right, cross-checking the instrumentation, making the necessary control adjustments with a greater precision than you are used to. Under instrument conditions you must perform flawlessly in a helicopter, otherwise people will be killed. Understand?"

"Yes, Chief. Got it."

"OK, so here's the deal. Lieutenant Bosterman . . ." he pauses ominously. "Well, let's just say that Bosterman's not as good a flyer as you. He struggled a little in Phase Two. But, as I said, it's going to get harder this phase. The two of you have been paired up." Again he pauses, but then seems to soften a bit, shrugs his shoulders and spits out, "I expect you to help Bosterman shore up his skill sets."

I had done this kind of thing before in my army training at Fort Knox and ROTC summer camp. Our platoon evaluator, a major, had paired me with a female cadet, Ruth Zeller, during our day and night land navigation training. It was a must-pass part of the summer's training and Zeller, crackerjack smart, a pre-med student at Boston College, was struggling. The major didn't tell me why he was pairing me with Zeller, he just did. And we both successfully got through the day and night land navigation courses. It wasn't until the last day of camp when the major finally told me why he put me with her. "I was curious to see how you'd handle the challenge. You didn't just tell her to follow you, Jack. You taught her how to think, how to use the compass and the map. So that approach to leadership is why you are the top cadet in the company and Haverman is second. He was given the same challenge with another cadet who was struggling. They both got through, but the struggling cadet told me Haverman told him to just follow him. There was no teaching, just a sheep following the shepherd."

I must admit, what Chief Lathrop is expecting of me is a bit daunting. My skills at flying one of these machines, while they might be better than Bosterman's, are still developing. I stammer, "I'll try, Chief, but . . ."

Lathrop, who has probably detected the tentativeness in my voice says, "Listen, I'm still the responsible party for getting you and Bosterman through this training, but I've been at this a long time and I know he's going to need every bit of help and encouragement you and I can give him to make it through."

I'm reminded of what Sergeant First Class Krasnowski, the army ranger I knew from my college ROTC days, had said to me. *Ranger training is as much a team effort as an individual one.* I look at Lathrop and say, "I'll do what I can."

"That's all that can be asked, Lieutenant. I'll tell you where I think he can use the help. But my guess is you are already a good enough pilot that you'll see it too."

"OK, Chief."

"The other thing I want you to know is I'm going to tell Bosterman what I've asked you to do and why. Again, my experience tells me it's best if he knows where he stands and knows help is available. It'll be up to Bosterman to step up and take advantage."

In this instrument phase of our training we will receive twenty hours of actual flight time in a TH-67 helicopter, all of it flying the aircraft under a hood, which restricts our vision to only our dashboard, or we will fly in actual instrument conditions. There will also be an additional thirty hours in a flight simulator. The classroom portion of Phase Three will also be more difficult. While there are always "rules of the road" when flying, those rules double or triple in number when flying under instrument flight rules, or IFR. My advantage: I had to learn the rules as part of my FAA fixed-wing instrument certification. Now they are second nature to me. A second advantage emerges from the first one: my familiarity with the procedures will allow me to concentrate more on just flying the helicopter.

September 13, 2006
Gerald Bosterman is at the controls. A hood is attached to his flight helmet limiting his vision only to the instrument panel in front of him. After his fourth attempt to pick the aircraft up to hover and execute an instrument takeoff, the tower directs, "Army three-seven-niner, there are four aircraft behind you. Please clear the Maltese," referring to the Maltese cross painted on the runway.

Lathrop, some frustration evident in his voice, replies, "Hanchey Tower, Army three-seven-niner, Roger." He then grabs the cyclic and collective, puts his feet on the pedals and snarls, "I've got the aircraft."

Gerald responds, "You've got the controls," and moves his hands and feet away.

Lathrop nudges the cyclic forward and the helicopter smoothly moves through translational lift, beginning to climb to altitude. I'm not sure what would come next and honestly I am surprised when Lathrop tries to be reassuring. "OK, we've got to work on those, but you've got to lighten up on the controls there, Lieutenant. You're choking the shit out of them. Light touch . . . light touch." It does little to quell Gerald's nerves.

I am sitting in the jump seat located just aft of the center console between the pilot and copilot. I am able to see Gerald's tentativeness, his death grip on the controls; his flight suit's shirt is soaked with perspiration. As the flight period went on, I could hear Lathrop losing patience with his student—and the frustration in Bosterman's voice—as he continues to veer too far off the assigned heading or altitude, miss a mandatory radio call, and take too much time in finding the information necessary for an upcoming instrument approach. I haven't flown with Chief Lathrop before, so I didn't know for sure what constitutes an unsatisfactory ride, but I am pretty sure I am witnessing one right in front of my very own eyes. I wonder if I can help Bosterman as Lathrop has asked.

Gerald and I switch places after refueling and I become the pilot under the hood. It takes me two tries to execute an instrument takeoff from the ground. My instrument cross-check is a little rusty because I have not flown instruments for a while, but as the flight period goes on, it becomes easier for me. An instrument cross-check is simply the pilot moving his eyes around an array of about five instruments on the dashboard. These instruments tell him exactly what the aircraft is doing. The pilot must then translate that knowledge into control movements that will correct any errors in altitude, heading, airspeed, rate of turn, etc. A good cross-check should only take five to seven seconds. My advantage is that I am already quite familiar with the procedures, the flight manuals, the protocols of IFR, and flight itself. So, all I have to do is concentrate on knocking off the rust on my cross-check.

As a matter of routine, we each sit through the other's post-flight debriefing. Lathrop is tough on Gerald and it is little surprise when Gerald gets a pink slip for his unsatisfactory performance today. As he and I are walking out of flight ops, his head is down. "I'm never going to be able to do this."

I try to reassure him. "Instrument takeoffs are tough. Neither one of us did them very well today."

"C'mon, Jack. You know as well as I do, it's not just the ITOs. It's every damn thing, from flying the helicopter, to working the radios, to cross-checking all the instruments. Lathrop's not the most patient guy either."

"Yeah, well, it's not just Lathrop. I overheard some of the other debriefings today. Doesn't sound like anyone's getting cut much slack. I looked around and yours wasn't the only pink slip given out today." We walk a few more yards toward the parking lot. "Listen, Gerald, why don't you and your wife plan on coming over to our apartment this Friday. We'll have dinner. Afterwards, I've got an idea. I think it might help both of us." He doesn't respond immediately, so I say, "Listen, man, we're all in this together. What do you have to lose?"

Friday evening, September 15, 2006
Dinner at our apartment has now grown from four to six.

Yesterday, Will Offerman and Paula Schlafferty came to me after flying and reported getting their first pink slips of this phase. Schlafferty brings garlic toast, Will brings two bottles of white wine, and the Bostermans bring two bottles of chianti. Annie's made a big batch of lasagna and we sit around the table talking mostly about flight training. Compared to my flight training in fixed wing aircraft in college, the army's helicopter flight training is much more intense, and it has consumed all of our lives, including those of our wives.

After dinner, the wives clean up while I pull back the area rug in our living room and place two dining room chairs side by side. I take two toilet plungers and stick them to the floor, one in front of each chair. I then tell Will and Paula, "OK, you two are first. Paula, you're the pilot; Will, you're the copilot," and hand each one a broom. "The plunger's your cyclic, this broom is your collective. Get in the cockpit." I point to the two chairs. They look at me like I'm crazy. So does Gerald. "Yeah, yeah, I know what you're thinking. This isn't going to work for control touch, but you need to practice the procedural stuff with something resembling the controls in your hands. Once you get the procedural stuff down pat, the control touch will come along." I can see the skepticism on their faces. But, I've talked this idea over with my instructor pilot, Chief Lathrop. We both think it might help. I play the part of ground control, tower, air traffic control, and IP. I tell them, "This procedural stuff is best learned by doing it over and over again. So, you're going to hate me before we're done with this, but we are going to do it until you can make these radio calls and run through these emergency procedures in your sleep. The goal is no more pink slips. Let's get started. We're taking off out of Hanchey Airfield. Paula, what's your first radio call?"

"I call for my IFR clearance."

"OK, tell me the frequency you should use and then make the call."

She looks down at her plunger stuck to the floor and, then, at the broom she's holding in her left hand and gives me a smirk. "Rigley, you're nuts!"

"So, I've been told. Now tell me the freq. What's the radio call sound like?"

"I call Hanchey ground control on 129.95."

"Do it," I say.

"Hanchey ground," she pauses for a moment. "What's my tail number?"

"Whatever you want it to be."

Hanchey ground, Army 1-2-3-4-5, request IFR clearance to MGM." MGM is the airport identifier code for the municipal airport in Montgomery, Alabama, a frequent destination for our IFR flights. Strapped around Paula's left leg is a metal pilot's kneeboard with note paper. She must write down the pertinent information Hanchey ground control will give her regarding her IFR clearance.

Now it's my turn as I play the part of Hanchey ground control, "Roger, Army 1-2-3-4-5 is cleared as filed to MGM. After takeoff, climb and maintain Flight Level 60. Contact Hanchey departure control on 126.1 after takeoff. Squawk 0204. Read back."

Paula must read this back almost exactly as I have given it to her, but she fails to include the transponder code she is supposed to *squawk*. Transponders are radios that emit a signal, also called a squawk code, which can be used by air traffic control to easily identify and track aircraft on radar. It is an important miss on her part. I tell her the critical mistake she's made and then tell her, "OK, so let's take it from the beginning. Call again for your IFR clearance. We're going to do this until we get it right." I offer her a tip I'd learned in college. "Write down the word CRAFT on your kneeboard like this," and I show her.

C MGM
R
A
F 126.1
T

Then I tell her, "The C stands for *cleared to,* the R, *route,* the A is for *altitude,* the F, *frequency,* and T is for *transponder code.* This is the information air traffic control is going to give you when you ask for your instrument flight clearance and it is the order in which they will give it to you. So, to save time as they are giving you this information you can fill in certain stuff in advance. For example, you expect to be cleared to Montgomery as filed, right?"

Schlafferty says, "Yes."

So, I write the letters MGM next to the letter C but then warn her, "It's rare, but sometimes you won't be cleared exactly as you've filed, so you need to listen carefully for any changes to your clearance. "Got it?" Paula nods. "OK, then the F is going to be Hanchey departure control's UHF frequency. That's almost always a constant 126.1." So, I write that next to the letter F. I explain to the three of them, "This way you will only have to fill in the information for route, altitude, and transponder code. If you miss something or aren't sure, ask ground control for clarification. They would rather you ask them to be sure you've got it right instead of reading back an incorrect clearance." I look at all three of them and ask, "Got it"

Bosterman, Schlafferty and Offerman all say, "Yes." And for the next hour or so, Will Offerman and Paula fly around our living room. I watch their movements with the plunger, the broomstick and their feet on simulated foot pedals to be sure their control inputs are correct. I tell them where they are and then wait for the appropriate radio call from them. If necessary, we "stop" the flight and I critique them. They shoot a simulated instrument landing system approach into Montgomery, Alabama's, airport.

The wives pop in from the kitchen in between flights. We all relax and have another glass of wine. I point to Gerald and Will and tell them they are next. "Will, you're the pilot; Gerald you're copilot."

Will starts to whine, but Paula tells him, pointing to her glass, "Stop it, Offerman. This is the only wine allowed around here." It gets a good laugh, as do the pictures Annie takes with her cell phone. They do look ridiculous sitting on kitchen chairs holding onto a plunger and a broomstick. It's after midnight before we conclude the final "flight" of the night. We're all tired, but I tell them, "We fly in the mornings next week, so plan on Monday, Wednesday, and Friday afternoons after class. Right here. More of the same." The three of them look at me as if I'm a slave driver.

One month later, October 15, 2006
Will Offerman had a progress evaluation ride today after getting his third pink slip for this phase yesterday. As he walks into the debriefing room with an IP I have not seen before, he looks at me, shakes his head and looks away. Gerald and I wait for him in the parking lot after our own debriefings. Offerman isn't the first in our section to wash out; there has been one other before him, but he is the first of my close friends to pay the price. Will sees us waiting for him and we watch his head drop. I'm sure he'd prefer not to talk about this, but I won't let him off the hook. I ask, "What happened?"

"Sorry, Jack."

"Hey, buddy. No apologies necessary. Tell me what happened."

"I screwed the pooch." Gerald and I just stand there. "Stunk up the instrument takeoff and things went downhill from there. Even I'd flunk me on that ride."

I look at Gerald and say, "How 'bout we scrap the living room runway stuff for tonight?" I turn my attention to my good friend. "You're comin' home with me, Will Offerman." Turning back to Bosterman I say, "Go get Denise. I'll call Schlafferty. We'll get some takeout from Blue Agave . . ."

"Jack, you don't need to . . ." there's a pause.

Gerald pipes up, "You're not goin' home to just sit around and mope about this, Will. Go with Jack." Bosterman looks at me and says, "I'll bring the beer."

I nod and lead Will to my car.

November 20, 2006

Things have moved slowly for Will Offerman over the past month. I've talked to him on the phone almost every day since he's been dropped from training, but today was different. His mood was upbeat. He suggested everyone get together tonight and he'd tell us what was going to happen to him. We're flying afternoons this week. I'll be tired tonight by the time I get home as will Gerald and Paula, but I give in to my friend's newfound exuberance.

Annie and I host everyone at our apartment with takeout from Smokin' Bones BBQ and Blue Agave Mexican restaurant. At about 7:00 p.m., there's a knock on our door, and I pull Will into the apartment. Annie; Gerald's wife, Denise; and Paula line up for hugs. Gerald offers a handshake that collapses into a hug. "Gonna miss ya' man," he says softly over Will's shoulder.

"Me, too, Gerald," Will replies, but then a smile breaks out all over his face. "But, it looks like I'm gonna come out of all this smellin' like a rose."

I blurt out, "You got orders!"

"I did." He looks at Paula Schlafferty. "The CG helped me out."

Paula blurts out, "No shit, Will," and then casts a sheepish look toward Annie and Denise. "Sorry, ladies." We all chuckle.

Annie shrugs, "Heard worse."

Denise asks, "What happened?"

"I dunno exactly, but I guess General McKenzie looks over the file of everyone that washes out. The school brigade commander told me the CG saw I was an electrical engineer and made a couple of phone calls. I'm being reassigned just up the road, Redstone Arsenal, in Huntsville."

I ask, "Any idea what you're going to be doing up there?"

He looks at me and then at Gerald and Paula, "I got one word for you helicopter studs and studette: *drones.*"

EIGHT

The Holidays

December 22, 2006

The thing about army schools is that they close for the holidays just like any other school would. Annie and I fly home, arriving just as a near blizzard is moving in. Danny and Rebecca Miller meet us at the airport and the trip to Empire takes twice as long as usual as the snow is pounding down.

We stay at the Millers even though my mom's lake house has an abundance of big bedrooms, nearly all with a view of the lake. In the days following the storm, the view over the pine trees on the dune between the house and the lake is dazzling, with the pine boughs bending under the weight of the heavy snowfall. But even though I am prepared for the worst, what we find at my mother's house is even beyond that. She is thin and frail. They say you notice changes in people more when you only see them infrequently. I try to allow for that in this case, but still—she is so thin. While the house is in reasonably good order, Annie and I agree, we are unable to remember her looking this bad. It's midafternoon, she is up, but still in pajamas and a clean, but well-worn chenille housecoat. In her hand is a half-empty glass of a clear liquid whose faint odor betrays it as vodka. She is happy to see us, but her words are slurred, and as we walk from the front door into the main part of the house, she stumbles. I wonder, *how long can she survive?* At one point, I see Annie looking at her and then wiping a tear away. We stay for two hours that first day and as we are leaving, I tell Liz Oxford, the cleaning lady I had found over four years ago, how thankful I am for the steadfast care she has given to my mother.

"Mr. Jack, can we talk?"

There is a gravity to her tone. From the expression on Annie's face, I can tell she hears it as well. I say, "Sure, Liz."

"There's a couple of things . . ." She pauses and then gets to her point, "My husband retired last year. He wants to do some traveling."

This isn't good news. Liz Oxford is the closest thing to irreplaceable that I am able to think of. "I see. So, you're thinking about retiring, too?"

Liz nods, "Yes, sir. I am. We are thinking we might want to go south for a few months this winter after the New Year, maybe February and March. That'll give you some time to find someone else to . . ." She takes a moment to choose her words carefully. "Mr. Jack, your mother is going to need some skilled nursing care soon. I can't get her to go to the doctor. She won't go. The party store in town delivers her liquor. I've had words with the owner, but he's a businessman . . . she's one of his best customers . . . well, you know the rest. It's made her incontinent, Mr. Jack; terribly so. She never leaves the house now for fear she'll . . . she wears Depends all the time and I have to change the bed linens almost daily. I've replaced her mattress two or three times just since you left for the army. It gets stained and smelly. I just let your dad know and he orders a new one and has it delivered."

"So, Dad knows how bad she is?"

"I don't know if he knows exactly how bad she is. I haven't told him exactly. It's hard for me to put it into words; but you're here now—you see. Your dad's been great. Whatever I tell him I need, he takes care of it."

I can't get angry with my father, especially after his reformation. Instead, I think, *he's paying the bills.* I've stopped blaming him for my mother's addiction. It wasn't his fault any more than it is my fault my mother has become a drunk. "OK, Liz. I'll call Dad. We'll talk about this. I'll let him know we have to find someone by the middle of January. Can I count on you until the end of January? I'm not sure we can ever find someone like you, and even if we come close, I would like for you to work with them for a couple of weeks before you head south. Would that work for you?"

"Yes, Mr. Jack. I'm so sorry to leave you and your dad in a lurch like—"

I put a hand on her arm. "Liz, you're not. You and your husband have earned your retirement. I'm happy for the both of you."

She paws away a tear. "Thank you, Mr. Jack. You're a good man, like your father."

I thank her again, tell her I'll be in touch and let her know what my father and I work out. I can tell she's grateful, but I am more so. She's been a true friend to our family. Quite honestly, I don't know what my mother would have done without Liz Oxford keeping an eye on her.

Saturday, December 23, 2006
I call my father's cell phone and Rita answers on the fifth or sixth ring. "Hey, Jack, it's Rita. Your dad's in the pool swimming laps."

I glance at my watch. It's one o'clock in the afternoon. I think, *he's swimming laps. Wow!* "You need him right now or can I have him call you?"

"No, just have him call."

Wednesday, December 27, 2006

Annie's brother, Pete, and I are playing a video game when my cell phone rings. It's my father. "Jack, got a minute?"

Pete was beating me like a drum. I am happy for the break. I hold up an index finger in Pete's direction and say, "Gotta take this." He offers to pause the game. I tell him he's too good; I forfeit. In Annie's old bedroom now, I close the door and say, "What's up, Dad?"

"Listen, Jack, Rita has been able to line up three home health care companies. How long are you going to be in Empire?"

"We fly back on New Year's Day. I gotta be back on the flight line on the second. Why?"

"I hate to do this to you, but each company has identified a candidate. Rita thought it best if one of us actually talks face-to-face with whoever's gonna take over for Liz. Since you're right there . . . well, I'm hoping you could do this. One candidate is scheduled for nine tomorrow, another for noon, and the third one is at three.

Our schedule is relaxed now that Christmas is over. We'd talked about a walk on the snow-covered beach, maybe using snowshoes, but nothing much beyond that. Without consulting Annie, I offer, "It's not asking too much. Happy to do it, but home healthcare . . . that's going to be a lot more expensive than Liz, isn't it?"

There's a pause and then Dad says, "Listen, Jack. Rita talked to Liz yesterday. Both of them think your mother's going to need some skilled nursing care, if not right now, then sometime in the near future. Rita thinks we should just get that ball rolling right now. Don't worry about the cost. We've got that."

January 1, 2007

Annie, Pete, Danny, Rebecca, and I rang in the New Year last night in a rather subdued celebration at the Miller house. We leave today. At the airport, it's a tearful goodbye between Annie and her mom. Danny and I shake hands; for now, at least, he's apparently resigned himself to my military service. As we settle into our seats on the airplane, I ask Annie, "You OK?"

She smiles and nods. "Mom wants to know if there's anything they can do to help out with your mom. I told her I'd let her know, but for now everything seems to be under control. I explained about the nurse. She thinks that's a good thing to do, Jack. She hasn't seen your mom, but she has talked to Liz occasionally. Apparently they run into one another around town."

I shrug my shoulders. "I wish she'd stop drinking, but honestly, I don't see that happening."

We feel the plane push back from the jetport and taxi for takeoff. Annie grabs hold of my hand as the pilot throttles up, releases the brakes, and the plane rolls to takeoff speed. We aren't in the air more than a few minutes before I feel Annie's head resting on my shoulder as she dozes off. I am ready to return to training, but I can't help but think this might have been the last time I'd ever see my mother alive. It's a sobering thought.

NINE

For the Good of the Service

P hase Four of our flight training is where we learn the techniques of flying a helicopter under combat conditions as scout pilots in an OH-58C. This is where I learned flying helicopters in the army isn't for the faint of heart. For the first eight to ten hours of training in this phase we learned the challenges of flying nap-of-the-earth, which is to say we were seldom over one hundred feet above the ground. Then things got even more challenging. The army's tactical doctrine is simple: the army that can prevail at night is the army that will win. After we became proficient at flying nap-of-the-earth during the day, we donned night vision goggles, or NVGs, and learned how to do it at night.

The technology surrounding night vision goggles can be compared to that of cell phones, in that it is constantly getting better. However, night flying using these things is dangerous. For me, the lack of depth perception was an immediate problem that required adapting to. The nearest comparison I can draw is that print on your car's outside rearview mirror saying, "Objects in the mirror are closer than they appear." That just begins to describe the challenge with NVGs. Not only is there a problem distinguishing how close or far objects are in front or behind you, in flight you also have the vertical dimension to take into consideration. So, "exactly how high am I above the ground" is the constant question. The tendency is to slow down. But the danger of doing that in combat is the helicopter then becomes an easier target to hit. Suffice it to say, I was scared shitless when I first began to learn the techniques of flying with NVGs. My IP, a veteran pilot of tours in both Afghanistan and Iraq, told me that was OK. "You'll get over the fear as your skill develops, but never lose your respect for the danger of flying with these things on."

This phase also brought on the first real challenge in Annie's and my marriage.

"Jack, I hate this schedule you are on. How much of this is there going to be?"

Annie hit me with this just as I walked in our apartment. I was mentally and physically worn out from the night's flight. Rather unpleasantly, I respond, "Jesus, Annie, there's going to be at least another two weeks. You got some better idea of how I'm going to learn how to fly at night?"

It was smartass, uncalled for, and plain rude; she lets me have it. "Go screw yourself, flyboy. *You* sit around here all night while I'm gone and see how well you like it." She slams the apartment door behind her as she heads to work, leaving me just standing there.

Selfishly, I think, *Dammit, what the hell do you want from me? I don't control the curriculum or the schedule.*

We both walked on eggshells for the next couple of days before we mutually acknowledged that neither of us liked this reverse training cycle, but there was nothing either of us could do except endure it. I think I speak for the both of us when I say,

"We're glad it's over for now!" But in the back of my mind is the sure knowledge that no matter where the army might send me after this, if it's a flying job, as I hope it will be, there will be more, maybe much more of this. But I stop short of telling Annie.

3:00 p.m., March 15, 2007
Yesterday we finished flying. Tomorrow there is a graduation ceremony for my class. The rumor is there will be fifty-six graduates. I am sitting in a comfortable leather easy chair opposite the well-organized desk of a petite middle-aged woman who just introduced herself as Ms. Bea. The nameplate on her desk reads, *Ms. Beatrice Womack* and then under that, *Secretary to the Commanding General.* I think I might have an idea why I've been summoned to this place where the air is almost rarified. But it's just a guess—a hunch. Ms. Womack has told me, "General McKenzie will be right with you, Lieutenant." So, I will find out the reason in due time.

From my vantage point through the open door, I can see there is someone in there with the general. My assumption is that when that individual leaves, I will be the next to enter. I know the protocol, walk in, assume a position of attention in front of the desk, salute and say, "Lieutenant Rigley reporting, sir," but still the adrenaline makes my stomach roil. A buzzer sounds on Ms. Womack's desk phone. I hear her say, "Yes, sir," and as she hangs the phone up, she looks at me. "Lieutenant Rigley, General McKenzie will see you now." So much for my earlier assumption. Whoever is in there is apparently going to be a part of my meeting with the CG. I get up, enter the office and execute the required protocol. My attention is solely focused on McKenzie.

General McKenzie returns my salute sharply, stands up, smiles at me, reaches across his desk offering his hand and says, "First of all, Jack," his familiarity surprising but also putting me at ease a bit, "Let me be the first one to offer congratulations. You are your class's distinguished graduate."

This was my speculation. I had hoped this was why I might have been summoned. Still, I'm stunned into silence for a moment. I think, *What about Haverman?* But then a voice from behind me—the other person in the room—brings me out of it. "Nice work, Jack."

I turn and shake Chief Warrant Officer Five Lathrop's outstretched hand, my IP during the instrument phase of training. "Chief, good to see you again. Thanks."

As the good news is still sinking in, General McKenzie says, "Sit down, Jack." Ms. Womack enters with a tray containing a coffee pot, a mug and bottled water. She offers me my choice. I take the water and say, "Thanks Ms. Womack." General McKenzie holds out his mug for her to fill with coffee and says, "Thank you, Ms. Bea." She does the same for Chief Lathrop who also smiles and says, "Thanks, Ms. Bea." When she's out of the room, the general tells me, "She likes to be called Ms. Bea. She should be called Queen Bea. She's served five commanding generals. Ever watch *M*A*S*H*, Jack?" he asks me.

I nod. That show is in perpetual reruns. "Yes, sir."

"That lady right there," he points toward the open door to his office, "is the real Radar. CGs will come and go from Fort Rucker, but she's the real institutional knowledge around here." Chief Lathrop offers, "Stay on her good side, Jack." Both men laugh, and I do too, but, truthfully, I have no idea why I would need that advice. With the news of my class rank, I'm confident I will attend

CH-47 training and then be on my way to Fort Campbell—or so I am foolish enough to think.

General McKenzie takes a sip of his coffee and begins, "I have a job for you, Jack, something I need you to do."

I say, "Yes, sir."

"Yeah, well, it's probably not what you're thinking, but frequently officers are called upon to do things for the good of the service, know what I mean?"

I nod as if I know what he might be alluding to, but I don't really. I'm too new at this stuff, so I just say, "Yes, sir."

The general says, "I know your preference is for CH-47s . . ." Feeling a bit like a bobblehead, I nod, again, "but I'm going to send you to Blackhawk training instead." He gives that a moment to sink in. "I know what you're thinking, 'C'mon General, you just told me I'm the distinguished graduate and now you're telling me I'm not going to get my first preference.' Am I right?"

He's absolutely right. So, the son of Ben Rigley gets his back up a little bit, "Yes, sir. I really want to fly the big boys."

"In my job, I have to look at things from the perspective of what's good for the army, what's good for army aviation. So, if I'm really doing my job here at Fort Rucker, I have to watch out for all the stakeholders. The old rule was, distinguished graduates and honor graduates got their first choice of what they want to fly and where they will be assigned. But when I looked at that rule carefully, I didn't like what I saw. The utility helicopter community was getting screwed. Over the last five years of distinguished and honor graduates, only about fifteen percent of them were assigned to flying utility helicopters, yet those are the helicopters the army has the most of, by a long shot. Seems like most of the hot sticks . . . like you . . . want to fly guns or heavies. So, it falls to me, Jack, to level that playing field. To make up for past poor practices, starting with your class, there's going to be a higher percentage of distinguished and honor graduates going on to fly Blackhawks. I know that decision doesn't make you happy, but do you understand what I'm trying to do here?"

I look to Chief Lathrop who offers nothing in support except an almost imperceptible nod. I screw up my courage and ask, "I understand, sir. Any chance I could go to the aviation maintenance officers' course after Blackhawk transition?"

I see Lathrop smile and the general chuckles. Something is up and the only one in this room that doesn't know what that is—is me. McKenzie looks at the Chief, nods and says, "You were right. You said that's what he'd want. So, Chief, why don't you tell him what we need him to do."

Chief Lathrop nods and turns toward me. "Listen, Jack, you are one of the quickest studies on helicopters I've had the pleasure to teach over the last two or three years, but," I get ready for more disappointment, "you're still just a novice when it comes to these machines. Doesn't matter whether it's Blackhawks, Kiowas, Chinooks, or Apaches, just coming out of your initial training and then a transition course, you don't really know the helicopter well enough to be a truly effective maintenance officer."

I am thinking, *Congratulations, Rigley. You're not getting 100% of anything you wanted!*

Lathrop turns to General McKenzie. "May I tell him about his follow-on assignment, sir?" McKenzie nods.

Lathrop says, "You're going to the 101st when you're through here at Fort Rucker. It's a fine outfit and you'll get a lot of real flying there, could be as much as five or six hundred hours a year; more if you get deployed somewhere." This perks me up; not just the news about the 101st, but the flying hours as well. Selective hearing loss allows me to tune out the part about getting deployed. The Chief continues, "Give the maintenance officers' course a few years, Jack, and a thousand, maybe fifteen hundred flying hours, and then ask for it. By that time, you'll really know what you're doing."

Looking back and forth between the two of them, I say, "Good advice. The 101st is where I'd asked to be assigned."

My attention focuses back on General McKenzie as he says, "I've spoken to Bill Foley. He's the CG of the 101st. He and I go way back. He's looking forward to you getting to Fort Campbell, but he's also said he's OK if I keep you here for a bit longer to do a job I have in mind. I'd like for you to do this job before you go to your Blackhawk transition class."

Now my interest is really piqued. "Yes, sir. What is it?"

"Remember your friend, Lieutenant Offerman?"

"Yes, sir. Thanks for helping him."

"Well, credit lies elsewhere, Jack. The decision to find Will Offerman that job at Redstone Arsenal was the work of Chief Lathrop here and four of his cronies. I call them The Committee of Fives. Explain that to him, will you, Chief?"

"Jack, you know as well as I do, flying—especially helicopters—isn't something just anyone can do. They're complex machines requiring not only good coordination but also a sharp, reactive mind. Your class saw four wash out and that's about the average. So, the question becomes, what's the best thing to do with the people who wash out? Maybe they can't fly, but is there something aviation-related they might do to benefit the army? Or should we just write them off, go back to the Department of the Army and say 'they can't fly,' so find something else for them to do, there's no room for them in aviation. If that's the approach we take, then there's every possibility your friend, Will

Offerman, wouldn't be at Redstone Arsenal today working on drones."

I say, "I've talked with him since he's gotten to Redstone. He really likes what he's doing there."

Lathrop continues, "So when your class started, General McKenzie brought together me and four other Chief Warrant Officer Fives. He named us The Committee of Fives and tasked us with looking at those students who wash out and advising him on what we think is the best thing to do for them, and, of course, for the army. So, me and the four other fives on the committee spend a fair amount of time interviewing them, picking their brains, and then we come together to make a recommendation to the General. In Lieutenant Offerman's case, we recommended he remain in aviation in some capacity, in part because of his engineering expertise, but also because of his attitude. He couldn't be an aviator, but he told us he wanted to stay in it to contribute to advancing aviation. We followed that same process with the other three in your class who washed out, and two of those three we've recommended to stay in the Aviation Branch. But, again, credit where credit's due. It was General McKenzie who found the job for Offerman at Redstone. He called the CG up there and made a recommendation. So, there you have it. That's what The Committee of Fives does."

It was fascinating stuff to me. It was a big, highly bureaucratic institution, taking the time to consider people as individuals with talent and value, and trying to figure out how to best utilize them, rather than simply chalking them off as failures. But, for the life of me, I couldn't figure out what any of this had to do with me until General McKenzie began to make that clear.

"So, Jack, here's the project I need your help with. I would like for you to write a policy and procedure guide for The

Committee of Fives to follow. I know this probably isn't something you're chomping at the bit to do. Writing policy and procedure wouldn't be my favorite gig either, but it's vitally important if The Committee of Fives is to become something more than just a bright idea of mine that will perish the day after my change of command here at Fort Rucker. Your work will help to institutionalize this kind of review process that maximizes the army's use of its human potential, the human potential of young officers and warrant officers who, for one reason or another, just aren't the stuff that helicopter pilots are made of, but still have great potential to serve in an aviation-related capacity."

I have truly missed Will Offerman since his departure, but I am thankful to these two men who gave him a second chance. I'm also humbled and inspired. "Sounds interesting. I appreciate your confidence in me."

Chief Lathrop breaks out into a smile. The general says, "The ninety-day clock will start next Monday. Chief Lathrop will be your primary point of contact. If either of you should need something from me, just let Ms. Bea know. I look forward to seeing what you come up with gentlemen."

The next day, 9:45 a.m., March 16, 2007
The graduation ceremony begins in fifteen minutes. I am in the first seat in the front row, and on my left are the six honor graduates of this class. Looking down the row, I notice Ross Haverman is not among us. I introduce myself to the number two graduate, Tom O'Reilly, whom I don't know at all because he was in the other section. After we congratulate each other, I ask him, "Any idea what happened to Ross Haverman? I thought for sure he'd be an honor graduate."

Tom chuckles and says, "Yeah, so did Haverman."

Haverman's reputation precedes him! Then, curiosity getting the best of me, I ask, "What happened?"

"He led our section coming out of ground school, but as soon as we started flying he faded slowly out of contention. Don't know the details of it. He and I never really got to know one another, but I am friends with a couple of the guys he flew with. He tended to piss off the instructor pilots with his 'ranger-dom.'"

"Ranger-dom?" I ask.

"You know, he was always trying to impress anyone within earshot with the fact he graduated from ranger training before coming to flight school, like that was some kind of pre-qualification setting him above everyone else in the class. It didn't work with most of us and it certainly didn't work with his IPs. One of his stick buddies told me he heard their IP unload on him once, 'Lieutenant Haverman, I could give a shit if you are the lone fuckin' ranger. You're here to learn to fly helicopters, not eat snakes. So put that shit in your duffle bag and concentrate on flying and you'll be better off.' I heard he was told that as the IP handed him a pink slip for the day. Sure seemed apropos to me. You a friend of his?"

"No, just an acquaintance. He and I were at ROTC summer camp together in the same company a couple of years ago."

Tom harrumphs, "Was he as big a pain in the ass then as he is now?"

I chuckle. "He doesn't lack confidence in himself, that's for sure. Any idea where he's being assigned from here?"

"Oh, yeah. He's been runnin' around thumpin' his chest. He's going to the 101st as a scout pilot."

I can only think, *What the hell do I have to do to get away from this fuckin' guy!*

Three months later, June 15, 2007

Time has flown. In Major General McKenzie's office, at a ceremony attended by Annie, Ms. Bea, Chief Lathrop, and the other four Chief Warrant Officer Fives comprising The Committee of Fives, Annie and the General pin on my shoulder boards promoting me to first lieutenant. Then, to my complete surprise, General McKenzie awards me an Army Commendation Medal for completing the project of regulating and standardizing the process of how flight school washouts are handled. The guide, written in close coordination with The Committee of Fives, is now officially known as Fort Rucker Supplement 1 to Army Regulation 600-8, Retention/Reassignment Policy for Initial Entry Rotary Wing Student Incompletions. The certificate accompanying the medal and ribbon reads:

> *First Lieutenant Jack Rigley is awarded the Army Commendation Medal for his outstanding performance of duty in coordinating the myriad details of reassignment procedures for students unable to satisfactorily complete Initial Entry Rotary Wing Flight Training. Working with a committee of experienced, senior warrant officers appointed by the Aviation Center's Commanding General, Lieutenant Rigley's work, completed in a timely and highly efficient manner, reflects great credit upon himself, the Aviation Center and the US Army.*

It is signed by General McKenzie

July 27, 2007

Since completing the special project assigned to me by General McKenzie, I have completed fifteen hours flying the UH-60

Blackhawk helicopter, a Sikorsky product. It is an impressive piece of machinery, with twin turbine engines, a completely different rotor system, and more sophisticated instrumentation than the TH-67 I'd learned to fly initially. All in all, I'd come to like flying this helicopter better than I thought I would. It has a wide variety of mission capabilities, including hauling external loads, and it is here that I had one of my more harrowing moments since learning to fly helicopters.

We are at an altitude of two thousand feet, and slung under our UH-60 is a cargo net full of cement blocks, their weight comparable to that of a combat-loaded, high-mobility multipurpose wheeled vehicle, HUMVEE for short. That's about six thousand pounds. We are flying at about one hundred knots into a headwind of about twenty knots, when suddenly we hit a severe downdraft. In less than a couple of seconds, the downdraft pushes our aircraft five hundred feet lower, and at the same time we suddenly develop an oscillation of the heavy load beneath our aircraft. Newton's law of physics applies here: for every action there is an equal and opposite reaction. So when the load under us oscillates to the right, our aircraft oscillates to the left. Conversely, as the load oscillates to the left, the aircraft tips right. Not only does the arc of the oscillations seem to be increasing, so does their frequency. I try to slow them down by reducing airspeed to 80 knots. Nothing! The IP takes the controls from me and he tries to slow them, but he is no more successful than I had been. Fortunately we are over open country, so the IP directs me to punch the load off. But when I pull the trigger that should release the load, nothing happens. As we continued to oscillate more and more, the IP yells through the intercom, "I said, punch it off, Lieutenant."

"I did Chief. My trigger's not responding." He tried his

trigger but had no better success than I. Our aircraft's side-to-side oscillations are now getting much worse. If this keeps up, it won't be long before the sling load we are carrying is controlling us rather than us controlling it.

My IP has over three thousand hours in the UH-60, and I can tell he isn't exactly sure what we've gotten ourselves into. He says, "I've got the controls. This is going to be dicey, but I think the only thing we can do is continue to slow down and hope that settles her. Here's what I'm gonna try. I'm gonna shoot an approach to that open field there." He points to a wide-open field straight ahead of us. I watch as the airspeed indicator drops back through eighty, then seventy, then sixty knots. The oscillating slows but is still bad enough that we feel our aircraft tip from side to side as the load sways beneath us. We are about one hundred feet above the ground, our airspeed is now below thirty knots and still decreasing. The load is still swinging. I hear the IP over the intercom talking. It sounds as if he's walking me through what he's trying to do. "OK, what I've got to do is stop us at a hover and let that load just touch the ground. Timing is everything. I need to let the load touch just at the same time I am at zero airspeed." His voice was calm. I watch his control inputs. They are nearly imperceptible. "Call out our airspeed, Lieutenant."

I begin, "Twenty-five knots . . . twenty knots . . ." Below twenty knots the airspeed indicator is less reliable, but I call out "fifteen knots . . . ten knots." We feel the load touch the ground directly underneath us just as the needle on the airspeed indicator lays against the peg at zero knots. There's a jolt and the IP reduces lift, putting some slack in the cargo net between the cargo hook and the ground. I watch him hover just slightly left of the load under us and then he puts the Blackhawk on the ground. "Wow!" is all I can think to say.

We are picked up by a recovery aircraft. Back at Hanchey Army Airfield at Fort Rucker, we are in the debriefing room at flight ops. I say to my IP, "I can't believe you were teaching me at the same time you were landing us."

He gets a quizzical look and asks, "Was I?"

"Yes, Chief. You were. You walked me through it, start to finish."

He laughs, "I'll be damned. Don't remember that at all. I was just trying to land the damned thing."

What I've learned today is even though the Blackhawk is a much more powerful helicopter than any I'd flown up to this point, power isn't always your friend, and the skilled pilot better know how to manage all that power with quick thinking and a gentle control touch.

By the time I'd completed my transition into the Blackhawk helicopter, I felt like I did after graduation from WMU. I was over school. I wanted to get into the ranks of a real unit, a helicopter unit at Fort Campbell, Kentucky.

TEN

The Real Thing

August 22, 2007

Today is my first duty day at Fort Campbell. I am assigned to Bravo Company, 5th Battalion, 101st Aviation Regiment. I am excited to start doing what I've trained to do the last six years: fly.

Haverman's here. I haven't seen him since flight school graduation. At least he'd offered a pro forma handshake and congratulations when I'd beaten him out for top cadet in our company at ROTC summer camp. At Fort Rucker, he'd left the graduation ceremony without a word to me. He's assigned to 2nd Battalion, 17th Cavalry, I'm told flying OH-58Cs. The cav guys are easy to spot. Their headgear is a black Stetson hat emblazoned in the center with gold crossed sabers. In the old days, cav guys rode horses into battle. In the modern army they ride in armored personnel carriers or fly in helicopters into combat. Fort Campbell's a big place, but Haverman's and my paths will cross—not something I look forward to.

Our move here was exciting. Annie and I figured we'd be here for a while, so we decided to buy a house. Rita put us in touch with a local realtor she knows who found us a place across the river from Fort Campbell, in Clarksville, Tennessee, advising that while real estate in Clarksville might be more expensive, Tennessee's tax structure was better and resale, if and when that time might come, would almost be guaranteed to be better. In preparation for moving in we have spent the last few days acquiring some furniture, bedding, groceries, cleaning supplies, and some yard equipment and supplies that Annie wanted, but she won't be going back to work.

Last night we'd gone to dinner, nothing special really, just hamburgers and fries. I'd ordered a beer, but I noticed Annie opted only for water.

"Jack . . ." I could always tell when something was on her mind. She'd say my name followed by an ominous pause and a look. "I . . . I don't know if this is a good time to tell you or not."

"Annie, what's wrong?"

She shakes her head, "No, nothing's wrong. I didn't mean to . . . what I'm trying to say is I'm pregnant."

It would take me a few days to realize the importance of that singular moment in our lives, another true inflection point. I have loved Annie almost from the moment I first met her, but now, at the announcement that our family is to grow, I love her even more.

August 27, 2007

I'm flying, but I have no idea if it's a lot or if this is just the standard orientation for newbies like me. The euphemism is "Peter Pilot," which I much prefer over the more salacious "FNG" or "Fuckin' New Guy." My battalion's SOP, standard operating procedures, requires me to take a check ride with one of its instructor pilots, which I easily pass. The instrument check ride, however, gives me some trouble. All of my flying time up until now is in the UH-60, but I have been flying under visual flight rules, VFR.

When it comes to instrument flying, procedurally I know exactly what to do, but I do not have any instrument flying time as yet in the Blackhawk. I am about thirty minutes into my instrument check ride today and we are shooting a precision approach into Campbell Army Airfield. As I pass the outer marker on an instrument landing system, ILS for short, precision approach into Campbell Army Airfield, I fail to take into consideration how much faster I am flying in the UH-60 cruising at 180 knots versus the TH-67 helicopter I'd flown for instrument training at Fort Rucker which cruises at about 90 knots. So, by the time I hit the middle marker beacon, I am way above the glide slope for the approach and fail to get down to the decision height. I begin struggling with the controls to correct this, but it's too late. We are over the runway and I am still several hundred feet above the altitude I should have descended to.

Over the intercom the IP says, "I've got the controls" and then tells the tower, "Campbell Tower, Army four-three-niner, executing missed approach."

"Roger, Army four-three-niner, contact Campbell approach control on 124.5."

The IP asks, "Know what you did wrong, Lieutenant?"

"Yep. Didn't get down to the decision height." If we had been in actual weather conditions with a low ceiling of cloud cover, there's a good chance we would never have made the necessary visual contact with the runway environment. In other words, I busted this instrument approach.

"Know why?"

"Yep." This kind of flight using strictly instruments to take off, fly, and land was like the ultimate video game. I tell him, "I wasn't thinking far enough ahead of the aircraft. Can we try that again?"

The IP says, "Sure. You've got the controls." We do three more instrument landing approaches into the airfield. Each one is better than the other one, but I'm still fighting the controls too much as I continue to lag behind the speed of the UH-60.

September 10, 2007
This is a melancholy time of the year for me as is the spring of each year since Charley Kimball and Zeke Hatch were killed. I'm proud of the decisions I have made to enter military service. I'm flying a lot, learning something new each time I go up. I truly believe this is what I should be doing at this point in my life.

However, I'm not sure Annie thinks along the same lines. For the next month, my assault helicopter company will go to reverse cycle training, which means we will fly at night, and this has my pregnant Annie upset. For the next month the family routine will be tossed to the wind. But I honestly don't think that is her biggest concern. She knows the stuff we are doing is dangerous. A year before we got here, four UH-60 pilots and sixteen soldiers were killed here at Fort Campbell when two helicopters, flying at night, collided.

These night flights using night vision goggles are intense. Sleep is a necessity in order to be ready for the challenges. Nourishment is equally important. Yet I will be sleeping and eating on an entirely different schedule than Annie. I will be asleep during her lunch and have to leave for the flight line while she is having her dinner. I offer to take her to breakfast occasionally before I sleep during the day. Her response is, "Stop trying to put lipstick on a pig, Jack. You better not be doing this when it's time for the baby to come or I'll . . ." Her voice trails off, probably because she cannot think of a punishment severe enough to match the crime of not being there when our baby is born.

Six months later, February 27, 2008
Rebecca Marie Rigley is born at nine o'clock in the morning, a healthy baby girl weighing in at eight pounds, six ounces. Like her mother, Becca is long and lithe. At twenty-three inches, the delivery nurse commented to me, "I didn't think she was ever going to stop coming out." Danny and Rebecca Miller and I are gathered around her bed in a semi-private room at Blanchfield Army Community Hospital on Fort Campbell. Becca, asleep, is laid across Annie's chest bundled in a blanket, looking like a little bullet. Lieutenant Colonel Critchfield, Annie's doctor, has just done a final examination of both mother and daughter. "We'll keep Mom here tonight, but barring any unforeseen circumstances, Anne and Rebecca will both go home tomorrow morning, if that is alright with you." It was the best news we could get. Ben and Rita wisely have stayed in Miami, deciding things will be hectic enough without them adding to the changes that must come.

10:00 p.m., February 27, 2008
It's late, this has been a busy day and the house has now gone quiet. I am standing in the nursery Annie and I have prepared for Becca. The Millers are asleep in the guest bedroom. I look around at everything we've done to prepare for our baby. I realize the quiet I am enjoying right now will change after tomorrow and Annie and the baby come home. Over the last few months, I've thought about this moment. I would be a liar if I said there was never any trepidation on my part about being ready for this next part of our lives to unfold. But now, after seeing Becca lying

across Annie's belly this morning, after putting my index finger into Becca's little hand and feeling her fold her tiny fingers around it, after watching Annie's parents dote over the two of them, I decide I am not only ready, I am eager.

Rebecca Miller is going to stay on with us for a few weeks while Annie and I adjust to life as new parents and Becca begins to settle into her own routine. I've logged about two hundred and fifty flight hours since arriving here. Last week I was signed off by one of the battalion's IPs as a PIC, pilot-in-command. Next week we are flying every night as part of a week-long tactical exercise in preparation for an expected rotation at the National Training Center at Fort Irwin, California. It's good Rebecca will be here to help Annie, who isn't happy about the nighttime exercise, as we continue to adjust to the newest addition to our family.

ELEVEN

Train Like It's War

Blount Island Terminal, Port of Jacksonville, Florida
1 August, 2008

I step down from the cockpit of my UH-60 Blackhawk helicopter after shutting down both engines and waiting until the main rotor is nearly finished coasting to a stop. Behind me are the four other helicopters in my platoon. It's early evening, but the ground crew at the port is hustling toward us. By this time tomorrow, our five helicopters will be broken down for ocean shipment from Jacksonville, through the Panama Canal, and then on to Port Hueneme, California, located about halfway between San Diego and San Francisco. We are not the first helicopters to arrive here in Jacksonville, nor are we the last. Five more will arrive in four hours, then five more after that, until the entire 101st Combat Aviation Brigade has closed on the port. What all of this must cost is inestimable to me—tens of millions—maybe even hundreds of millions. But this is exactly what we would do if the aviation brigade would ever have to deploy from Fort Campbell to someplace else in the world.

From behind me, Chief Warrant Officer Five Stan Hodges approaches. "OK, Cap'n, looks like the wrench-benders got it from here." Pointing, he continues, "Van's waitin' to take us to the hotel. Let's get out of this flight gear, get cleaned up. I know a little fish camp not far from here. Best fresh shrimp, fried catfish, and jambalaya you ever put in your mouth and the beer's real cold. Good place to celebrate those new railroad tracks you're sportin'. Your money's no-good tonight. Me 'n the rest of the platoon got this." I begin to object. Chief Hodges puts up a burly hand, shakes his head and firmly says, "No arguin' Cap'n. There'll be plenty of time for that in a few weeks, after we get to the NTC." NTC is the acronym for the National Training Center at Fort Irwin, California. "Tonight though, your money's no good!"

I'd been promoted to captain this morning before leaving Fort Campbell. Annie and Becca were there for the ceremony, and to see me and my platoon off. But before we'd left home, Annie and I had gotten into a bit of a tiff over this trip. "Why do you have to go? Isn't there someone else who can take your place? You're just delivering helicopters? It's going to be bad enough when you have to leave for Fort Irwin in a few weeks. Jack, I'm not sure I can handle all of this by myself—the house, the baby."

Tomorrow we will fly commercially from Jacksonville back home to Clarksville, Tennessee. It will be three weeks while we wait for our gear to transit from the east coast to the west coast. A helicopter company without its helicopters just doesn't have a lot to do. But this interim will give all of us some much-needed time with our families before we head to the west coast. I'm hoping I can use the time to heal Annie's spirits.

Fort Irwin, California
2200 hours, 27 September, 2008

We've been here for nearly a month. In that time, I've logged nearly seventy-five flight hours; about half of those have been daytime flying under visual flight rules, the other half has been night flying, most of it using night vision goggles. Tonight is our final test: my company of fifteen UH-60 Blackhawks will insert an infantry company into various landing zones, or LZs, under the cover of dark. The operations briefing is simple, straightforward, no surprises. The LZ assigned to my platoon of five Blackhawks is large enough to easily accommodate a flight of five.

Tonight, certain LZs will be defended by opposing forces, or OPFORs. We have no idea which ones, so each LZ has to be handled as if it will be defended. This is like the ultimate game of laser tag. The enemy's weapons, instead of firing bullets, will fire bursts of laser lights. Our helicopter's guns will also be capable of firing laser bursts. Each of our birds are equipped with laser sensors placed in critical locations. The OPFOR will wear laser-sensing vests as will the infantry we deliver to the LZ. Each laser sensor, if lit up by a laser strike, will register on a computer monitor at range control. The computer will record the time of the hit, the LZ in which the hit occurred, and will provide an assessment of the damage inflicted by the hit as either *fatal* or *non-lethal*. It's pretty sophisticated stuff, and just as I'd been told, it seemed to me to be as close to actual combat as one could get without actually getting shot at.

The aerial tactics are simple, dating back to the Vietnam War, but improved upon with more sophisticated helicopters and better technology. Each LZ will be penetrated first by a scout helicopter, an OH-58C equipped with thermal imaging gear. This equipment is sufficiently sensitive to detect the presence of any OPFOR from just their body heat. Loitering near each LZ will be an AH-64 Apache attack helicopter. If the scout detects any suspected enemy presence, it calls on the gunship to roll into the LZ with guns ablazin'. My platoon, and the other two platoons in my company, won't deliver our cargo of troops until we get an "all clear" from our respective scouts. All of us fly in total darkness, no navigation lights, no landing lights, in a reasonably tight formation; we are little more than a noisy shadow. All pilots are flying with night vision goggles. We've trained for this; we have confidence in our equipment and in ourselves, but perhaps most importantly, we have confidence in one another. An operation like this requires every member of the team to do their job and when that breaks down—well, everything goes to hell quicker than the blink of an eye.

My platoon has been airborne for about fifteen minutes. I'm flying in the left seat as the pilot-in-command. My copilot is a Chief Warrant Officer 2 with just a few less hours than me. I glance at the GPS; it tells me we are about five minutes from the LZ. I check the FM radio to make sure it's dialed into the right frequency, key the mic and say, "Night Hawk 1, this is Rover 26, over."

Within a matter of two or three seconds, my copilot and I hear, "Rover 26, Night Hawk 1, over."

Our radios are good, reliable, but even the best of them distorts the voice; yet I think I recognize Night Hawk One: Ross Haverman. There's no time to ponder this. I'm only four minutes from the LZ. I key the mic and say, "Roger, Night Hawk 1, Rover 26 is four minutes out.

"Roger, 26. Night Hawk 1 is short final into LZ Charlie."

"Rover 26, Night Hawk 1, Night Hawk 2 is standing by."

Night Hawk 2 is the Apache gunship assigned to our LZ should close air support be needed. Haverman and I both acknowledge Night Hawk 2's advisory.

I am reassured. Everything is on schedule. Everyone is where they should be. I glance at my GPS. Three minutes out—plenty of time. Me and my flight of five are in a shallow descent into the LZ. A short time passes; GPS indicates we are about a minute and half from touchdown. "Hawk 2, this is Hawk 1. Nothing here. Relocating to loiter position." Hawk 2 responds, "Roger." Then Night Hawk 1 reports to me, "Rover 26, Night Hawk 1, LZ Charlie is clear." GPS tells me we are one minute out. Through the green glow of my night vision goggles, I can see the LZ ahead of me, an open desert area somewhere in the nether region of Fort Irwin. Every helicopter in my platoon reports they have the LZ in sight.

At thirty seconds out, I slow the aircraft in preparation for touchdown. We are all about one hundred feet above the desert floor. At somewhere around fifty feet of altitude and less than twenty knots of forward airspeed, the air is filled with green laser lines shooting up at us from the desert floor. We are under fire. Door gunners on either side of all five ships return fire. Our green lasers now criss-cross the OPFOR's lasers. I key the FM radio, "Night Hawk 2, Rover 26 taking fire."

The gunship comes back, "Roger, Rover 26. Call clear of the LZ." He is loitering less than a minute away, but he can't come after the enemy until he is sure we are out of the way. In the meantime, I am committed . . . we are just seconds away from touchdown as are the other four aircraft in my platoon.

My copilot keys the intercom in our aircraft and says, "What the hell. The place is crawlin' with OPFOR."

I reply to him, "Sure as hell is." Then I key the FM radio and tell the other four aircraft, "Too late to back out now. Get in, get out." We touch down and the dozen or so infantrymen in the back of the aircraft bail out, returning laser fire with the opposing forces.

The crew chief tells us, "Troops are out, sir." My copilot is at the controls. I tell him, "Pull pitch, Chief. Let's go." Out of my peripheral vision I see him snatch the collective lever up. I shift my attention to the instruments, but I can feel it in the aircraft as he applies power, tips the rotor disc forward, and the blades bite into the still, night, desert air. The other four Blackhawks in my platoon report they are airborne behind me.

I can hear Night Hawk 1 and 2 talking over the FM radio frequency we share. I key the mic and advise Night Hawk 2 we are clear of the LZ.

Then we get the sickening call from Range Control, "Rover 26, Range Control, over."

I key the mic, "Range Control, Rover 26, over."

"Roger, Rover 26, metrics indicate three of your birds shot down at LZ Charlie. Stand down three. The remaining two may continue to participate in the exercise at the direction of your battalion's headquarters."

No one died, but the sick feeling I have in the pit of my stomach makes me feel otherwise. I think, *What the fuck, Haverman! Was that you? You called the LZ clear.*

0300 hours, 28 September, 2008
Debriefing Room, Range Control, Fort Irwin, California
Three of my five helicopter crews have been here for the last three hours after getting "shot down" at LZ Charlie. The room is full of people, but seated at the table at the front of the room, in front of a wall-to-wall display showing the total operating area

for tonight's exercise, are the brigade commander and his subordinate battalion commanders. The exercise's chief umpire, a lieutenant colonel sporting a pair of master army aviator wings on his uniform, begins with the bottom line up front. He looks at the brigade commander and says, "Sir, the umpires agree that the Brigade's performance this evening is rated overall at 'marginally successful.'" I'm still a rookie at all of this and I'm an optimist by nature so I interpret that as about a C-. But CW5 Hodges, who has a ton more experience than me, is standing next to me. He destroys my illusion. "The old man's not going to like that. Marginally satisfactory is just another way of saying 'we're all fucked up.'"

The chief umpire continues, "Sir, we realize this score is, well, it's low, but it's based on the overall accomplishment of the Brigade's mission which was to insert an infantry battalion across a wide front to defeat an opposing force." He uses a laser pointer to show the front and where the OPFOR were located for tonight's exercise. "This point right here," again he uses the laser pointer, but for me, I've had enough lasers for one night. "This point right here, in the middle of the front is the main cause of the low score. Three birds were lost at LZ Charlie as well as seventy-five percent of the infantry delivered to that LZ."

There was no finger pointing, no arguing; the results were what they were. The enemy's front at LZ Charlie was not disrupted and that allowed the OPFOR to outflank the infantry battalion sent in to defeat them. I expected an ass chewing of monumental proportions to come my way after the debriefing. I look around the room for Ross Haverman to ask if he was Night Hawk I, and if he was, why the hell did he call the LZ clear when it wasn't, but he's nowhere to be found.

October 4, 2008

It's been a long six days since my platoon's failure in the desert; still no ass chewing. Chief Hodges is sitting next to me
on the charter commercial flight from San Francisco back to
Fort Campbell. Hodges is a veteran of flying in both Iraq and
Afghanistan and is the senior warrant officer in my platoon. I've
come to respect his opinion and advice. He tells me, "Aw, Cap'n,
don't worry over it. Doesn't do any good. Think of it as a learnin'
experience. Somebody didn't do their job and it wasn't you.
Nothin' you could have done would have changed anything."

Nearly a month later, October 31, 2008

Our birds had made the ocean trip back to Jacksonville, Florida,
from the west coast. Maintenance teams had reassembled them
and now we were retrieving them. The flight from Jacksonville
to Campbell Army Airfield is a long one, necessitating a stop at
Pope Field at Fort Bragg, North Carolina, for refueling. It felt
good to get back in the cockpit again. The entire flight home
was done in V-formation with my Blackhawk in the lead and two
staggered behind each other slightly aft of me and on either side.
It was difficult for me to see exactly how tight our formation was,
but both of our formation landings, the first at Pope and the last
here at Campbell, received compliments from the tower. Our aircraft performed flawlessly on the flight home, no one reporting
any discrepancies that would ground their bird. I'm tired, but it's
a Friday night and I've told Annie I'm taking her out to dinner.
Date night.

Edward's Steakhouse in Clarksville is busy, but Annie had
made a reservation for the two of us at 7:00 p.m. We're a little
early and are enjoying a drink at the bar while we wait for our
table when I feel a tap on my shoulder. It's Stan Hodges and his

wife, Betty. I stand up, shake his hand, and give Betty a hug while Stan does the same to Annie. While the women talk, Stan asks, "Heard the scuttlebutt?"

"About?" The army's big, but when it comes to scuttlebutt, sometimes it can be small, like a bunch of old men sitting in front of a general store swapping lies.

"You told me you thought the scout pilot at our LZ was some guy named Haverman?"

I nod. "Yeah, Ross Haverman."

"Well, apparently you are correct. Rumor is he was in a bit of trouble after that evening's clusterfuck." He's lowered his voice to cover the vulgarity.

"Really?"

"Yeah, he didn't do his job. Never got below about four hundred feet. Never gave the thermal imaging gear a chance to work. He's a brand-new pilot-in-command and somehow got paired up with a brand new Wobbly-1. The Peter Pilot didn't know what to do and Haverman didn't trust his training to get down and dirty, so they called the LZ clear without really knowing what was what."

Annie is still engaged in conversation with Betty Hodges. I lean in toward the chief, "No, shit. What's going to happen?"

"Heard there was talk of an FEB," Hodges says. Flight Evaluation Boards are no-shit serious business and can result in a pilot losing their wings if found to be incompetent. Before I can say anything, however, Stan continues. "But apparently this guy's got a guardian angel."

"He sure does," I say. "Daddy's a retired four-star general." I am furious Haverman's incompetence is looking like it's going to be excused.

"Well, that might explain it," Hodges says. "Apparently, he's been booted upstairs to the brigade's personnel shop. He's going to be an assistant to the lieutenant colonel who's in charge there. The colonel isn't a rated aviator, just a personnel weenie. I guess they expect Haverman to advise his boss on 'all things aviation.'"

"He's not gonna be flying anymore?" I ask.

Hodges shrugs his shoulders, "Don't know the answer to that one, Cap'n." His tone turns to one of pure sarcasm. "But here's another rumor. Apparently the division chief of staff is a Citadel graduate and so's Haverman. Maybe a little ring-knockin' is gonna save his ass."

The hostess calls our name. Without the slightest regard of Annie's feelings, I ask her if we can have a table for four instead of two, but she says that would necessitate a wait of a little over two hours. Stan says, "Go ahead, Cap'n. Enjoy your dinner. We can talk about this some more next week. Bottom line, what happened in the desert that night wasn't your fault, it was his." I thank him. Annie and Betty say their goodbyes and we take our seats at a table for two near the fireplace.

The waitress takes our drink order and Annie says, "Jack, you should have asked me if I minded if anyone joins us for dinner. This is a date night, or supposed to be one." Annie's had a lot on her plate while I was gone to the NTC. I've noticed a certain irritability since I got home. This most recent three-day trip to Jacksonville to retrieve our helicopters hadn't helped. She does know, though, how we screwed the pooch on our final exercise at the NTC. On the way home I begin to broach the news about Haverman, but it's soon obvious to me Annie is not the least bit interested in discussing any of the politics swirling around Haverman and what should happen to him. It hits me then just how much my absence has strained our relationship. I make a silent vow I will somehow make it up to her.

TWELVE

Deployment

It's been three months since returning from the National Training Center. I haven't seen Ross Haverman and that is probably for the best. In my mind he is the one solely responsible for our poor performance that night. My opinion is he should not be flying, but no one has asked me. On the other hand, I am flying quite a bit and enjoy what I'm doing. But the news I must carry home today is not good.

It's early afternoon, so I'm not expected home. I enter through the garage into the laundry room and then into the kitchen. Through the window above the sink, I see Annie and Becca on the patio. It's a beautiful day, sunny, mild for January. Annie's wearing a bulky sweater, and Becca is bundled up. At first I think she's protecting her against a gusty wind, but then I realize that's not Annie's intention. Becca's toddling now, but sometimes her forward momentum outruns her ability to keep her legs under her. The winter wear, in addition to keeping her warm, will protect her if she should fall on the patio's unforgiving concrete. It suddenly strikes me that, while I may have been here to see her begin to walk and hear her utter her first *Mama* and *Daddy,* I likely will not see those steps turn into her first run or hear her first words turn into sentences. I've been put on alert for deployment as part of a team from the 101st headed to Iraq. I tap on the window. Annie looks up, surprised at first, but then she smiles at me, scoops up Becca and heads for the slider where I meet her and pull the two of them close to me.

"You're home early," she says as she sets Becca down and begins to pull off the winter wear. "It's such a beautiful day, I felt like we just had to get outside."

"Yeah," I say.

My tone betrays me. Annie asks, "Everything OK?"

I can't detect any real concern in her voice, but she knows I'm rarely home early. "Uh, Annie . . ." *Shit! Just get it over with.* There's no sugar-coating this, "I'm being deployed."

Without a word, she continues to get Becca's winter wear off revealing a onesie that says on the front of it *Daddy's Girl.* Seeing that, the already large lump in my throat grows larger.

I know her so well. When she starts to get angry, her speech gets clipped and I can sense her aggravation. "When?" she asks as Becca crawls off in the direction of the family room.

"Not exactly sure, but sometime within the next six months."

"Iraq?"

"Yeah."

I watch her move to the sink, busying herself with some dishes there. She says, "Well, that's just great, isn't it, Jack. First the training center for a month and now a year. That's right, isn't it? You'll be gone a year this time?"

I cannot think of anything that will make this whole thing seem better than it is, so I shrug and say, "Most likely."

"Jeez, Jack. Why you? Why now?" Then, she says, "I can already hear my father." I am fully aware of the ripple effect this news is going to have. Annie has frequent communications with her mother and father. Even though I am privy to only one side of these conversations, I know when she talks with her father, he is critical of "the surge." Two years ago, in early 2007, a bunch of generals, Vice President Cheney, and Secretary of Defense Donald Rumsfeld convinced President Bush we could position ourselves for withdrawal from Iraq by making one last push which would include US troops committed to battle, and training the Iraqi Army to stand on their own. Annie's father was livid. I recall her holding the phone away from her ear and turning it toward me. I could hear him ranting, "The damn dummies don't remember a thing. We tried something like this in Vietnam. All the generals were telling everyone we were winning the hearts and minds of the Vietnamese. We needed to stay the course. We needed more men. And what happened? Tet, '68 happened. They killed your Uncle Max. The North Vietnamese and the Viet Cong weren't finished fighting then, just like the Sunnis and the Shiites aren't finished fighting in Iraq. Their differences are tribal, going back thousands of years. What the hell makes us think a few thousand more American troops are going to turn all that around?" What's more, Annie's father was right. The surge in 2007 hadn't made a difference. Americans were getting sick of the war there, just as they'd done with the war in Vietnam. There was a lot of talk amongst the politicians in Washington, DC, of a pullout.

The walls in our kitchen seem to be closing in around me. I just stand there, looking at Annie, at a loss for words. Her cheeks are stained with tears as she takes a few steps in the direction of the family room to check on Becca who is sitting in the middle of the floor surrounded by several of her stuffed toys. I say, "We're going to be retrograding . . ."

She angrily interrupts, "I don't care what you're going to be doing. It's all dangerous over there, Jack! I watch the news, just like you do."

Now that I'm standing in the middle of this minefield, I say, "There's more." I watch Annie cringe. She throws her hands up and drops them against her legs, "Great! Sure, there's more! What is it?"

"They want me to go to the aviation maintenance officers' course and then to the test pilot course after that." If there was anything at all about this news that was uplifting, this was it. I was finally going to get my shot at aviation maintenance thanks to, of all people, Ross Haverman. Annie says nothing as tears still flow. "Ross Haverman apparently pulled some strings."

Her anger flares some more. Glancing in the family room at Becca who is playing on the floor paying no attention to the drama unfolding in the kitchen, Annie stomps her foot, and says, "Let me get this straight. The guy that screwed you once has just done it again. Is that right?" Before I can answer, she steels her eyes on me and asks, "Is he being deployed?"

"No. You know he's in personnel now . . ."

Annie rolls her eyes. I could tell she could care less what might have motivated Haverman. All she could see is he was now responsible for our upcoming separation. "When do you leave?"

"Two weeks."

Annie holds her hands up as if she's pushing me away, leaves me standing in the kitchen, and sits down with Becca in the middle of the family room floor. Becca smiles and moves toward Annie's lap as Annie wipes away her tears and tries to smile at her. I've followed her into the adjoining room and say, "I have an idea."

"Look, Jack, we knew this was going to come and I know

maintenance is what you want to do." A silence draws out between us and then she says, "So just go. We've managed before without you. We can do it again."

Those words cut like a knife. I say, "I want you and Becca to come with me to Rucker while I'm in school there."

"But—"

"Listen, Annie. I know this is a lot. But between the maintenance officers' course and the test flight course, it's sixteen weeks. That's sixteen weeks we can still be together."

"What about the house?"

I had an answer to that. I wasn't sure it would help to salve her anger, but I had nothing to lose at this point. "We'll close it up for the sixteen weeks. We can ask the neighbors to keep an eye on the place." For the moment, I notice the tears abate. "At the briefing they told us that everyone deployed on this mission would be coming back to Campbell after the tour." I gave her a moment to digest this information and then added, "I know we talked about you going home to Empire if this should happen. You can still do that. You and Becca can go home whenever you want. Just close up the house and go. And when I come back home after the tour, we're right here. Already settled in." She won't look at me, but she's stopped the tears. After a respectable amount of time, I muster sufficient courage to ask, "What do you think, Annie?"

I never really get an answer to that question. She goes to bed without telling me. Another sign of her anger. I shower and slip into the bed next to her. She doesn't move, doesn't acknowledge my presence at all. While I had expected the news of my pending deployment to upset her, I am saddened and a bit angry to be getting such a cold shoulder. Though we hadn't talked about it extensively, we both knew something like this would likely happen at some point. Now that the time has come, she seems to have become unwilling to deal with this reality of military life.

Four months later, June 15, 2009
Annie, Becca, and I made the most of our sixteen weeks together at Fort Rucker for my training. Army schools offer a routine that is easy, almost laid back, compared to the hustle and bustle of life in the aviation brigade at Fort Campbell. While we were at Rucker, we took advantage of our time off to see and do everything we could as a family, together. On one occasion we took the opportunity to stop in at the post's headquarters. Major General McKenzie had changed command, gotten his third star and is now Lieutenant General McKenzie, currently serving as the Deputy Chief of Staff for Operations on the army staff at the Pentagon. But the ever-present Ms. Bea greeted the three of us with open arms, especially the youngest Rigley, Becca. The new commanding general at Fort Rucker is the seventh she's served as executive secretary. I also had the opportunity to see Chief Warrant Officer Five Lathrop who is now retired, but is still an instrument instructor pilot. He is a civilian contractor, flies five days a week, and seems to be happy in this new/old role. He told me the new CG still uses The Committee of Fives to determine the best way to manage students who do not successfully complete initial entry rotary wing flight training, although there is only one of the original CW-5s still on the committee. The sixteen weeks has flown by, and now Annie and I must face the hard part: deployment.

I'm sitting in the aisle seat of a chartered commercial airliner provided by Choctaw Transportation Services, whom I'd never heard of. Other than the plane's registration stenciled in black letters and numbers on the fuselage just forward of the tail section, it is unmarked; I saw their name stenciled some-where on the inside of the door as I boarded. It's some version of the 737, an older aircraft. The seat I'm sitting in is threadbare along its edges. My mind briefly wonders how many other sol-diers have sat in this same seat as this aircraft carried them off to a war zone. We are bound for Ramstein Air Force Base in Germany, where the aircraft will refuel, and then continue on to Joint Base Balad in Iraq, which we are told will be our primary base of operations. Our mission has been clarified several times over since we were first alerted, but it still boils down to the same thing: we will be in charge of preparing army helicopters of one sort or another for retrograde, the army's term for *shipment,* back to the United States.

The plane, filled with one hundred and fifty soldiers, mostly all from the 101st Combat Aviation Brigade's 96th Aviation Support Battalion, is eerily quiet an hour into the seven-hour flight to Ramstein. I lay my head back on the headrest and close my eyes, and in the pit of my entire being I have never felt more alone in my life. It could be a year or more before I see my sweet Annie and Becca. I'm not optimistic that the disconsolation I feel will abandon me anytime soon, no matter how busy we might be in the coming months.

THIRTEEN

My Plight as an Army Wife

The Rigley home, Clarksville, Tennessee, noon, June 15, 2009
He's gone. The garage door rolls up and I pull in alongside Jack's truck. A lump swells in my throat and I want to cry but I stifle that urge. In the rearview mirror I can see Becca, strapped into her car seat, kicking her legs up and down, pointing at the video screen Jack had bought and installed for her as an aftermarket feature our daughter had come to love. Giggling, she coos, "Dora, Mama, Dora." Dora the Explorer had replaced Big Bird as her favorite, and she'd been enthralled in the video since I'd put it in for her as we left the airfield after my tearful goodbye with Jack.

I lift her out of the car seat and instead of simply carrying her into the house, I set her down. She's old enough now to prefer navigating on her own. I take her hand and the two of us nego-tiate the two stairs from the garage floor to our laundry room door and into the house. I hated opening that door and entering our home . . . a place I loved, but knew would somehow not be the same without the slightest prospect of Jack's presence for the next eternity. The house felt as empty as I did in the pit of my stomach. I wonder where he is now, *somewhere out over the*

Atlantic Ocean. What's *he* thinking about? *Does he miss Becca and me as much as I miss him?* The baby brings me back to reality. "Juice, Mama." I smile at her, get her sippy cup and fill it half full of cranberry juice, her favorite.

When she's done, I say to her, "OK, let's get you down for a nap." She reaches up, takes my hand, and we head for her bedroom.

With Becca asleep, I sit down at the kitchen table, cradle my head in my hands, and begin to sob. The loneliness, the emptiness I feel is palpable; nothing like what I'd felt on those occasions when Jack had left Empire to return to school in Kalamazoo, or when he'd gone that summer to ROTC camp. No, this was a loneliness tinged with a real fear of the dangerous possibilities of him spending a year in a combat zone. There were a hundred ways he could be hurt or killed and after considering only the first couple of them, I found myself crying harder and harder. I had to snap out of this. Raising our child, keeping the home fires burning . . . these were now my jobs, and I had to get back to the business of carrying out *my* duties just as Jack would carry out his.

4:00 p.m., June 15, 2009

Becca's noon nap was a short one and we'd spent an hour or so in the backyard. It was a hot, humid day, but I puttered in the small vegetable garden Jack and I put in. I pushed Becca in the swing Jack had installed just a few weeks earlier. Now back inside, she was playing with her Dora the Explorer doll on the family room floor while I began putting her dinner together. The ringing doorbell startles me. It's Nancy Capaletti, a neighbor, two-doors down and on our side of the street. We'd met at several parties; once last Christmas at Fort Campbell, at the home of the commanding general, an opulent place provided by the US government to the man and his family who had the distinction to lead this historic combat unit, the 101st Airborne Division (Air Assault). The other time was at a neighborhood get-together just before we'd left for Jack's maintenance training classes at Fort Rucker. Her husband, Ron, was a major. Jack had explained he was a "snake eater," a term I, at first, thought derogatory, but as Jack explained its meaning, I found he meant it with a degree of respect. "Major Capaletti's a ranger—"

I recalled interrupting him when he'd told me that. "Like Ross Haverman?"

"Uh . . . no . . . not at all. Ron's a real ranger. Haverman somehow got the patch, but he's working in personnel now, about as far away from being a ranger as you can get," Jack had explained to me. "Ron Capaletti's the executive officer for one of the battalions in the 1st Brigade Combat Team."

I remember putting my hand up and saying to him, "Whoa. Hold up. What's all that mean?"

He smiled at me and relented, "Yeah, you're right. Sorry." Jack always was patient with me and my slowness—maybe one could call it *reluctance*—to try and understand how the army was organized, how it worked. "What it means is he's a real boots-on-the-ground guy that jumps or rappels out of our helicopters and meets the enemy eye-to-eye, rifle barrel to rifle barrel. Haverman's a phoney. His daddy got him into ranger school. But Ron Capaletti—he's the real deal, a real ranger, not just a wannabe like Haverman."

Nancy Capaletti has a casserole dish in her oven-mitt-clad hands. I open the door and invite her in. She smiles at Becca, still sitting on the floor and engrossed with her Dora doll, and says, "Well, hello, sweetie." Becca returns her smile and then Nancy turns to me and extends the casserole dish, "This is for you. It's a chicken pot pie, just out of the oven. Where would you like me to put it?"

I motion for her to follow me into the kitchen. Pointing to the stove top, I say, "Nancy, this is very thoughtful of you. Just set it down here."

A long moment extends out between us and then she asks, "How are you doing?"

I put up a false front. "OK."

She must see right through me. "It will get easier, Anne." Tears form in both my eyes. She continues, "I've been where you are right now, twice, so I know how tough these first few days can be; coming home to an empty house, everything around you a reminder of Jack." She is so spot on. The tears reappear. She embraces me. After a silent moment, in which my emotions and her empathy are somehow traded between us, she says, "I have a small group of women. We've all been through deployments. In fact, two of our husbands are deployed now, like Jack. We get together every now and then just to check in on one another. We're meeting next week at my house, Wednesday evening at seven o'clock. You're invited to join us, and you don't have to decide right now. Just give it some thought. We're a good group of gals. Lots in common." The embrace ends.

I explain to her I was just getting ready to feed Becca to which she responds, "Oh, go right ahead. I remember when Lyndsey was that age, and there is no such thing as patience when it comes to a hungry toddler. I simply nod and return to the counter where Becca's food sits half ready. Nancy adds, "Listen, Anne, Lyndsey is fifteen now and I've given her permission to babysit. I'm sure she'd love watching Becca when you need to get away, like next week when the wives are getting together."

It was good to know. Jack and I had struggled with finding babysitters and now it turns out there's one that lives practically next door. I relate that irony to Nancy, then I add, my tears subsiding, "You're sure this gets better?"

"Guarantee it. But it helps when you have some help. So let me help—let *us* help—the other wives I mean, and the offer includes Ron. You need some help with some odd job Jack would do, let me know. He'll be here ASAP."

I thank her and offer, "You're right about the place feeling empty."

She smiles, "Want some advice?" Then she quickly adds, "If you don't then that's OK, too."

I figure, *what do I have to lose?* and then say, "Sure."

"Get a dog or a cat. I happen to think a dog is better, but it's a matter of personal choice. Point is, it'll be something for you and Becca to come home to, something to make the house seem not quite so empty. A dog'll greet you at the door with its tail wagging every time."

I remember my dog, Samantha, at home in Empire. The thought makes me smile and I think, *Sam must be at least sixteen years old now.* I feel a sudden affection, a sense of gratitude toward this woman who, in the last few minutes, has migrated from *acquaintance* to *friend*. "Thanks. I'll give that some thought." I thank her again for the casserole.

She says, "Hope to see you next week. But I'll check in on you from time to time regardless. This is *the* toughest thing about being a military wife." There's a pause in the conversation and then Nancy adds as she continues to make me feel a little better, "Ron says he's only heard good things about Jack."

Somewhat surprised, I comment, "But I didn't think Ron . . ."

She breaks in, "No, Ron's not a pilot, but he rides in those helicopters Jack flies. You think those guys don't talk about which pilots they like and which they don't? Oh, no, they talk, and Jack's got a reputation as one of the good ones."

As she leaves and I close the front door behind her, I feel better already . . . not quite as alone.

FOURTEEN

PLA
N AH
EAD

17 June, 2009

I had expected better. Our arrival at Joint Base Balad, located about thirty-five miles north of Baghdad, is a complete cluster-fuck, as if no one told them we were coming, or no one there cared to admit they knew. Task Force Iraq Retrograde seemed to be the ugly stepchild no one wanted to see, talk about, or admit to. It was so bad our first night there that all one hundred and fifty of us were herded into an empty hangar and told we were "allowed" to spend the night there. At some point an air force pickup truck arrived with some meals-ready-to-eat, or MREs. These are plastic packets of dehydrated "stuff" to which water, hot or cold, could be added to create a mixture with a flavor akin to cardboard, but which would sustain us. At least that is what we are assured by the Department of Defense-approved labeling on the damned things. The problem now was there was no water to add to them. There were no water fountains in the place and signage above the sinks in the latrine read WARNING: NON-POTABLE WATER. Some phone calls were made, some voices raised with the net result that, a few hours after the MREs arrived, the same pickup truck returned with cases of bottled water.

The more experienced in our group came prepared with bottles of hot sauce squirreled away in their rucks. The less experienced got stern looks as this precious liquid was somewhat reluctantly shared when asked. By morning, portalets were anonymously placed in front of the hangar after we'd completely overwhelmed its one female and one male bathroom, which were never meant to accommodate this number of troops turning the place into a barracks. There were no shower facilities unless one counted the emergency decontamination shower permanently installed as a safety measure. We'd been warned not to use it because it was hardwired to an alarm at the base dispensary that would dispatch an ambulance immediately. If there was any upside to this bitter welcome, it was the air mattress each of us had as part of our personal gear, providing welcome relief from the cold, hard hangar floor.

I had not been a part of the advance logistical planning for our deployment to Iraq, nor had I had any hand in selecting who would be part of Task Force Iraq Retrograde. If I had been, I think I would have suggested that an advance party be sent at least two weeks, maybe even a month, ahead of the main party's arrival. That would have precluded all of this confusion. But, I had been away at maintenance officers' school and test pilot training when all of the planning was taking place. There was no point in going over what should have happened. We are here. Now we have to make something happen.

I realized after only a couple of hours in Balad that Lieutenant

Colonel Richard Westfield, our task force commander, was a force to be reckoned with. Over the last three days, I'd listened while he went to war with the powers that be here to finally get our basic needs satisfied in a more permanent way. It turns out the US Air Force, the service responsible for things like barracks, messing, and work facilities at Joint Base Balad, knew our Task Force was coming, but claimed ignorance on the exact date and on exactly what our work facility requirements were going to be. The air force further excused itself by claiming a tremendously heavy mission workload, causing the details of preparing for us to be simply OBE or "overcome by events." Westfield didn't hesitate to tell them he thought that excuse was pure bullshit. He'd become quite cynical after our poor reception.

Bluntly, he tells me, "The truth of the matter Captain Rigley is—and you will need to remember this—this is a fuckin' US Air Force Base. Don't let that word *Joint* fool you at all. The air force is gonna take care of their own before anyone else."

I listened intently to what he was telling me. This would be my first time interfacing with another service. The closest thing I'd ever been to something even remotely considered a *joint operation* was inserting a US Air Force Red Horse Team into some remote spot at the National Training Center when we'd been there. There were eight of them on that team and they had some equipment with them; all I was told was where to fly them. They were a rapid-response civil engineering team, and they acted like if they told me what they were doing in the godforsaken spot where I dropped them, then they'd have to kill me.

I am to be the production control officer for Task Force Iraq Retrograde. The position description simply reads that I am "responsible to receive, prepare, and retrograde eligible aircraft from the theater of operations and ship them back to CONUS."

CONUS stands for Continental United States. I am the only other commissioned officer assigned to Task Force Iraq Retrograde besides Lieutenant Colonel Westfield. There are eighteen chief warrant officers assigned, six of whom are either CW5s or very senior CW4s. The remainder of the Task Force, about one hundred and thirty soldiers, are quality control inspectors, mechanics and a couple of supply people.

Westfield and I are in his office, located in the hangar we'd used as a barracks three nights before. Now it will be the primary building assigned to us for our mission work. Because of all the confusion surrounding our arrival, this is the first time my boss and I have really had a chance to talk about the reason we are here: moving helicopters back stateside. "Jack, I'm gonna be straight with you. We are under a microscope here. Our mission is going to be looked at closely by the army staff. I don't have to tell you, aviation assets are some of the most expensive lines in the army's budget. We took a lot of flak from Congress about all the stuff we left in the sandbox after Desert Storm. So, the army is going to be more careful this go-round. Our job is to move a bunch of aircraft back to the states in a short period of time and have them ready to go into service as soon as they get back there. You're the guy that's gonna orchestrate how that's to happen. What's your connection to General McKenzie?"

A light bulb begins to glow dimly. "I did a project for him after I graduated from flight school."

"Well, I had another guy I liked for your job because he had a little more maintenance experience, but I got overruled. You know McKenzie's the Deputy Chief of Staff for Operations on the army staff, now, right?"

"Yes, sir."

"Well, apparently General McKenzie called the 101st Division

Headquarters and told them you need to be assigned to this task force. When a three-star general tells a two-star general who he thinks is right for the job—well, everyone else down the line listens. So, I've got to trust that what you lack in experience you make up for in smarts."

I'd be lying if I said I didn't have some jitters about all of this. Hell, I am just out of the maintenance officers' course and test pilot training. I make a mental note that, someday, if I ever get the chance, I'll ask General McKenzie what the hell he was thinking! Maintenance experience is not my strong suit. But what I do have is an ability to look at something, figure out all the moving parts—or at least the ones that are most important—and then talk the planning over with those who do have experience, get their input, modify the plan and then work together to get things done.

Just before Westfield and I break up our meeting, he adds, "Some factory reps from Sikorsky and Boeing are assigned to you. You will also have a rep from the US Department of Agriculture and US Customs at your disposal. The factory reps don't come cheap. Use them often. Pay attention to the customs and ag guys. They'll be the long pole in your tent. If they don't sign off on the customs and ag clearance paperwork, the aircraft won't ship until you make them happy. Be sure you give them everything they want, OK?"

I respond with a quick, "Yes, sir."

Westfield looks around. "Nice of the air force to give us this hangar." He was being sarcastic. "You've got twenty-four hours to come back to me and tell me what else you're gonna need—wash racks, water supply, ramp area, staging areas—things like that. I'll get you those facilities. It'll be up to you to make it all work. Are we on the same page here, Jack?"

I give him a confident nod and say, "Yes, sir." But inwardly, I only hoped I had what all of this was going to take. There was never a mention of *aircraft retrograde operations* in my aviation maintenance officers' course, yet here I was, one of its most recent graduates and essentially the officer-in-charge of these preparations in a combat theater.

I needed to talk to Annie. I needed to hear her say, "You've got this, Jack!" Though we both had cell phones, they were no good internationally. I asked around. There's a United Services Organization, USO, service center here on Balad. I could get on a list to place an international call, which is exactly what I did after leaving Lieutenant Colonel Westfield's office.

Mid-July, 2009

We've been at it for about a month now. Aircraft are arriving at Balad daily for us to prepare for shipment stateside. Using my "advance party" idea, a couple of the senior warrant officers fly to a unit a few weeks before they are to begin bringing their aircraft to us at Balad. We let them know what our expectations of them are, and we answer their questions to the best of our ability. This has worked out well. It allows the unit owning the aircraft to finish what maintenance it can before the aircraft arrives for retrograde. For example, UH-60s require a periodic maintenance inspection at the end of each one hundred hours of flight time. If a particular helicopter is within ten flight hours of requiring this inspection, the unit is instructed to do it before delivering the aircraft to us. This way we don't have to worry about it, and by the time the aircraft arrives back to its stateside unit, they won't have to immediately ground it for this inspection.

We have twenty-five helicopters that are ready to be retrograded stateside parked in our staging area: sixteen UH-60s, four CH-47s, and five AH-64s. Our average time from reception to ready-for-shipment is two weeks on the UH-60s and AH-64s. It takes us three weeks to get a CH-47 ready to go. The first thing that happens when we receive any helicopter is an intensive records review. Helicopters have a lot of components known as *time change components*. These are things like engines, transmissions, and gearboxes. If a helicopter's records indicate any of these time change components is within fifty flight hours of needing replacement, we will do it, test fly the helicopter and certify it as mission ready once it reaches the states and is properly reassembled.

Disassembly for shipment is perhaps the easiest step in our process. Main rotor blades and tail rotor blades are removed and mounted on a crib that ships along with each helicopter. Main rotor blades, front and back, are removed from the CH-47s, placed on a crib, and that crib is lashed down inside the helicopter itself. Once the helicopter is disassembled, the hardest and most time-consuming part of the process then takes place— cleaning the aircraft to the satisfaction of the US Agriculture Department and US Customs Department. All access panels are removed and cleaned behind, sometimes requiring the use of a steam generator to remove oily messes. Floorboards are removed and spaces below them are thoroughly cleaned. This step gets extra attention on aircraft used for medevac purposes to be sure such things like traces of blood or human remains are removed.

Shipping is the last step in the process, and it has been one of the most challenging tasks we've had to deal with. The Military Sealift Command owns and operates several ships we could use to retrograde army aircraft from Iraq. The problem was we either had to provide a full shipload of helicopters or they wouldn't play ball with us. Their claim: it is too expensive to operate a ship unless it contains a full load. They proposed we simply prepare the aircraft one by one, keep them at Balad until we had a full shipload, probably somewhere in the neighborhood of three hundred aircraft, then load all of them at one time onto their ship, which they would position at Umm Qasr.

This "full-load concept" was shot down by the agriculture and customs inspectors, and the air force. Customs and agriculture didn't like it because once an aircraft was cleaned and declared cleared for shipment to the US, they didn't want it sitting around collecting dirt and dust for months before it shipped back to the US. The air force's objection was space. They were adamant there was not room on the already-crowded Balad airfield for us to mothball dozens of aircraft while we accumulated a full shipload.

Our option at this point was to figure out a way to use American President Lines' container ships, the only US flagged ships calling at the port of Umm Qasr. The problem with this option: none of our disassembled helicopters would fit inside of a standard ocean-going container.

We are huddled around the conference table in Lieutenant Colonel Westfield's office: me, CW5 Denney, a rep from American President Lines—APL for short—a rep from Boeing and a rep from Sikorsky. Westfield looks at me, "What are we gonna do, Jack?"

"We've got a plan, sir." I look over at the APL rep and say, "Show the Colonel what we have to do."

He unrolls a sheaf of drawings, showing modifications the shipping line will make to four container shafts on the two container ships they have making stops at Umm Qasr, and walks Westfield through them. There's also a second set of drawings depicting a flat steel panel—he refers to it as a "flat rack." It is the exact length and width of a standard shipping container, but only about two inches high. Our aircraft will be attached to these. Another drawing depicts a lifting sling, adaptable to a dockside container crane, that will be used to lift the flat rack-mounted helicopter up, over the side of the ship, and then lowered into the container shaft.

Westfield listens intently, looks over the drawings carefully, and then asks, "What the hell is this going to cost, Captain Rigley?" Before I could answer he adds, "I just got the bill from the air force for the two other wash points you needed. Wanna take a guess what they gouged us for those?"

I didn't but took a stab. "Fifty grand."

"Nice guess, Jack. Forty-five thousand. So, what's the price tag for the shipping?"

I broke it down for him. "There are one-time costs of half a mil to design and fabricate the equipment needed to load the helicopters. There is also a half million-dollar cost for modifications required to each of the ships. Boeing and Sikorsky charged us a total of a quarter million dollars to design and build the lifting slings for the three different types of helicopters." I saw him grimace. That bothered me a bit because the news was going to get worse before it got better. When he didn't say anything, I continued. "Shipping costs with APL are per aircraft and they don't care what type of aircraft because regardless of type it will take up the same space in the ship's container cell."

He brightened a bit, "Well, that makes sense. What's that number?"

"The Military Sealift Command negotiated that rate. It's going to cost us about forty K per aircraft. So, if we move five hundred birds, that will run us about twenty million." I waited for Westfield's head to explode just as mine had when I first heard that number, but it didn't.

Instead, he asks me, "Does that seem a reasonable number to you?"

The fact of the matter is, after I'd studied it quite a bit, it did. One UH-60 costs the army about six million dollars to procure new. For an AH-64, an Apache gunship, the price soars to fourteen million, and a CH-47 Chinook heavy lift helicopter—wait for it—comes in at a whopping thirty million new. When you considered shipping costs compared to procurement costs, forty million in shipping seemed a bargain. "Given what we pay for these things brand new, sir, forty million's a fair price to get them back to the states.

Two weeks later, 0700 hours, 28 July, 2009
CW5 Ryan Denney and I land our Blackhawk at the Port of Umm Qasr, Iraq's deep-water port closest to Balad. We are here to meet the first fifteen UH-60 Blackhawk helicopters that we have prepared for ocean shipment back to the United States. The aircraft are being trucked here on flatbed trailers from Balad. We still have to work out some details on the trailers that will move the CH-47s to port because of the height of these behemoth helicopters. The air force has some low bed trailers, called lowboys, that will work. The problem: getting our hands on them is going to be a fight. As we flew into Umm Qasr, we were able to see the convoy stretched out on the highway about fifteen miles away from the port's entrance.

The day wasn't without its issues. The stevedoring contractor providing the labor at the port had no one with more than a limited ability to speak English. So it was a real challenge to make the laborers who would hook up the specialized lifting harnesses understand how they were to work. Then the crane operator had to learn that slinging a flat rack with a helicopter clamped down on it required a bit more "gentle handling" than simply slinging a container up and over the side of a ship and down into a container hold. But by mid-afternoon, a routine had been established that worked for both labor and management, "management" being me and Chief Denney, who about shit our pants the first time the crane operator slammed one of our flat racks into the side of the ship by lifting it too quickly.

2000 hours, 28 July, 2009
CW5 Denney and I crank up our Blackhawk for the thirty-minute flight from Umm Qasr to Balad. The first fifteen UH-60s from Iraq were safely loaded and lashed on board the *President Kennedy*. The ship would sail on the next tide. In fifteen days, APL's *President Eisenhower*, the second of the company's ships configured to carry our helicopters, would call at Umm Qasr. Both of us felt a real sense of accomplishment as we reached an altitude of about two thousand feet, and I dialed in the frequency for our task force's operations center on the FM radio. "Retrograde Operations, this is Retrograde Three, Over."

The response from Ops was immediate, "Three, this is Ops, over."

"Roger, Ops. First shipment is secure onboard *President Kennedy*," I was not prepared for Ops response back.

"Uh, Roger that, Three. Retrograde Six needs to see you as soon as you land. He said to tell you he'd be in his office." Retrograde Six was Lieutenant Colonel Westfield's radio call sign.

My immediate thought was, *What the hell went wrong while I was gone?* Not liking surprises, I am tempted to ask what he wanted, but we were less than twenty minutes away, and chances are the person on the other end of this radio exchange was merely the messenger.

On intercom, Denney says, "Wonder what the fuck went wrong while we were gone?"

I see him looking over at me, so I just shrug, then key my mic and respond, "Ops, three, Roger that. Out."

We land and taxi to our tiedown spot at Balad. Ryan Denney tells me to go see what the old man wants; he'll take care of shutting down the aircraft and getting it refueled. I unbuckle and head for Westfield's office.

It's about a quarter of a mile to the well-lit hangar. We work a 24-hour shift in disassembling helicopters. The cleaning and washing, however, has to take place in daylight so customs and agriculture inspectors can see every nook and cranny on the helicopter. Colonel Westfield's office door is open, and I can see him at his desk. I knock on the door and enter with a smile, "The first loadout went well once we got the contractor to see how the lifting gear worked, and the crane operator got the feel of the flat racks. Next shipment should be about twenty Blackhawks and six Chinooks fifteen days from now, if we can get the air force's cooperation on those lowboys."

I expected a smile and congratulations, instead I get a frown and the directive, "Sit down, Jack. I've got some bad news. I received a Red Cross notification. It's your mother. She's passed. Your family has asked that you return to Empire for the funeral."

It's not as if I hadn't expected this, yet when it finally comes, it's a blow of gigantic proportions. I just sit there with a blank expression on my face.

Lieutenant Colonel Westfield continues, "I've checked with the Air Mobility Command terminal here. There's a C-17 departing Balad in four hours to Dover Air Force Base in Delaware.

You've got a seat on that bird. There's a travel office at Dover where you can make a commercial reservation to Michigan. I've made arrangements with the USO for you to make a call to your wife tonight. She's expecting it. Just go over there, they will connect you. Take a week. Let me know if you need a little longer, but Jack, I don't need to tell you how important you are to this operation."

I knew, of course, that I was leaving him in the lurch. I nod. "I understand, sir. I won't be any longer than—"

Westfield interrupts me, "Jack, I'm sorry, sorry about your mother, and sorry that I can't say to you 'take as long as you need,' but it is what it is. I hope you understand."

"I do, sir. I do."

I find my way to the USO. Annie picks up on the second ring on her cell phone. She's already in Empire with Becca, staying at her mom and dad's. It's comforting to hear her voice, to hear her say how sorry she is. I tell her, I'll be on a freedom bird, what we call any aircraft heading back stateside, in just a few hours. I'll call her when I get to Dover. After we've talked, I find my way back to my hooch through rote memory; my mind's in Empire. I shower and then lay down, but I can't sleep. I get up, pack a few things into my duffle bag, and then sit on the end of my bunk, thinking of Annie, Becca, and Empire.

FIFTEEN

It Matters!

Cherry Capital Airport, Traverse City, Michigan, 10:00 a.m.,
July 30, 2009

I have told Becca her daddy's coming home. She's babbled about little else since, but I've made the decision not to take her to the airport with me to pick Jack up. She is home with my mom, whom she has forever named Mima, with a short *i*. Purely by coincidence—certainly with no insight as to how seriously ill my mother-in-law, Anita Rigley, was—Becca and I came home to Empire about a month ago along with our new dog, Sophie, a shelter dog, whom our vet estimated was two, maybe three years old. A stray, she's an odd mixture of hound and terrier.

It's been just a little over twenty-four hours since Jack and I spoke on the phone. Even though we've been together nearly a decade, he's a hard read on exactly how he feels about his mother's death. In some respects I feel like he's been expecting the news long before this. Yet, in our brief phone conversation the other evening, I felt his sorrow. He'll be here soon. We will talk some more, and I will get a better feel for where he is right now.

I'm standing in the main corridor just outside the TSA

security checkpoint at Cherry Capital Airport in Traverse City, Michigan. A young woman standing a few feet away from me in the airport's corridor holds an infant in one arm and a sign in the opposite hand. It reads: WELCOME HOME, SFC JIM REEVES. WE LOVE YOU! WE'VE MISSED YOU!! I ask a question even though I think I already know the answer, but I nonetheless plow ahead, "Waiting on your husband?"

She responds, "Yes, ma'am. He's been in Afghanistan for a year." She bounces the baby on her hip, smiles at the infant and says, "He hasn't even seen her yet. She was born six months after he deployed."

I can feel her eager sense of anticipation and it leaves me at a loss for words. Her hero is coming home. I am happy for her, and I suddenly feel quite lucky. At least Jack had been at my side when Becca was born. And, if I am honest, the sudden surge of happiness is much better than the way I have been feeling. First of all, I hated that Jack had to come home to the tragedy of his mother's death, and in my own grief I had somehow mixed all that together. I was very eager to blame somebody—something—and that just happened to be the army. Then there was a purely selfish feeling on my part that he would be home for only a few days and then would have to leave again. Again, I blamed the army. I knew what he was doing in Iraq was important work. I tried to absorb an understanding of it as we talked on our weekly calls, but I fully admit, much of it was beyond my comprehension. Honestly, his attempts to explain what he was doing left me in a bit of a funk because I had the distinct impression that, while he missed Becca and me, he was enthralled with the challenge he faced in Iraq.

Passengers on the arriving flight from Detroit begin to stream toward us. Soon, I'll be able to hold him, to kiss him, only to have to let him go again in a few short days. I hated this about the army. While the reunions were dazzlingly romantic and heroic, there was always the lurking presence of a heart-rending goodbye.

Jack owed the army four years for his scholarship. I honestly think he's completely unaware he has no further service obligation beyond the summer of 2011, but it's certainly been on my mind. If there is any awareness there on his part, he certainly hasn't expressed it to me. I, on the other hand, hate this separation the army has forced upon us much more than I ever thought I would. It was something that nagged at me. This wasn't like the years we'd endured apart when he was finishing college in Kalamazoo and I was waiting on him in Empire. This was different. He was in a dangerous place, and even though there was talk about the US withdrawing from Iraq, there was the constant question of where else in the world might he be called to duty. I have vowed to myself that I'm going to address this now, while he's home on this emergency leave.

I see them at a distance on the other side of security. The woman waiting on her husband next to me sees them at the same time; both men are in gray camouflage fatigues, and they are talking to one another. She looks at me and exclaims, "There he is."

I tell her, "I see. That's my husband he's talking to."

"Your husband is coming home too?"

"Yes. From Iraq, but he's on emergency leave. His mother just passed away." Then I think, *Well, nice work Annie. Talk about raining on her parade!*

For a brief moment the woman's exuberance changes, her face slackens to somber and she says, "Oh, I'm so sorry."

Before I can say anything to her, both soldiers are heading

toward the two of us at a dead run. Sergeant First Class Reeves scoops up his wife and daughter in a bear hug that completely engulfs them. My tears are flowing as Jack does the same to me. The two couples, one with a six-month old pressed between them, stand there for an interminable minute as two statues of American military families reuniting. We break apart only because we hear applause. We are ringed by people, some passengers just off Jack's and SFC Reeves's flight, others waiting on someone, some heading for the TSA checkpoint. I even notice a shopkeeper from the nearby convenience shop, and they are all applauding Jack and SFC Reeves—they are applauding us. They've stopped in their travels long enough to recognize what is happening right there in front of them. Mrs. Reeves's baby smiles and waves her arms seemingly in response to the applause and that strikes laughter, cheers, and greater applause. We look around. I want to acknowledge their kindness, their respect, but words fail me. Then actions speak louder than words as Jack and SFC Reeves each offer a salute to the crowd.

As the crowd slowly disburses, Jack grabs my hand, SFC Reeves takes his baby from his wife and holds her close to him, and we head to baggage claim. In that all-too-brief moment, whatever anger I hold against the army fades and an overwhelming sense of guilt sweeps over me. On the way to the airport's short-term parking lot, several people offer their thanks for his service. Politely he thanks each one and says, "It's my privilege."

I say, "Have you ever seen anything like that?" referring to the applause and cheers in the corridor.

"Naw! But it was kind of nice of them wasn't it?"

"People should respect your service, Jack. God knows it isn't easy."

"Well, it's nice when they do, but you know, Annie, I think

I'd be happy doing what I'm doing even if no one ever said anything."

That comment speaks volumes to me. *He has no idea his service obligation is ending!*

8:00 p.m., August 4, 2009

A funeral mass was conducted this morning for Anita Rigley at Grace Episcopal Church even though Anita herself had never once attended services there. She was buried in Maple Grove Cemetery, and a celebration of life, such as it was, was held at the Lake Michigan house on Storm Hill where Anita had spent most of her final years in a drunken stupor. The funeral service had been lightly attended. Jack and I, my Mom and Dad, and Jack's dad and stepmother were the only ones at the graveside service. Ben and Rita were leaving Empire shortly to meet a NetJets flight at Cherry Capital Airport. If I were to be perfectly honest, I would describe today as pretty pro forma. We'd done what we, the living, felt was needed to help alleviate our grief. For a long time now, all of us knew she was drinking herself to a slow death. None of us labored over whether or not we'd each done enough, either individually or collectively, to stop her. All of us knew she wasn't going to stop. She was seeking solace after her divorce. She couldn't find it in money. Sadly, she couldn't even find it in her son's successes. Unfortunately, she seemed to find what she was looking for in the bottle, and it eventually killed her.

My mom and dad have gone home to allow us to be alone with Jack's father and stepmother, Ben and Rita, before they must leave. As we sit in the fading light of day, looking out at a magnificent Lake Michigan sunset through the house's wall of windows overlooking the bluff, it's Ben who says, "Rita and I have been talking about what to do with this house."

Jack didn't immediately respond. I think it's perhaps because he didn't have a lot of good memories of his time in this place.

Ben continues, "It needs some renovations. The kitchen's out of date and so are the bathrooms. Rita's got an eye for these kinda' things and we think there's some walls that could come down, rooms could be enlarged, some floors could be replaced with wood or tile . . . the whole place needs a fresh coat of paint, maybe some new carpet in the bedrooms. What do you think?"

I watch Jack shrug his shoulders. He wasn't snarky, but he asks, "Then what Dad? Put the place up for sale?"

Rita chimes in. "We could do that, Jack. But that's not what I had in mind. I've come to like Empire in my couple of visits up here, and this is the place you and Anne both call home. It's where you were both raised, and this is where Anne's parents are. I know the army tugs you away, but it's also some place the both of you have come back to—will keep coming back to. So, why not let Ben and me fix this place up and keep it as a family retreat? You two don't have to respond now. Give it some thought and let us know. Ben and I will do whatever you want us to do."

10:00 p.m., August 4, 2009

Jack crawls into bed next to me in my old bedroom in my parent's home. Ever since we were married, this is where we stay when we come home to Empire. It still seems somehow strange— almost forbidden—to have Jack here next to me in bed, the very same bed we couldn't even sit on together during those nights he'd come over for dinner and we'd study in my room with the door open. I like the idea of fixing up the house on Storm Hill and keeping it in the family. Jack has been silent on the subject since it came up. He snuggles in next to me and pulls me close. I know he wants to make love and that is what I want as well, but I have to ask first, "So, what do you think about Ben and Rita's proposal?" Through the now-closed bedroom door, we both hear my father open the door to my parents' bedroom and walk down the hallway past our room toward the kitchen. I feel Jack's embrace ease up a bit.

I watch him glance at the closed door. He says, "I think it's probably a very good idea."

I nudge him and laugh, "Is that because you are afraid to make love to me with my parents so close by?"

"Afraid? No. Cautious? Yes. And, for the record, I know that's crazy. We're married for cryin' out loud. And I have to leave in two days. If we were in the lake house, we could throw caution to the wind."

We wait until we hear my father close the bedroom door behind him and then we are both consumed by each other's passion. Tomorrow, Jack will call Rita and tell her to go ahead with renovating the Lake Michigan house.

8:00 a.m., August 7, 2009

At the very same spot and in the very same corridor at Cherry Capital Airport in Traverse City where we were united just six short days ago, I cling to Jack with all my might. Becca holds on to his leg for dear life. She is talking a little now, but tears are her only expression as she knows her daddy is about to leave us again. I feel Jack's grip on me relent.

He bends down and gently wipes the tears from his little girl's eyes and says, "Don't cry, sweetie. Daddy will be home before you know it." He stands and then must wipe my tears away as well. "Unless, things have changed since I left—and that isn't impossible—we might be able to wrap this goat rope up in nine months rather than a year. I love you, Annie." He kisses me one last time; another painful goodbye. And then he steps away. Through my tears, I watch him go. After a few paces, he turns around toward me and swipes at something below his left eye with one hand while offering a final goodbye wave. I watch as TSA checks his ID, after which he places his duffle bag and rucksack on the rollers at the security checkpoint and steps into the metal detector.

I never did mention to him my frustration with these goodbyes. I never did ask him whether he intends to resign his regular army commission or stay in. We might have that discussion in nine months or a year, but for now, I blow him a goodbye kiss, grab Becca's hand and say, "Come on, sweetie. Let's go see Mima." His service to our country truly matters!

PART III

Field Grade

Military rank applying to
mid-level army officers as major,
lieutenant colonel and colonel

thefreedictionary.com

2011–2022

SIXTEEN

Stay the Course

July 28, 2011

I have been home from Iraq a little over a year. Task Force Iraq Retrograde was highly successful in accomplishing our mission, even though it took the full year. We would have wound things up sooner, but operational necessity intervened and army aviation assets, especially the AH-64 Apache gunships, were needed longer than anticipated. Every member of the task force was awarded the Bronze Star for our duty in Iraq. Every enlisted member received the Army Commendation Medal. Every warrant and commissioned officer received the Army Meritorious Service Medal, and Lieutenant Colonel Westfield, our commander, was awarded the Legion of Merit. Warrant officers and commissioned officers who performed flying duties in Iraq received multiple awards of the Army's Air Medal. In the civilian world, efforts like ours typically result in cash rewards of varying amounts. The medals we received, on the other hand, are purchased by the army by the thousands every year at a price probably below five dollars each. Yet the pride we take in wearing them cannot be measured—they are priceless.

While I was gone, my battalion underwent a change of command

and the battalion's maintenance officer was reassigned to the Pentagon just before my return from Iraq. The new battalion commander heard what we'd accomplished there and was impressed enough to appoint me as the battalion's maintenance officer, a job I considered a promotion and something I really wanted to do.

When it came to adjustments on the home front, however, I was pretty "obtuse"—Annie's word, not mine. In retrospect I would describe myself as downright selfish.

Annie had been on her own for a year and she, Becca, and the dog had created their own routine, both here at our home in Clarksville, and in Empire where the three of them had spent a lot of time while I was in Iraq. I returned expecting all to be the same as before I left, and it turns out, that is a completely wrong-minded expectation. Annie was not shy in pointing out that they had gotten along quite nicely despite my absence, and it was her expectation I would adapt to their routine rather than vice versa. Sadly, there were some shouting matches between us.

My right-hand man in Iraq, Chief Warrant Officer Five Ryan Denney, became my sage advisor. A veteran of three year-long separations, he made me realize the truth in the saying, "Happy wife, happy life." Denney pointed out, "You know, Cap'n, it probably took your wife more'n a week to get used to being the only one raising that child after you left. Setting a routine and making that a part of your daily life may not sound hard, but try it when you are the only adult in the room. My advice is if you mess with the routine she's set up, you are playing with fire."

It took me some time. Annie was not bashful about telling me when I overstepped the boundaries worked out during my long absence. All of this has demonstrated to me that marriages in the military only survive when give-and-take is the rule rather than the exception.

Clarksville, Tennessee, the Rigley home, August 1, 2011

Annie and I have, for the most part, reintegrated ourselves into a family unit again. As a battalion maintenance officer, I don't fly as much at night as I did as a platoon leader in an assault helicopter company. But I still have to stay proficient, so there are those weeks, as opposed to months, where I am flying at night—and last week was one of those weeks.

I've just walked in the door at home and Annie says, "Jack, I don't feel like cooking tonight. How 'bout if I see if Lyndsey Capaletti can babysit for us and we go out for dinner."

It is the middle of the week and usually Annie keeps to a strict routine of dinner for the three of us at six o'clock. If for some reason I miss that time, I can expect her to keep a plate for me, but she and Becca would have their dinner on time.

Dinner is followed by an hour of play, and then Becca is off to bed at eight sharp. It's five-thirty, I am in a sweaty flight suit and need to clean up first, which means we won't be leaving before six or so at the earliest. Yet, she was the one asking to break her and Becca's routine. She asks these kinds of things so infrequently, I feel compelled to say yes. Lyndsey, now seventeen, our neighbor's daughter, arrives at six-thirty, gets brief instructions from Annie because Lyndsey was very familiar with Becca's bedtime routine, and we are out the door. In the car as we back out of the driveway I ask, "Any place special?"

"Ummm . . ." Annie ponders momentarily and then says, "Let's go to the Liberty Park Grill. It shouldn't be crowded on a Wednesday night. I'm hungry for a good juicy steak."

This strikes me as a bit odd because she rarely eats beef and I can't recall the last time she ever ordered it in a restaurant. But I say, "Liberty Park Grill it is."

I order a glass of red wine. Annie demurs and tells our waitress, "Just a glass of water with lemon for me, thanks."

I ask, "Sure you wouldn't like a glass of wine?"

"No. Water's fine."

When my wine comes we order our steaks, mine medium rare and, again, to my surprise, Annie orders hers prepared the same way. She proposes a toast to the two of us, and as we clink glasses, Annie looks at me and, with that incredible smile of hers, announces, "Jack, I'm pregnant."

Nine months later, 12:30 p.m., April 30, 2012

Annie's second pregnancy, like her first, has been textbook. All four grandparents and I surround Annie's hospital bed at Blanchfield Army Hospital. Becca is being entertained by our neighbor, Nancy Capaletti, at the Capalettis' house. Hours-old Rita Jacqueline Rigley, whom everyone has agreed will be called RJ to avoid confusion, lies across Annie's stomach. I put my arms around the two grandmothers. Rebecca presses her head against one shoulder as Rita presses against the other. RJ's eyes open. A moment later her mouth parts in a cavernous yawn. Both grandmothers squeal with delight. Annie's father and I smile, and Annie shoos us out of the room announcing, "OK, she's awake. She's hungry. Everyone excuse us while this little one takes some nourishment." I wonder how life could get much better than this.

October 15, 2012

Six months after having a sister introduced into her life, Becca has made a quick adjustment to things. RJ is a good baby and is on a sleep schedule that corresponds well with that of her parents. Annie and I, together, have established the new daily routine required by the addition of RJ to our family.

At work, however, nothing is ever routine. Helicopters are maintenance nightmares. Somewhere I read about a report by Harry Reasoner, longtime American journalist who visited most American living rooms via CBS or ABC while reporting on the Vietnam War. He'd been interviewing some helicopter pilots about their experiences flying in Vietnam. The quote from one of these pilots went something like this: "These machines are one hundred thousand moving parts, each one trying to break away from the one they are attached to." And that is a pretty good summary description. For every forty hours a UH-60 Blackhawk helicopter flies, it requires twenty hours of maintenance.

If I were to summarize my job as battalion maintenance officer in one word, it would be "readiness." The operational readiness rate, or ORR as it is commonly referred to, of the helicopters assigned to the 5th Battalion, 101st Combat Aviation Brigade, forms the basis of my efficiency rating. And I'm not the only one measured in such a way. Every aviation company commander, each battalion commander, the brigade commander, and ultimately the division commander's efficiency rating relies heavily on the ORR. Monthly it is reported directly to the Department of the Army, and it is the microscope we all live under. I am proud to say, the 5th Battalion's ORR has been consistently the highest in the 101st Air Assault Division for the last six months.

It's been hot for October at Fort Campbell, and I am ready to call it a day. I began about midmorning, performing a preflight inspection and maintenance operational checks on a Blackhawk just coming out of a periodic inspection in which one of the main rotor blades required replacement. During my first runup to full operating RPM—revolutions per minute—of the main rotor blades, I noticed a distinct one-to-one vibration, which meant one or more of the four rotor blades was out of track with the others. This is not an unusual condition when changing things out on the main rotor hub, but it had taken me several hours of adjusting here and tweaking there to eliminate the vibration. Then, during the test flight, the main transmission chip detector light came on. I returned immediately to the airfield, shut down, directed the crew chief to remove the access plate, pull the chip detector plug, and let me look at it. Sure enough it had a very small piece of fuzz on it, very likely introduced into the system when the oil was drained and replaced as a regular part of the inspection. That little piece of fuzz was sufficient to break the continuity of the electrical connection between the plug and the light on the aircraft's dashboard. I wiped the plug clean, had the crew chief reinsert it, and when I cranked the aircraft up again, the light did not illuminate. I completed the test flight just as dusk was settling in at Fort Campbell. As I was hovering into the aircraft's spot on the maintenance ramp, the FM radio crackled. "Army 63425, Ground Control."

I replied, "Ground, 425, over." I was expecting them to tell me to reposition to another spot or something like that.

Instead, "425, Eagle Assault Six requests your presence in his office ASAP. Over."

Eagle Assault Six is Lieutenant Colonel Swanson, the 5th Battalion's commander—my boss. *Shit!* I thought. It was five-thirty. I was already late for dinner by the time I got shut down, completed the test flight paperwork and drove home. *It's gonna be another plated dinner. No time to see the kids. Annie sitting at the dinner table watching me eat. Shit!* But, I have no choice. "Ground, 425, Wilco." The word *wilco* in radio lingo means "will comply." I understood the message. My tone, however, may have also conveyed to the person in ground control I wasn't very thrilled at the news.

Sweaty, disheveled, and anxious to find out what the ol' man wanted and get on my way home, I enter battalion headquarters only to be met at the door by the Command Sergeant Major. "Geez, sir. Where have you been?"

I almost get smart with him but back it off a notch. He's the top enlisted person in the battalion and everyone—including me—respects him. "I had to sign off—"

"It's OK, sir. I'm just hasslin' you a little. Let's go. The Colonel's waitin'." He hustles me down the hallway toward Lieutenant Colonel Swanson's office. I step through the door to a crowd of folks packed in there including the aviation brigade's commander, Lieutenant Colonel Swanson, his wife, and Annie and Becca. *What the hell?*

Swanson bellows, "There he is. Finally! We've been waiting since you landed."

"I—I'm sorry, sir. I didn't know . . ." I truly didn't know what I was supposed to know.

Swanson must have read the confusion on my face. "It's OK, Jack. All's good. In fact it's better than good. Seems that you are gonna soon be one of the army's newest majors."

That took a minute to sink in. I knew I was approaching the zone of consideration for promotion but hadn't had a lot of time to carefully examine just how close. Promotions in all of the military services are a function of time-in-service and time-in-grade/ rank.

"You were selected below the zone, Jack," meaning I was not yet in the primary zone of consideration for promotion; in other words, the promotion board had selected me for an early promotion to major ahead of my peers.

"What?" was the best I could do, as Annie and Becca sidled close to me.

Annie says, "Congratulations, Jack." Becca wraps her arms around my legs.

Still befuddled, I stammer, "Where's RJ?"

Annie laughs. "She's at home with the sitter. She's a bit too young for this kind of celebration."

Lieutenant Colonel Swanson says, "I think the army's made a great choice." The next thing I knew, the brigade commander, Colonel Bannion—whom I'd met, but didn't really know—hands me a glass containing a brown liquid. It was then I noticed everyone else in the room had one as well. Bannion raises his glass in a toast, "To early promotion and to Captain Promotable Jack Rigley!"

Turns out the brown liquid was Woodford Reserve Kentucky Straight Bourbon Whiskey. I am not a straight liquor kind of a guy, but have to admit, I didn't even notice the burn in my throat as Annie pulled my face close to hers and kissed me, as everyone in the room erupted in cheers and applause.

We're on our way home after the celebration, and I've secured Becca in her car seat and turned on another of Dora the Explorer's endless adventures for her to watch on the seat back. Annie drives home while I look over the entire promotion list of captains who've been selected by the army to become majors. Colonel Bannion had graciously supplied me with it. I recognize many names on it and quietly approve of most of them until I get to the list's bottom where those selected for early promotion are listed. Three names above mine I see *Ross Haverman*. I look over to Annie, "You aren't going to believe this."

"What's that?"

"Ross Haverman's on this list. Selected below the zone."

Incredulous, Annie glances at me, down at the list in my hands, and then back to the road ahead, "No way."

I look back at the list to confirm. "Unless there's two . . . no . . . wait a second, this says, 'Ross Haverman, AG.'"

Annie responds, eyes still on the road, "What's that mean?"

"AG stands for Adjutant General's Corps. Last I knew he was Aviation Branch, like me."

"Is he even still here at Fort Campbell?" she asks and then adds, "I haven't run into either him or his wife, but then again, I'm not a big golf, tennis, or bridge player."

I laugh. "I don't know. I haven't seen him, but then again, I don't go around seeking out Ross Haverman. I'll have to make some inquiries."

Annie asked, "What does the Adjutant General's Corps do anyway?"

"Mainly personnel management, but they also get stuck with a lot of the administrative ash and trash that keeps the green machine running."

"Like what?"

I give that a second to think of an example and then come up with a perfect one. "Remember that Fort Rucker Supplement to the Army Personnel Regulation General McKenzie asked me to write for him just after flight school?"

"Yeah."

"Well, before that could be published as a supplement, it had to be approved by someone in the Deputy Chief of Staff for Personnel's office at the Pentagon. They wanted to make sure it didn't somehow change any of the army's policies outlined in the basic regulation. See what I mean when I say 'ash and trash?'"

"Do you think it's the same Ross Haverman?"

"I don't know, but it could be. After he screwed me over at the National Training Center that night, instead of a Flight Evaluation Board, he got kicked upstairs into the Brigade's personnel office.

So, could be. Maybe he branch transferred. Like I said, I'll have to ask around."

We get home. I'm beat, and so is Annie, as we crawl into bed. Lyndsey Capaletti had gotten RJ to bed right on schedule. She never woke up after Lyndsey put her down for the night. Becca, however, was another matter. She had gotten some of the cake and ice cream Lieutenant Colonel Swanson's wife had made for the promotion celebration and she was still flying on a sugar high. It probably isn't the best time for me to bring up something about this promotion that Annie wasn't aware of, but it had been on my mind for a while even before the events of today. "Annie, you still awake?"

"Yes."

"Can I ask you something?"

"Sure. What is it?"

"This promotion, once I pin on the new rank, incurs another two years of obligated service. Right now, I don't owe the army anything. Flight school, the advanced course, maintenance officer's and test flight training—it's all paid back. You OK with us taking this promotion?" I emphasized the word *us* because this was a decision that impacted the four of *us*, not just me.

She asks me if I remember the day I came home for emergency leave and what happened in the corridor at Cherry Capital Airport. I tell her I do. Then she turns, puts her arms around me and says, "I was feeling sorry for myself before that happened. That was stupid. You make me proud everyday I'm married to you and it won't be long until Becca and RJ are old enough to feel that same kind of pride. Take the promotion, Jack. This is what you were meant to do."

SEVENTEEN

The Accident

Fifth Battalion Headquarters, 1500 hours, December 12, 2013
Three months ago, I pinned on the gold oak leaf, officially making me an army major. Two weeks ago, my office moved from the flight line to battalion headquarters, where I am the 5th Battalion's executive officer, or XO. I am reviewing the daily operational readiness report for the battalion when the Command Sergeant Major pokes his head into my office doorway and announces, "Sir, there's been an accident." Those are words no one associated with aviation wants to hear. I look up as the Sergeant Major steps in. He says, "Not one of ours, the 160th. One of their Chinooks. There's fatalities, sir," and with that he confirms my worst nightmare, even though it wasn't one of our battalion's aircraft involved.

"What happened, Sergeant Major?"

"Not a lot of details yet. I just got a call from a friend of mine in airfield operations. He says it went down about thirty minutes after takeoff."

The Chinook, or the CH-47 helicopter, is a massive machine capable of carrying a lot of equipment or up to as many as thirty-six passengers. Equipment is expendable. People are not. "Passengers?" I ask.

He lowers his head, "Yes, sir. About twenty-five of 'em including the crew.

Shit! I think, and then I say it, "Shit!"

The 160th Special Operations Aviation Regiment (Airborne), commonly referred to as the 160th SOAR, is an elite unit. Every member has volunteered. Every member has undergone extensive additional training in combat operations in order to qualify for this duty, which is most often short notice, dangerous special operations missions conducted under extremely austere conditions. Perhaps their most famous mission was in 2011 when they flew navy seals into a mysterious compound in Abbottabad, Pakistan, aboard two Blackhawk helicopters in the middle of the night. One of the birds was damaged during the daring raid and rendered unflyable. The crew of that bird and the second aircraft managed to secure the outside of the building while the seals moved inside and eventually killed Osama Bin Laden, the mastermind behind the 9/11 attack on America. Everyone got out and they took Bin Laden's body with them. After DNA confirmed the corpse was indeed Bin Laden, President Obama directed them to dump the body overboard at sea, rather than give any terrorist group the opportunity to call Bin Laden's burial site *holy ground.*

The 160th's pilots, crew members and support staff are considered the best the army has when it comes to helicopter pilots, crews and support staff. Their aircraft are all equipped with the most recent technologies, modifications, and improvements. Maintenance on their aircraft is both frequent and meticulous.

December 19, 2013
Christmas this year for the families of twenty-one members of

the 5th Special Forces out of Fort Bragg, North Carolina, and four families of the 160th SOAR will not be a merry one. Their sons, husbands, fathers, aunts, and uncles, perished in a fiery crash of a CH-47 Chinook helicopter into a farmer's field twenty-five miles north of Campbell Army Airfield. CW5 Denney, who has remained a fast friend ever since our work retrograding aircraft from Iraq, knew both of the pilots who were killed. Even though now my work as battalion XO means I don't see him very often, Ryan Denney and I still talk periodically. This day we plan to meet at a convenient watering hole on our way home to have a quick libation and catch up. After we exchange Christmas greetings, I ask him, "You knew the Chinook pilots?"

He nods, "Yep. CW4 Chuck Fielder and CW3 Bill Spicer. Between the two of them I'd guess they had about fifteen thousand hours. Fielder'd been with the 160th for about seven years and had maybe twenty-five hundred—three thousand hours of that sneaky-pete type of flyin'. He was on the CW5 promotion list. The army's gonna make that happen posthumously for his family. Spicer's a bachelor, so no wife and kids involved, but it still sucks for his family."

"Jeez, Chief. I'm so sorry. Any idea what happened?" I had heard only bits and pieces—rumors really—more than facts, and I figured if anyone knew more of the straight skinny, it would be Chief Denney.

He shakes his head. "Naw. Haven't heard anything yet. The 160th's being pretty tight-lipped about it. I've got some friends over there and if they knew they'd tell me, but no one's talking."

This was my first experience with a helicopter accident involving fatalities. I'd been involved in mishaps before where an aircraft was slightly damaged, but no one was even injured, much less killed. "So, what happens next?"

"That's a good question, Major." He flashes me a smile and says, "It's sure strange calling you that. Shit, I remember when you were just a wet-behind-the-ears Cap'n askin' 'what's *retrograde* mean again, Chief?'" We both have a good laugh and then he gives me what he knows. "What I am hearin' is that there's an accident investigation team coming from the Combat Readiness Center at Mother Rucker." *Mother Rucker* is how army aviators sometimes refer to Fort Rucker, the home of army aviation. Sometimes it was used fondly, other times not so much. "I guess they ain't just gonna let us less-informed folk here at Campbell determine what went wrong."

I ask him, "Is this the worst aviation accident in army history?"

"Worst one I've heard of in a training scenario. We've had a couple of bad shoot downs in combat in Iraq and Afghanistan, but that's different. Some fool with a rocket propelled grenade or a heat seeking missile pulls the trigger and gets lucky. That's a combat loss. This one here—well, I don't know what they'll find out, but in the end most of these things get blamed on pilot error of some kind."

EIGHTEEN

People in High Places

5th Battalion Headquarters, 0900 hours, December 21, 2013
Specialist Donna Hayes, the 5th Battalion's indispensable admin clerk, appears at my office door. "Major Rigley, you've got a call waiting on line five. A Major Haverman from the Pentagon." And with that, the mystery of 'what happened to Ross Haverman?' is cleared up. I thank her, pick up line five wondering, *What the fuck!* I don't like this guy, so I let my tone intimate that, "Been a while."

"Jack, what are you doing right now?"

It's an odd question, but, then again, it is Ross Haverman. So, I cautiously reply, "Not much. I'm the XO at 5th Battalion. Less flying, more paper shuffling." I try to veer the conversation in a different direction and get answers to a few more of my questions about him. "What are you doing these days?"

He responds, "I'm the aide to General Smith, the deputy chief of staff for personnel." I think, *So maybe you did branch transfer to the Adjutant General's Corps.* A possible answer to another question I'd had about him. But that thought is soon overtaken by a more urgent question, *Why the hell would the aide-de-camp for the army's deputy chief of staff for personnel be calling me?* I didn't have to wait long for the answer.

"Listen, Jack. I told General Smith you were a friend of mine." That surprises me. *Friend . . . he thinks of me as a friend!* He continues, "He asked me to make this call. You're gonna have a lot of questions, and I'm not sure I've got the answers. I don't think General Smith does either."

Now my internal caution alarm was blaring. "Uh, OK Ross. What's up?"

"General Smith got a call from General McKenzie, the vice chief." The vice chief of staff of the army is a four-star general. I think, *Holy shit! General McKenzie has his fourth star. How the hell did you miss that?* My thought is interrupted by Haverman, who asks, "Do you know General McKenzie?"

Without going into any detail, I respond, "I did a project for him right after flight school."

"Well, he remembers you. His note to my boss was, "I want Jack Rigley PCS'd to the DCSOPS immediately. Let him have Christmas and New Year's at home, but then get him up here to Washington by 2 January, not later than the third. Tell Rigley I'll explain when he gets here. His orders should read 'report directly to the vice chief upon arrival.'"

This was a lot to take in. First, PCS is military lingo for *permanent change of station* . . . permanently reassigned. That means the whole kit and kaboodle known as the Rigley family was going to move to Washington, DC. DCSOPS is the Deputy Chief of Staff for Operations. Finally, all of this is apparently being directed by the vice chief of staff of the army, General McKenzie. Perplexed would be a kind word for how this was all settling with me. "Shit, you've gotta be kiddin' me."

"Not in the least," he replied seriously. "I honestly can't give you much more than that. I asked General Smith if he knew any-thing more. He's as baffled as I am. Smith even told McKenzie you were assigned as a battalion XO at Campbell—not exactly a slacker's job, but it didn't dissuade the vice chief. He's got some-thing in mind for you, Jack, and whatever it is he's not telling anyone else—at least not right now."

Grasping at straws in some desperate attempt to at least give me a reasonable amount of time to get things rolling on a major move like this I say, "You know my boss isn't going to like this."

Haverman's response was sympathetic, but also very practi-cal. "I know. If I were you, I wouldn't say anything to him about this until the news works its way down the chain of command, which will be only a matter of hours. General Smith is calling the division commander as we speak to start your orders moving along. By this afternoon, you'll have PCS orders in hand. It isn't going to matter how much anyone objects. Four stars will win out every time."

He was right. Within a couple of hours I'd been called to the Division Chief of Staff's office where I was handed my orders. Colonel Jarvis, the Chief of Staff, says, "Don't know what any of this is about, but you've been summoned, Jack. Good luck."

This was another one of those days when I hated going home, much like the day I had to tell Annie I was being deployed to Iraq. I refrained from calling her with the news, feeling like it was something I needed to do face-to-face. When I'm driving home I actually wish I lived further away. This isn't going to be easy.

As I enter through the laundry room door into the kitchen, I'm greeted by two squealing daughters whose exuberance over Santa's upcoming arrival is boundless; I'm cheered, but only slightly. Annie's at the kitchen sink cleaning some lettuce for a salad she plans to serve as part of our dinner this evening. I bend down and give each of the girls a fleeting hug before they bound off into the great room with Sophie, our dog, to watch some children's Christmas special on TV. I walk over to the sink and give my smiling Annie a kiss. "Got some news today."

"What's that?"

I decide direct is best. There's no way any amount of lipstick on this pig is going to make it any prettier. "How do you feel about moving to Washington, DC?"

She drops the romaine leaf into the sink and turns toward me. "What?" Before I can clarify she also asks, "When?"

Two one-word questions, but each delivered with an intensity borne out of a combination of surprise and incredulity tempered by a tinge of frustration. I reach in the baggy pants-leg pocket of my fatigues and produce my orders, the ink on them barely dry. She takes them from me. I watch her as she scans. When she looks up to me, her voice is hushed so as not to disrupt our girls at this most happy time in a kid's life, but she clearly is not pleased with what she's read. "The second of January? You have to report on the second of January?" I nod. "But what about us, Jack? The girls and me, Sophie, the house. We can't just pick up and move like that. What the hell is the army thinking?"

"I don't know. Haverman . . ."

"Him again," she interrupts. He's got a hand in this?"

"He was just the messenger. General McKenzie has asked for me. I'm to report directly to him on January 2."

Annie is not happy, but we agree not to discuss this in front of the girls. Christmas is a special time of year for kids this age. We weren't going to spoil it for them with talk about a move to someplace neither of them had ever heard of.

0630 hours, January 2, 2014

A little over a week later, I'm on the division commander's C-12 airplane headed for Davison Army Airfield at Fort Belvoir, Virginia, just south of Washington, DC. This courtesy afforded by the commanding general has allowed me to enjoy New Year's Day with my family. At Fort Belvoir an army sedan with a driver delivers me to the Pentagon. General McKenzie's aide meets me at the entrance and escorts me quickly through security.

It has been, to the best of my recollection, seven years since I last saw General McKenzie in his office at Fort Rucker as he promoted me to First Lieutenant. I'm waiting in his outer office to be told to report, but this morning there will apparently be no formal reporting. His office door opens, he steps out, offers his hand and says, "Welcome to the Pentagon, Jack. I'm glad you're here." He hasn't changed much in the intervening years, with the exception of some graying around the temples, which only adds to his already distinguished appearance. He motions for me to follow him into his office and closes the door behind us. "Anne still speaking to you?" he asks and gives me a laugh.

"Spoke to her just a little while ago, sir. Just after I landed at Davison. She told me to tell you two things." He smiles. "First, she says hello. Then she wanted me to remind you, you owe her more notice on our next move." I'm only partially joking with him. Annie is still at Fort Campbell to sell the house, pack it up and get her, the girls, and the dog moved to Washington, DC. My job, in addition to doing whatever the hell the General wants me to do, is to find us someplace to live up here.

"I know I've probably ruined your holidays, but I've got something I need for you to do for me. What do you know about the Chinook accident that took all those lives last month?"

I'm honest. "Not much, sir. That was a 160th bird. I've asked around, but other than knowing a little about the pilots, everything is just rumor."

McKenzie puts the palm of his hands on his desktop, "Yeah, there's a million of those flying around. The Chief of Staff is really worried about them spiraling out of control. He's not an aviator and he's asked me to take a good hard look at how this thing happened, how it's investigated."

I nod and tell him what Chief Denney had told me. "I hear the Combat Readiness Command is sending a team to Fort Campbell."

"That's right. That team is due to arrive there today to start the formal investigation, but . . ." He stops there for a long moment. When he continues, there's a sense of urgency I had not previously detected in his voice. "This accident is getting a lot of play on the Hill. Representatives, senators, they're all piling on, questioning everything from the rigor of our training, the risks our pilots are put through, what we expect of them, and the airworthiness of our aircraft."

I let my naiveté show, "Investigations like this take time. Don't they understand that?"

He shakes his head, "No, they don't. They want answers. Now. We lost a lot in that accident, Jack. Those twenty-one Green Berets represent years of training, decades of experience. The pilots—well, I don't have to tell you. This accident has Congress asking a lot of questions about the Chinook. Some are claiming it's too old, outdated. They want to know why the army can't use the Osprey like the marine corps uses. So the Chief of Staff has asked me to get on this investigation, to get to the bottom of what happened, and that's where you come in, Jack."

I had a million questions coming into this meeting this

morning, but right now, I couldn't recall a single one of them. I just sit there.

"I want you to get back to Campbell as a member of the accident investigation team. I've sent a personal back channel to the Combat Readiness Command's commander directing him to have his team chief include you on the investigation team." He hands me a note. "This is my personal cell phone. If you have any problems with anyone—I don't care if it's the 160th, the team chief, it doesn't matter—call me and I'll get it handled."

I ask, "Sir, can I give Annie a call and tell her I'll be home for dinner tonight?"

He chuckles, "You certainly can. Maybe this'll get me out of the doghouse with her. And while you are at it, apologize on my behalf for all the difficulties I've caused with this move." Then he holds up an index finger. "But it's still a permanent change of station move for you. When this investigation is all wrapped up, you'll come back here and serve on the staff of the DCSOPS as the aviation readiness officer. In the meantime, let's keep your work on the accident investigation team close to the chest. You can tell Annie what you're doing, but not anyone else. I know I don't need to tell you this, but I will. You're not there to cover anything up. You're not there to make the army look good. You're there to get to the bottom-line cause of this accident. OK?"

I'm more experienced now, and with that has come self-confidence. But, I must admit to some concern. I've never been involved in an accident investigation, especially one in which so many fatalities are involved. Then there's the pressure from Congress. "Got it, sir. Anything else?" He shakes his head and stands. I take this as a signal our meeting is over. I stand and salute.

General McKenzie's aide puts a call into Davison Army Airfield. The C-12 that brought me to DC is still there. He has them hold it. It will return me to Fort Campbell. On the sedan ride back to Fort Belvoir, I place a call to Annie, "Hey, here's a surprise. I'll be home for dinner tonight."

Shocked, she replies, "What's going on, Jack?"

"I'll tell you when I get home. Pick me up at airfield ops. I'll call you when I've landed at Campbell. OK?"

"Uh, yeah, OK . . . I guess. I mean, I'm happy, but very, very confused."

"Yeah, I get that. We're still going to DC, but there's something General McKenzie wants me to help with at Campbell before we go. I'll tell you more later."

"OK, but you've got to tell me what's going on as soon as you get here. I'm dying to know."

The next day, 0800 hours, January 3, 2014
The accident investigation team has been given office space inside a hangar at Fort Campbell Army Airfield where the charred remains of the ill-fated CH-47 have been stored. The main hangar door has been opened to help clear out a distinct smokey smell, but it still lingers. I ask a chief warrant officer who is on the hangar floor looking over one of the heaps of twisted metal, "Can you tell me where I might find the team chief?" He gives me a quick once-over. I suspect he's about to tell me I'm not allowed in here because he doesn't see an ID around my neck similar to the one he's wearing. Before he does that, I tell him, "I'm Jack Rigley. I'm being assigned to the team."

Apparently, I'm expected. He replies, "Yes, sir. You're the guy from the Pentagon." He points, "Colonel Spencer's expecting you. He's in the last office along that wall."

I thank him and head off in that direction. I knock on Spencer's open door. Reading my name tag, dripping disdain, he snarls, "Major Rigley, our savior from the Pentagon, come in, please. You and I need to have a talk." Military courtesy requires me to salute upon entering his office. His head is bent down as he shuffles through papers on his desk and he doesn't return my courtesy. I excuse this by thinking he doesn't see me, so I drop the salute and stand there. Without looking up, he says, "Colonel Westfield tells me you're a water-walker, Major. Is that right?"

My back is up already. Not returning a salute is poor military manners on his part. Also, I don't consider myself a water-walker, a military euphemism for someone who is perceived as perfect. I'm not. Just ask Annie. But I remain calm and ask, "You know Colonel Westfield, sir?"

"He and I go way back. Gave him a call yesterday when I got the word you were descending from on high to join us mortals."

Can you see now why my back is up? I didn't ask for this fuckin' job. I was assigned to it. Spencer might be my superior in rank, but his rudeness in the span of only seconds requires my response. I interrupt, "All due respect, sir, I didn't ask for this assignment any more than I expect you did. I was told to report to you this morning. Here I am. I am not looking for your approval nor do I expect your condescension. Rather, I'd prefer we have a constructive discussion of how I can help. As to Colonel Westfield, he's a former commander of mine. I was his operations officer on a task force assigned duties in Iraq. We got along well, and we got our job done. I neither consider myself a water-walker nor a deity. I consider myself a part of your team and am looking for your guidance on how you would like me to proceed."

He's quiet for a long time, his head still bent down, still shuffling papers on his desk. I suspect he was trying to determine exactly how he was going to handle this upstart *water-walker.* When he looks up, he says, "Westfield said you weren't one to hold back, and that was one of the things he liked best about you. All right, Rigley, but there's one thing I want to get straight with you. I don't need a spy on my team. Do you have a direct reporting responsibility to anyone at the Pentagon as far as this team is concerned? If so, I want to know about it, right now."

This surprises me. It sounds as if he knows General McKenzie has handpicked me for this job, but McKenzie said he wanted that kept as closely held information. I think, *Fuckin' Haverman called this guy!* But that's just paranoia speaking. Haverman didn't know what McKenzie was going to ask of me. Spencer's question is straightforward and deserving of an equally straightforward answer. "I met yesterday with the vice chief, General McKenzie. He's the one primarily responsible for my assignment to your team. But I'm not here to be a spy, Colonel. General McKenzie's only specific direction to me was to let him know if I run into any problems getting the information this team needs to properly investigate this accident. I don't anticipate having to use that power, but the two of us should take some comfort in knowing he's willing to go to bat for us, if we should need him. Other than that, I foresee no need to speak to General McKenzie. When we've completed our investigation, our team's final report of the accident's cause should speak for itself."

He's staring at me as if evaluating—perhaps reevaluating what he sees. "All right, Major Rigley, let me ask you where would *you* like to begin?"

"Could I start with the paperwork? I'd like to take a look at all of its maintenance records, as well as the aircraft's logbook if it wasn't destroyed in the crash."

He reaches into a desk drawer and pulls out a green notebook labeled CH-47G. 160th SOAR, Tail Number 03-08003. "We caught a break. Somehow this thing was thrown free of the aircraft on impact. The recovery crew found it about fifty yards away from the wreckage." He reaches across his desk and hands me the logbook. "The maintenance folks at the 160th have been alerted that someone from the team is going to comb through their paperwork on this bird. Looks like that'll be you, Major Rigley. There's a daily meeting this afternoon at 1600." He points toward the front door of the cavernous hangar, "Two office doors down we've set up a conference room. We'll meet there. I've found it best if we each keep one another updated on our findings each day. Helps to keep everyone on the same page. I'll introduce you to everyone else then."

I didn't expect him to apologize for the chilly reception, but we'd progressed from "water-walker" and "savior" to "Major Rigley." Progress, no matter how small, is still progress.

1200 hours, January 9, 2014
It's been a little over a week and I've been combing diligently through everything the 160th has in the way of records on the doomed aircraft. Colonel Spencer is in his office. I'd been looking for him for the last couple of hours. I knock on the door. "Come in, Jack."

He'd started calling me "Jack" yesterday as the thaw between the two of us continues. "Sir, I think I've found something," and I lay out a spreadsheet I've created. It contains the comparative records of three aircraft's spectrometric oil analyses records for the last three years. The army has an acronym for nearly everything and sometimes they make more sense than others. In army aviation, spectrometric oil analysis is referred to as SOAP: Spectrometric Oil Analysis Program. Every aircraft in the army's inventory is enrolled in it, as was the CH-47G that is the subject of our current investigation.

SOAP is a non-destructive testing measure to determine the internal wear and tear on aircraft engines, transmissions, and gearboxes by measuring, in parts per million, the number of microscopic bits of metal contained in the oil used to lubricate these various mechanisms. My comparison had taken nearly a week to create because the CH-47 helicopter has a total of five transmissions, two engines, and a variety of gearboxes in the forward and aft pylons. My discovery involved the doomed aircraft's combining transmission, a critical component that synchronizes the rotation of the three rotor blades on the forward pylon with the three rotor blades on the aft pylon. The important fact is that in this heavy lift helicopter, even though the aft pylon is higher than the forward pylon, when the forward and aft rotor blades rotate, they actually overlap each other. The combining transmission is the mechanism that prevents them from colliding with one another, an event that would be catastrophic. I point to a row of numbers under a column marked, Combining Transmission-003 SOAP, and say, "Look at this increasingly high progression of microparticles on 003." Spencer nods. I continue, "Now look at the progression on CH-47F 012 and then at the same progression on CH-47F 005." I gave him a few minutes to do a quick comparison.

"003's progressing at a much higher rate," he concludes, then follows up, "Our bird's a G-model, these others are F-models. Is it the same transmission in each type?"

I assure him the transmissions are the same and then add, "I chose the comparison aircraft, 012 and 005, because their combining transmissions are about the same age and hours as the combining transmission on 003. We need to get 003's combining transmission pulled apart and see what was going on with it. It was definitely wearing at a higher rate."

"Why didn't someone in maintenance catch this, Jack?"

I shrug, "I don't know for sure, but I suspect because the SOAP samples all came back within normal limits, no one bothered to look to see the faster progression, the faster increase in parts per million. I'm a maintenance guy, sir, albeit on UH-60s, not Chinooks, and I'll be honest with you. All I ever looked for in a SOAP report was whether or not the parts per million were within normal limits. If the sample was WNL, then the bird is good to go."

Spencer asked, "So, if you were to speculate at this point, what do you think we are going to find if we tear that combining transmission apart?"

"Again, I can't be sure, but my bet is, something came apart. A teardown will tell us. Let's get the combining transmission down to Corpus Christi Army Depot and let them look at it."

Spencer asks, "Are you ready to brief this to the rest of the team at the 1600 meeting today?"

"Yes, sir. I think so."

"Good. You may have just shortened this investigation by months."

This accident investigation team is a good one, full of experience, and all of them have been briefed on the importance of their work on this particular accident. They will look at my work critically, but I am confident in what I've found.

That afternoon my colleagues concur with my comparative analysis of SOAP results. The civilian in charge of preserving the wreckage tells us, "The combining transmission case shows it's been in a fire, but it's still intact. I'll get it ready for shipment to Corpus Christi."

As we are leaving, Spencer pulls me aside, "Jack, maybe you should give General McKenzie a call and let him know what you've found. Ask him if he can make sure our transmission gets Corpus Christi's first and foremost attention."

"Yes, sir. Will do."

"And, by the way, Westfield was right about you. So was I. You are a fuckin' water-walker!"

While I still don't like the term, in this context, I take it as a compliment rather than a slight.

1600 hours, January 19, 2014

The results of the teardown and inspection of 003's combining transmission arrived just a few hours ago. Colonel Spencer and I have gone over them. I am about to brief the team. It won't take long. The first key finding was that one of the reduction gears showed shearing of a dozen gear teeth, completely disabling that gear's ability to mesh. The second key finding was when that gear couldn't mesh with its mate, the accompanying imbalance set up a shimmying effect within the transmission that ultimately resulted in the shaft connecting all the reduction gears to snap. Bottom line: the combining transmission disintegrated internally, a fatal flaw for which there is no tested emergency procedure.

As a pilot, I know the extent to which we are all trained on emergencies. We not only know in our heads what to do, we've continuously practiced the necessary control moves needed to correct the situation. But in the back of our minds we always know there are certain things that can happen for which there is no preparation. Since getting these results back from the depot, I've tried to imagine what was going through the heads of the pilots of 003. *What were you thinking? What did you do to try and correct what was happening?* I can almost sense both their fear and their frustration as their aircraft was falling out of the sky.

NINETEEN

Karma

1800 hours, May 1, 2015, Office of the Aviation Readiness Officer, Deputy Chief of Staff for Operations, the Pentagon

It's been a long year, but I am only recognizing this during a moment of reflection as I am cleaning out my cramped Pentagon office. At home in Woodbridge, Virginia, a close-in suburb of the District of Columbia, I called Annie a couple of hours ago to tell her I would be late, that I would miss dinner with her and the girls—again—that I was tying up loose ends. In this past year, since arriving at the Pentagon and working on the army staff, I've missed dinner at home as much as I'd made it. Tonight, whatever they have will be simple fare eaten on paper plates and using plastic knives, forks and spoons. Our home is in a moving van on its way to Fort Leavenworth, Kansas.

Becca is now seven and in second grade. RJ just turned three. While my work here at the Pentagon has been important and I feel like the army has benefitted from it, I have hated the incessantly long hours that have kept me away from Annie and the girls. But tomorrow, all of us will set out for our next adventure. I have been selected to attend the army's Command and General

Staff College, or CGSC. My reporting date is June 1. Tomorrow we will clear out of our rented house and turn the keys over to the management agency. On the way to Fort Leavenworth, we will stop in Empire for twenty days of leave, which both Annie and I feel we've earned at this point.

Ross Haverman and I will be classmates again as he has been selected for CGSC as well. But there has been a rather odd reconciliation between the two of us—or maybe it's just me reconciling—over this past year. After all, Haverman once told his boss, "we're friends." Bottom line is I've buried the hatchet.

* * * * * * * * *

It didn't happen easily, however. A year ago, within a day or two of my arrival at the Pentagon, he turns up at my office door. "Hey, Jack, welcome to the puzzle palace."

I recall not being in the mood for pleasantries. I was having trouble finding a place for us—Annie, the girls, the dog. The dog, Sophie, was the impediment. There were lots of places to rent, but none that I'd found so far would rent to us with a pet. But I'd been given my marching orders: Sophie comes, or we aren't. Making matters worse, while my title was *aviation readiness officer*, this position was not a rated position, which means I would not be flying, and flying was my primary reason for being in the damned army. So, I say to him, "Yeah. Wish I could say I am glad to be here."

Things go downhill from here. "It's a ticket punch. Fast movers like you have to work on the army staff at some point. You're lucky General McKenzie's taking care of you."

He's pissed me off now. *Fast mover* is just another term like *water-walker*. I bristle, "Jesus, Haverman, is that all the army is to you, just a ticket punch. Get the fuck away from me." I hoped that would be it, that I'd never see him again. This wasn't just a hint. I was out and out right rude to him. I literally didn't want to see him again. But, while the Pentagon might be a big place with a lot of people working there, it can get small at times.

I joined the Pentagon Officers' Athletic Club, POAC for short. I made it a habit to visit it for at least an hour every day of the work week. The place was jammed at noon, so I started to work through the noon hour and then hit the gym around 1500. My fuckin' luck, that was when Haverman was in there. I avoided him at first, but he was the one who first offered the olive branch, "Listen, Jack, I know we've been competitors . . ."

I rudely interrupt him, "We were competitors at ROTC summer camp and again in flight school, but those were like games. What you did at the NTC that night wasn't a game. You were one part of a team, a critical part of it at a precise point in time. I don't know why you called that LZ clear that night, but you let everyone down and I, for one, haven't forgotten it."

"I don't fly anymore."

"Yeah, I know. You transferred to the Adjutant General's Corps. Good for you. Maybe you won't get anyone killed there." It was as harsh as I'd ever been to a fellow officer, but I had lost all respect for him.

We didn't speak for a few months—until *karma* became that bitch that sometimes catches up to us. I needed some help from the deputy chief of staff for personnel's office and I was directed to see a Major Haverman. So, there's a lesson about not burning bridges.

He was helpful, and when I got what I needed quicker than I had expected, I decided to personally thank him. And that is when the two of us finally began a détente. I was standing in the door of his office when he says, "Sit down, Jack. I've thought a lot about what you said to me in the POAC."

I didn't really have the time, but something told me maybe I should make the time. I sat down.

Haverman tells me, "Truth be told, I'm not a very good pilot. I never got comfortable with the aircraft or my ability to manage all the dimensions of flight. I'm not sure if it was lack of confidence in the aircraft and its instrumentation or lack of confidence in myself. It didn't matter. I let everyone down that night at the NTC. I know that."

I felt like a priest on one side of the confessional with him on the other. *Maybe I've been a bit too hard on him. Maybe he is sorry for what he did.* But there's a lot there to forgive. Instead of saying, "Say three Marys and two Our Fathers," I say nothing.

His confession continues, "I was going to have to face a flight evaluation board, but my father knew the division's chief of staff." I think, *yep, dear ol' Dad'll bail you out!* But I'm surprised at what he says next. "There was a deal worked out. I would branch transfer to the adjutant general's corps and avoid the FEB. I took it. My father was furious. He was a combat arms guy and really only thought my going to flight school and then to the 101st was an acceptable substitute for not being in the infantry, armor, or artillery. When he found out I was going to become "a personnel weenie," that's exactly what he called me—a personnel weenie— we parted ways and rarely speak anymore. I know I'm a disappointment to him, but I would have been a bigger disappointment had I stayed in aviation."

At one point in his office/confessional Haverman tells me he's divorced. When I brought that bit of news home to Annie, she said, "I'm not surprised. Elizabeth was as shallow as a puddle. I mean, c'mon, Jack! You heard her: bridge, tennis, golf! The woman had no ambition beyond that?"

I agreed with her. Breaking the cardinal rule of the confessional, I tell her about his admission of guilt for what happened that night at the NTC and his acceptance of the fact he isn't suited to be an army helicopter pilot. Annie suggests perhaps we should have him over for dinner and get to know him better. That was Annie, her cup always half full; the Annie who can see the better part of people.

Me? I was surprised at his reformation, but there was still the point about his ambition—or my perception of it as over-ambition. His comment to me on my very first day at the Pentagon, "It's just a ticket punch, Jack." That still bothered me, so I tell Annie, "I don't know about dinner. I think he's still too much of a climber for me."

It was a few weeks later and I'd gone back to see him in follow-up on the project he'd helped me with. When we'd accomplished the original point of my visit, I decided to let go with my niggling reservation about him. "Can I ask you a question?" We would use his office this time as a classroom rather than a confessional. Haverman would give me pointers on the reality of moving ever upward in the army.

"Sure."

"You recall telling me, my job is a *ticket punch?*"

"I do."

"Do you really mean that—I mean, is that what you really think you and I are doing here?"

"I think that is an important reason for the two of us to be here, in the Pentagon. You don't?"

"No. It seems pretty cynical to me."

He gives that a minute to sink in and then says, "Yeah, I

guess I can see that. But I also know the reality of it is this: guys like you and me, doing the jobs we are currently doing, will move up in the ranks, and it's important that people who are good at what they do in the army are allowed to move up." I just sit there as I realize that less-cynical spin makes some sense. "Listen, Jack, we both know you'd rather be someplace where you are flying, but even if you don't want to admit it, the army has bigger plans for you. That's why you got that job in Iraq. That's why General McKenzie put you on that accident investigation team." I am surprised he knows my service record about as well as I do. "You're being groomed, Jack, like it or not, for bigger and better things. Now this is going to sound very conceited, but I think I am, too, just not in aviation. I'm a personnel guy now, and this is where I need to be if I'm going to learn, if I'm going to move ahead in that field."

When I go home and tell Annie about all of this, she says, "I hope you weren't surprised by any of that." Truth is, I wasn't. It's flattering to be handpicked for jobs and I'd been handpicked three times; once for the project at Fort Rucker following flight school, once for the job in Iraq and, last, for the job on the accident investigation team. Annie suggests again, "You know, maybe we should have Ross Haverman over for dinner. Maybe we'd both like to get to know him better now that he's shed that suck-up ex-wife."

A week or so later, I extend him an invitation to dinner at our home. He accepts. If the hatchet isn't fully buried, there's only a little of the handle sticking out of the dirt. The last time we'd had him over for dinner was just before the movers packed us up for this move to Fort Leavenworth.

A year later, 1000 hours, June 7, 2016,
US Army Command and General Staff College,
Lewis and Clark Center, Fort Leavenworth, Kansas

Our year here has flown by. My class is lining up to enter the main auditorium for our graduation ceremony. I am number two in line; Ross Haverman is our class's Distinguished Graduate. I must admit, he deserves the distinction. It was his Master's thesis, I think, that separated the two of us. It was well-written, expansive, and, in my case, timely. In it he makes the point that every one of the army's current list of two hundred and thirty-one general officers have one thing in common; successful completion of both battalion and brigade command. But if one studies those selected for these sought-after commands, there is an exceedingly high failure rate while serving in command at the battalion and brigade level, suggesting a better method of selection, one with a more rigorous screening, might be in order. He even went so far as to put a dollar amount as to what this new system might cost, along with how much it might save the army in the long run.

While we have been here at Command and General Staff College for this past year, forty-five of us have been selected for promotion to lieutenant colonel; Ross and I are the only two selected early, and both of us have also popped on the selection list for battalion command. Classmates are good-naturedly calling us "water-walkers." While Ross will have to wait a year to go to his command, I am headed there immediately, due to an unanticipated and unfortunate series of consequences that, it would seem to me, proves the point of Haverman's thesis.

My battalion command will be in Afghanistan. Annie and the girls will not be accompanying me, something Annie is not happy about. I will be working once again for Colonel Richard

Westfield, who has just assumed command of a combat aviation brigade, replacing a colonel who was caught in a compromising relationship with a subordinate; a fatal leadership flaw.

I will command an assault helicopter battalion, which is part of Westfield's brigade, and the lieutenant colonel I am replacing has been relieved of his command by Colonel Westfield. I am not privy as to whether or not Westfield has requested me by name for this job, or if all of this is just coincidence. But, I have the feeling I have been handpicked, yet again. Westfield and I have talked, and he's not offered up this detail, nor have I thought it appropriate to ask. I am not unhappy to be working with Rich Westfield for a second time. I just wish it didn't have to be in Afghanistan, away from my family, again. The battalion's current executive officer will hold down the fort until I get there, but I have been briefed that the battalion's operational readiness rate is in the dumper, the Inspector General is constantly receiving complaints about the lack of leadership at all levels, and morale in the battalion is generally low. Any one of these failings means trouble, but all of them combined are fatal to remaining in command. The officer I am replacing is no one I know, but I'm told he's a West Point graduate described to me by Westfield himself as "brilliant," but, apparently, completely lacking in people skills. Again, it seems the point in Ross's paper is proven; the army needs a better method of selecting those officers chosen for these important command positions.

1900 hours, January 16, 2017, Officers' Mess, Bagram Air Base, Afghanistan
I have been in-country for about ninety days. I miss Annie and the girls, but the work associated with reviving an assault helicopter battalion whose training, maintenance, morale and about

everything else has been off track has been intense to say the least. I am having dinner this evening with Rich Westfield to discuss my battalion's improving-but-still-lagging operational readiness rate. We've gone through the chow line and gathered our food and just as we are about to sit down, I look up and lock eyes with a woman I vaguely recognize. As she walks the short distance toward me, I struggle to recall the who, when, and where of our knowing one another, but as she sticks out her hand in greeting, it all comes back to me. "Jack! Jack Rigley!" I remember her. It's Ruth Zeller.

She is dressed in camouflage fatigues; in her other hand she holds her fatigue cap. Her brunette hair is pulled back along the sides and top of her head and rolled into a bun, but I can tell that if she let her hair down, it would be long—very long, well below shoulder length. On her fatigue jacket and on her cap is the distinctive insignia of a full colonel. "My God! Ruth Zeller! How long has it been? What are you doin' here?" Before she can answer, I realize my rudeness and introduce her to Westfield, "Sir, this is Colonel Ruth Zeller. She and I were in the same platoon at ROTC summer camp at Fort Knox about a thousand years ago." Turning to Ruth, I say, "Colonel, I'd like you to meet Colonel Rich Westfield, my boss, commander of the 1st Combat Aviation Brigade."

Pleasantries now behind us, Westfield motions toward the chow line. "Why don't you go get your food and join us?"

"I'm not interrupting anything, am I?" He assures her she is not.

When she returns, I ask, "So, Colonel Zeller—"

She interrupts me, "Jack, if you call me *colonel* one more time I'm . . . " Without completing her threat she turns to Westfield and says, "Jack Rigley is the reason I'm still in the army."

It's flattering to me, but I know the army and I know she wasn't just given that colonel's insignia. So I ask, "Ruth, what are you doing here in paradise?"

She takes a drink of her ice tea and replies, "Right now, I'm doing double duty. I'm the commander of the 344th Combat Support Hospital at Forward Operating Base Salerno. I flew in with a patient of mine from there. I'm also the resident neuro-surgeon until another one arrives from the states."

I remember from our conversations at summer camp, she'd wanted to be a doc. I say, "So, you did become a doctor!"

Ruth nods, "I did. My day job is Chief of Neurosurgery at Massachusetts General Hospital in Boston. But I kept my reserve commission. This is my second tour in Afghanistan. I've been here about nine months now. The 344th's a trauma hospital. We save lives every day. My patient today was the victim of an IED. He's stable, but still in very critical condition. I flew in with him on a medevac chopper and got him on a C-9 medical transport headed to Ramstein Air Force Base. I just wanted to make sure he got loaded as a priority and that he was in good hands. He is, but I'm stuck here overnight. There's a helicopter headed back to Salerno in the morning, and I've got a seat on board. The air force is putting me up for the night in their VIP quarters. Have you seen those? You'd think it's the Hilton."

Westfield cracks smart about the air force just as his cell phone rings. He takes the call and then says, "Ruth, it's nice to meet you. Thanks for the good work you do. Jack, I gotta go. One of our attack helicopters had to make a precautionary landing in the boonies with a transmission chip detector light after taking some small arms fire. The pilot got the bird on the ground, but radioed he was getting a lot of control feedback. Maybe the fire they took penetrated the transmission case and the damned thing is coming apart. I need to get to ops and make sure everyone's OK and find out what's the plan to get the crew and the aircraft back here to Bagram."

I say, "Let me know if you need us. I've got two crews on standby."

He leaves Ruth and me to catch up. As we sit, I jokingly say, "So, catch me up on the last thirteen or fourteen years."

I can't help but notice that she has kept herself in good shape in those intervening years, but as she begins, it doesn't take me long to determine her life hasn't been without its challenges. She is divorced, never remarried and has no children. By her account she is devoted to two institutions: Mass General Hospital and the army. Then she asks, "How 'bout you, Jack?"

She sits and listens as I tell her about Annie, Becca, RJ—even our dog Sophie. When I finish, she surprises me a bit. She says, "You know I meant it when I told your boss I likely wouldn't be here today if it weren't for you on that navigation course at summer camp."

I think, *Night nav course! I've just told you about my life, my wife, our kids, our dog, for Christ's sake!* Then I say, "C'mon, Ruth. Let me ask how many times you've used those navigation skills over the last fourteen years?"

She laughs. "OK, point taken. But you really helped me with my confidence that summer at Fort Knox, Jack." We linger over coffee for a while and reminisce some more, but it's getting late and I have some office work to do before turning in. As I start to wind things up for the evening, I'm surprised again when she says, "You never called."

I flash back to the piece of paper she'd given me the last time we'd seen one another all those years ago at Fort Knox. On it she'd written an address and phone number. Still trying to keep things light, I smile at her and say, "Ruth, I . . ."

She smiles at me. "I know, Jack. Annie. That's what you told me then and I can see that she's still the center of your universe. But, this is Afghanistan and we're both thousands of miles from home. I'm in room 6 in the VIP quarters, if you'd like to carry this evening a little further." With that, she stands, we shake hands, she gathers her tray and leaves.

When I get to my office, I call Annie. We usually schedule our calls. My daily routine is a jumble. Annie's, because of the girls, is more rigid. This call is off that schedule. When she answers, I detect a hint of concern in her voice, "Jack? Everything all right?"

I smile, "Yes, everything's just fine. I was just missing you and the girls. How's your day been?" It had been good seeing Ruth. I am glad she'd become a doc, even happier she was an army doc, but, as Annie tells me about a funny thing that had happened to her and the girls today, I honestly hoped Ruth Zeller's path and mine would never cross again.

TWENTY

Another Aviation Accident

2000 hours, 20 March, 2017, Bagram Air Base, Afghanistan

I am tired, hungry, and now, just now, a bit irritated. We are the last remaining assault helicopter battalion in-country and our daily mission load is heavy. This is the third day out of the last seven I have been pressed into flying an all-day mission. After shuffling papers at the Pentagon and studying for a year at the staff college, it's good to be back in the cockpit again. But the downside about flying all day—and I am being very selfish to point this out—it means there is a stack of papers, phone messages, emails, etc., that are piling up in my office that will require tending to before I turn in for the night. It is a relief I won't have to fly tomorrow. Though the mission load tomorrow is heavy, I have sufficient pilots and helicopters to cover it.

My current irritation is because, as was the case in Iraq at Joint Base Balad, I am an army unit on what amounts to a US Air Force base, and generally speaking, air force priorities often clash with mine. Most of our missions require two birds, and today was no exception. I have called for fuel for me and the other aircraft. My battalion's designated call sign is Chukker. I am not in the habit of pulling rank, but I had the thought it might help expedite our fueling requirement. "Bagram Ground, Chukker Six." The "Six" identifies me as the battalion's commander.

The response is immediate; a good sign. "Chukker Six, Bagram Ground, Over."

"Bagram Ground, Chukker Six and Six Alpha require fuel at Chukker Ramp, Over."

"Chukker Six, Ground, Roger. Be advised you are sixth in line for fuel. Estimated wait time, one hour." My attempt to pull some rank has failed miserably. I look over at my copilot and mouth the word *Fuck*. He shakes his head. Over the aircraft's intercom, he says, "Go ahead, Boss. I've got this." The crew chief in the back echoes my copilot's help. I tell them both I appreciate it. After all, they are both just as fuckin' tired as I am. Flying in a combat zone is more taxing than any other flying I have done—even though the threat is somewhat diminished by the enemy's lack of sophistication. The Taliban have only small arms for the most part, and once we get to fifteen hundred feet or so above the ground, their rifles and pistols are ineffective. Still, once in a while, they get lucky with a rocket propelled grenade or a mortar, but these are the proverbial one in a million shots and have happened mostly when the aircraft are on the ground.

We shut down, but leave our navigation lights on, so the fuel truck, when it does get here, can spot us. I crawl out of the cockpit, remaining crouched down as the ever-slowing orbit of our rotor blades causes them to droop at their tips. When I'm clear, I straighten up and quicken my pace. It feels good to stretch my legs after flying all day. A few minutes later, I walk into my battalion headquarters and check with the battalion staff duty officer who assures me it's been a quiet evening, so far. Proceeding to my office, I walk in and sit down behind the desk just as my cell phone rings. These convenient devices have revolutionized communication, making unaccompanied tours of duty like this one a little more tolerable. Annie and I use WhatsApp, so we are able to talk and text internationally with ease and regularity. I smile into the phone and say, "Good mornin'." With the time difference, it's about 9:30 a.m. in Empire. The girls and Annie are living in the Lake Michigan house on Storm Hill until I finish this unaccompanied tour and we find out where our next assignment will be.

"Jack . . ."

"Yes, Annie. I'm here. What's up?" I ask cheerfully.

"Jack, it's your Dad."

I don't like this. Caution in my voice, I ask. "What's happened, Annie?"

"He's gone, Jack." I hear her crying.

There's nothing to compare to the feeling that overtakes you when you so suddenly, so unexpectedly get this kind of news. Even in the case of my mother's death, where I knew she was at high risk, I wasn't prepared when the news did come. My father, since his marriage to Rita, was a new man, and that included how he took care of himself. He swam almost daily. Wine was about the only alcohol he consumed. I could not imagine how this could be. I manage to sputter, "What—What's happened?"

A moment passes like an eternity as she composes herself. "Rita called. He and a client were flying to Bermuda to look at a yacht the client was interested in. Their private jet went down. They've told Rita the Coast Guard has mounted a search but, so far, they can't find any wreckage. They're saying no survivors. I've asked the Red Cross . . ."

Just as she tells me this, my staff duty officer appears at my doorway, a note in his hand. I put my hand over the cell phone's microphone and motion for him to come in. He hands me a note and says, "Sorry, sir. It's a Red Cross notification about your father."

7 April, 2017

Annie met me at the Miami Airport a week ago. Tomorrow I must catch a flight from Miami to Dover Air Force Base, and from there a C-17 will return me to Bagram Air Base and my battalion. Rita is a mess, but less of one than she was when I got here. Sudden loss like this is so hard to deal with, and she has done a remarkable job, but closure is still a long way away for her—for all of us.

Dad's body was not recovered, but everyone flew down here from Empire—including Annie's parents—for a memorial service. The Millers and Becca and RJ will fly back to Empire tomorrow after I've left. Annie will remain in Miami for a while and stay with Rita as she sorts through this sudden, unexpected tragedy. I am thankful Annie can stay to comfort Rita. I'm also comforted to know that our two girls are in the loving care of their grandparents.

TWENTY-ONE

Time to Say Goodbye . . . Again

8:00 p.m., June 13, 2018, Rigley family quarters, the Army War College, Carlisle Barracks, Carlisle, Pennsylvania

I returned about a month ago from Afghanistan and am currently attending the year-long Army War College. This school is the next logical step—the next ticket to be punched—in my career, and it's a must if I am to progress to what I want to do next: command an aviation brigade. In a perfect world, that would be the 101st Combat Aviation Brigade, at Fort Campbell, Kentucky, that has just been redeployed back to the states from Afghanistan. But for now, I am looking forward to getting to know my family again. School is a pleasant respite after commanding an aviation battalion in a combat zone for a year. The routine is eight-to-five and some days, I'm even home just after noon. This evening, we've eaten together as a family at home and now are settled in our living room streaming a movie on Netflix when Annie's cell phone rings. I ask if she wants me to pause the movie, but she shakes her head. "It's Dad," she says. Becca, RJ, and I stay put, while Annie steps into the kitchen to take the call from her father. When she returns she is crying and has a stricken look, "Jack, it's Mom. She's had a stroke."

Both girls see their mother in tears. Becca is old enough to know what a stroke is, RJ isn't but begins crying along with her mother and sister. I grab Annie in a hug and tell her, "We'll be in Empire tomorrow morning."

11:00 p.m., June 13, 2018
A Red Cross message confirms for the Army War College that there is a medical emergency involving the mother of a student's wife. I am granted leave immediately and we are now on the road from Carlisle, Pennsylvania, to Empire, Michigan. Packing was quick and light. Most of what we need is already at the Lake Michigan house. According to Annie's father, her mother is in the hospital, comatose. For the girls' sake, Annie bravely holds back her tears. We are prepared for the worst, but we calmly tell Becca and RJ that their grandmother is going to be OK.

1:00 p.m., June 15, 2018, Munson Hospital, Traverse City, Michigan
I am en route back to the war college. Annie's mother appears to be in stable condition. Annie, Becca, and RJ will remain in Empire until, well—no one knows how long they will be there.

9:00 p.m., June 15, 2018, somewhere on the Pennsylvania Turnpike
My cell phone rings and I press the button on the steering wheel to answer the call, hands free. Annie is in tears, but through the sobs she is able to tell me, "Jack, Mom's gone." I'm first stunned at the news, and then ashamed that I'm not there to hold her, to comfort her and the girls. I am approaching a turnpike exit and I take it. I tell Annie, "I have to pay a toll." I wasn't prepared for either this news or this toll. My money is in my wallet which

I am sitting on. I'm the first in line at the toll booth, but there are four or five cars behind me. *Dammit!* "Let me get through this toll and I'll call you right back." A minute later I punch in her number and a sobbing Annie answers. I say, "I'm so sorry." Then I ask, "What happened?"

"They think she had a brain aneurysm."

I, of course, couldn't see her, but I know how much she loved her mother. I know she's bereft. I hold back my own tears because I feel like I need to be strong right now for my family. "Annie, I'm so sorry. I'm turning around. I'll be back there as soon as I can."

12:00 p.m., June 20, 2018, the Lake Michigan house, Storm Hill, Empire, Michigan

For the second time in just a little over a year, grief gathers us together. Annie, Rita, Danny, Becca, and RJ were with Rebecca as she breathed her last. Her funeral service this morning was attended by at least a hundred people, many of them faithful customers of the family business, Empire Feed and Grain. She was buried in Saint Philip Neri Catholic Church Cemetery, a feat that took a little string-pulling since the Millers are Episcopalians . . . decidedly not Catholic. But several of the family's friends who are Catholic intervened with the bishop and with an additional fee of a thousand or so dollars, Rebecca found her final resting place. This was Danny's wish. The cemetery is within walking distance of their house and he wanted to be able to "visit her every day."

Rita is here and she has been invaluable in taking care of Becca, who is now 10, and RJ, age 6, giving Annie and me the time we needed to make most of the arrangements. Both girls are grief stricken, having spent nearly every summer here in

Empire with their grandparents, not to mention the entire time I was deployed to Afghanistan.

Everyone is staying in Empire for a while except me. My absence from my studies at the war college has been long enough. I give Rita a hug and thank her for everything she's done. After I've given each of the girls a goodbye hug and kiss, Rita shuffles them off to the kitchen with the promise of baking some chocolate chip cookies. In an impossible attempt to try to console the inconsolable, I put my arms around Annie's father and tell him once again how sorry I am, and that I love him. Annie walks with me to the car. "Listen," I tell her, "you and the girls stay here as long as you think you need. It's best for your dad if all of you can be around for a while." Her tears begin to flow. We are both struggling with the conflict of doing what we know is the right thing to do, and what we want to do, which is stay together. Her tears tear me apart, but I have no choice; I have to get back to the War College. I wipe them gently from her cheeks with both my thumbs as I cradle her face in my hands. "I love you, Annie."

TWENTY-TWO

More Years Apart

June 4, 2019

Our year together at the Army War College is nearly over. A month ago, Annie and I made the most difficult decision of our entire married lives together. Neither of us know if it is the right choice. Instead of trying to make that judgment at this point, we have chosen to call it the necessary decision. Today I went to the transportation office here at Carlisle Barracks and made arrangements for our household goods to be shipped to Empire, to the Lake Michigan house, where Annie, Becca, and RJ will live to care for the still-grieving Danny Miller.

I, on the other hand, am one of only two army officers selected to attend graduate school at Harvard University. Honored? Yes. It seems I've been handpicked again. Does this make me happy? Not particularly. Annie and the girls remain in Empire.

A long year later, July 2020

Graduate school was what it should be: a learning experience. Harvard is a big school in an even bigger place, Boston. I spent the entire year, however, looking over my shoulder, hoping I wouldn't run into Ruth Zeller. Crazy, I know!

After graduation, I was able to spend a wonderful month with everyone in Empire at the Lake Michigan House. It was difficult, to say the least, when it came time for me to say goodbye. I am returning to the Pentagon to "punch another ticket" in my military career. On July 25, 2020, I will report to the Office of the Director of Operations for the Joint Chiefs of Staff. The key word in this descriptor is *joint*. Senior officers—that's how I prefer to be known rather than *water-walker or fast mover*—from all services are now expected to have at least one year in a joint duty assignment. In the last decade or so there has been a real push, much of it from Congress, for the Pentagon to get its act together and for the services to begin cooperating with one another instead of squabbling over money and turf like junkyard dogs. The main point of Congress's argument is based more on economics than anything else. It's cheaper if things that work for one of the military services can also be made to work for all the others. The concept is called interoperability, or developing the ability of a system to work with or use the parts or equipment of another system. It is something long overdue, in my opinion, which, by the way, no one has asked. My opinion, however, derives from having worked at Joint Base Balad in Iraq and Bagram Air Base in Afghanistan, where interoperability was sometimes foregone to meet the air force's priorities. So, I think I have some practical experience to bring to the table.

Annie and I have looked at our own finances to see what impact living apart will have on us, and we have determined we are blessed to have the mortgage-free Lake Michigan house, which Rita has done a bang-up job of renovating over the last few years.

I anticipate this assignment will be as much of a rat race as my last tour in the puzzle palace was. I already know I won't be spending a lot of time in whatever living space I can secure close to the Pentagon, an area in which the words "affordable" and "apartments" cannot be used in the same sentence. If I'm lucky I might find a one-bedroom, or even an efficiency apartment. We will use my Basic Allowance for Quarters, a part of my pay, to cover at least part of my rent.

It's been over a year since Annie lost her mother. We still believe our separation is a necessary decision at this point, maybe even the right decision. I had read somewhere that grief has five phases. Even though I know not everyone grieves the same way, I've watched my father-in-law's grieving from afar over this past year. Annie has experienced it up close and very personal while living in Empire. We both think he is stuck in the fourth phase of his grief—depression. Becca, RJ, Annie, and even I have noticed he has visibly lost weight, and sometimes he appears addled. While we went to some lengths and expense to get the necessary permissions for Rebecca Miller to be buried in Saint Philip Neri Catholic Cemetery near their home so Danny could "visit her every day," none of us expected this would last. But it has. Annie and I are convinced this habit he's developed, rather than helping him recover from his grief, is, instead, prolonging it. Even in the dead of this past winter, he's trudged through the deep snow to be at her graveside.

He's so distracted with his grief that if it weren't for Martha VanWert, Empire Feed and Grain would have closed its doors six months ago. Marty, as she is widely known, is perhaps Annie's oldest friend, their friendship dating all the way back to elementary school. She started working for Danny and Rebecca Miller a month after Annie and I left Empire for the army when she replaced Annie as the store's primary bookkeeper.

August 30, 2020

The Director of Operations for the Joint Chiefs of Staff is a marine corps three-star general. He's tough, demanding, but known to take care of those who work hard for him. I've been unexpectedly summoned to see him, and when I arrive, I'm stunned to find a smiling Annie there as the general's secretary ushers me into his office. Ross Haverman, whom I haven't seen since we parted ways at the Command and General Staff College over three years ago, is there as well. I am not usually at a loss for words, but Annie's presence has sucked the wind right out of me. I am so happy to see her. As she rushes into my arms I manage to ask, "What are you doin' here?" It's a stupid question, I know that as soon as I've asked it. Her smile, her kiss, *she's not here because something is wrong. Whatever this is, it isn't bad news. Who cares what she's doing here! She's here!*

After he sees I'm over my surprise, the general says, "Congratulations, Jack, you're on the army's promotion list for colonel. Well deserved!" He extends his hand to me.

I keep Annie close, my left arm still around her as I shake his hand.

He continues, "The army's given me permission to frock you." *Frocking,* in the military's use of the term, means that an officer selected for promotion to the next rank may be permitted to wear the insignia of that next higher rank even before his or her number on the promotion list has come up for official promotion, as long as the position that officer is filling calls for an officer of that higher rank. The "frocked" officer is entitled to all the courtesies and entitlements of that higher rank with one notable exception: pay. The general asks, "Anne, will you help me make this official?" He walks over to his desk, grabbing two black colonel insignias. Removing the clasps on the pins on the back of one of them, he hands it to Annie. Then he removes the black oak leaf affixed to the center of my fatigue shirt and tells her, "Pin it right there." When she's done, Annie gives me another kiss, the general shakes my hand, and hands me the other black, metal insignia of rank. "Here's one for your fatigue cap, Colonel. Congratulations, again."

I look at Ross. "Are you—"

Before I can finish he nods his head and says, "I am."

From that I infer we have both, again, been selected for early promotion—this time to colonel. Ross adds, "But I'm only in a lieutenant colonel's position, so . . ."

I interrupt, "Me, too." I give that just a moment and then direct a question to no one in particular, "So, how can I be frocked?"

Ross demurs, "You should tell him, sir."

"Lieutenant Colonel Haverman got my request to frock you and run through the army DCSPER's office quick." He gives a nod in Ross's direction and thanks him. "Here's what I want you to do, Jack. Take a couple of days off and show Anne around town. When you come back to work, you've got the desk in that little office just outside my door." I know the office he is talking about. It's been vacant for a few weeks after the marine corps colonel who was the general's executive officer departed to take command of a marine corps regiment on Okinawa. "I want you to be my next XO, Jack. You up for that?"

It was a demanding job, especially working for him, but I am both humbled and honored. "Yes, sir."

1800 hours, October 30, 2020

I've been the Executive Officer to the Director of Operations for the Joint Chiefs of Staff for about three months. It's early evening, and the general has left for the day as has his secretary. Since assuming duties as the XO to the JCS Director of Operations, I have two favorite times of the day. One is in the early morning before anyone, including the general, has arrived at work. The other is this time of day, after the phones have stopped ringing and the hustle and bustle of a jam-packed Pentagon day has slackened. Outside the Pentagon, parking lots are slowly emptying and filtering onto the crowded interstates that give way to the crowded northern Virginia suburbs. I put a call into Annie's cell phone, and she answers on the third ring. "Hey, Jack."

I've been trying to call all day, but every time I thought I had a moment, I was interrupted. I'm bursting with some news. "Hey, sweetheart. How's everything in Empire?"

"We're fine. The girls are fine. Becca's at basketball practice. RJ's at the stables with Rigley. That horse has become her life." Becca is our all-round athlete whose plan is to play three sports at Glen Lake Middle School. RJ has become a young equestrian.

"I have some good news . . ."

Annie interrupts me, "You've been selected for brigade command."

Deflated somewhat, I ask, "How did you know?"

"A month ago, maybe a bit longer, you told me the selection board had met. I figured it's about time for the results to be released. Proud of you, Jack!" There's a momentary pause and then Annie asks, "How about Ross?"

"Yep. He's on it as well."

"Any idea where you'll go?"

This was the best part of the news. "101st Combat Aviation

Brigade, 101st Airborne Division (Air Assault), Fort Campbell, Kentucky."

"Oh, Jack! Exactly what you wanted. I'm so happy for you. When?"

"Dunno exactly, but sometime next summer."

"How 'bout Ross?"

"The Adjutant General's Corps doesn't have any brigade commands, per se, but it looks like he's going to be the J1 at Headquarters, European Command in Germany. That's a good assignment for him. He can kill two birds with one stone. The J1 job is handling all the personnel at EUCOM. It's a joint-duty position, so he'll get joint-duty qualified while he's doing the equivalent of a brigade-level command."

Nine months later, Fort Campbell, Kentucky, July 20, 2021
I assumed command of the 101st Combat Aviation Brigade a week ago. Annie, the girls, Danny Miller, and Rita Rigley were all here for the ceremony. They left a couple of days ago to resume their lives elsewhere. I have settled into a four-bedroom house on Fort Campbell, Quarters #4, and, quite honestly, I feel somewhat ashamed of myself. I know there's a military family like mine here at Fort Campbell that would love to live in these quarters rather than be told there are no government quarters available for them on post. Instead, they will have to either buy a home or rent one. But it is a matter of policy—actually several policies. First, it is a policy of the division that brigade commanders reside on post in order to facilitate their quick response to any emergency that may arise. Second, Fort Campbell's housing policy is that certain houses on post are designated for brigade commanders. So, I have settled into this monster place and rattle around in it like a peanut in a boxcar.

August 8, 2021, Headquarters, 101st Combat Aviation Brigade, Fort Campbell, Kentucky

Today, I have encountered my first real test of handling a serious and unusual situation. I was visited by two FBI agents accompanied by the division's judge advocate general, a lieutenant colonel, whom I had not yet met. Their interest was in a senior noncommissioned officer assigned to one of my brigade's subordinate battalions. After summoning my command sergeant major, the two of us were shown video evidence of that soldier at the US Capitol using a piece of barrier material to break a window through which he then entered the building. The date time stamp on the video was *2:00 p.m., January 6, 2021.* In the video he is wearing a bulletproof vest and has a handgun strapped around his waist. He is wearing a baseball cap with the words "Oath Keepers" emblazoned on the front. The crimes he is charged with are numerous, and the agents indicated they were there to place him under arrest, which they did. As soon as they've left with him in handcuffs, my sergeant major knocks on my office door and asks if we can talk.

"By all means. I was just about to come see you. C'mon in, Top." It has always been my custom to refer to first sergeants or command sergeants major with whom I've served, by the term *Top,* referring to their status as the senior-most noncommissioned officer in their assigned unit . . . the *top sergeant,* if you will. I only use this term with them after I've gotten to know them. It is my way of being both friendly and respectful.

Solemnly, he begins, "He's not the only one who's mixed up in this group calling themselves Oath Keepers, Colonel."

I am not surprised by this news. "How many more do you think are involved?"

"Rumors have been flyin'. I checked with admin. This guy

was on leave from January 1 to January 10. His battalion's command sergeant major and I have had a conversation about him. He'd seen him wearing the hat before . . . the one that says Oath Keepers on it."

I comment, "So he wasn't at all hesitant to show his affiliation?"

"No, sir. The battalion's sergeant major told me about the hat. I didn't think much of it at the time. Until this thing at the Capitol, no one had ever heard of them." I'd heard rumors of various militia groups around here, but never heard a name associated with them. The sergeant major says, "Since January 6, I've had discussions with all of the sergeants major and the first sergeants in the brigade. These guys, the Oath Keepers, I mean, have been careful up to this point. We suspect they're recruiting our soldiers, but the NCOs tell me they don't think any of their recruiting or meetings happen on post."

I am pleased my command sergeant major seemed to have his pulse on the brigade's noncommissioned officers, or NCOs as they are commonly called. NCOs are truly the heartbeat of any military organization. In every army school I have attended we studied the importance of delegating responsibility: give a person a job to do, the resources to do it, and then let them tackle it.

"How many are involved?" I ask.

He shrugs, "Don't know for sure. But, sir, I don't think it's a very big number."

"Are we dealing with the Proud Boys, too?" The Proud Boys are another militia group, this one made famous when President Trump referred to them in a debate before the 2020 elections. Then, of course, there was their participation in the January 6 incursion at the US Capitol.

"No evidence of them yet, but where there's smoke, there's fire."

"Any idea if anyone else was at the Capitol on January 6?"

He smiles at me and shakes his head. I know as soon as I ask the question, if he had that information, he would have already passed it on to me and to the FBI. "Can't be sure but, it looks to me like the FBI is combing through a lot of video." Then he asks me a tough question, "You think the feds will let us deal with our boy or will *they* keep him for trial?"

Now it's my turn to shake my head. There were multiple charges under the Uniform Code of Military Justice I could charge this NCO with, every one of them serious enough to warrant a general court martial. But before any of that could happen the federal government would have to remand him to the military for discipline. "Good question, Top. I guess we'll just have to wait and see. In the meantime, all we can do is keep our ear to the ground."

October 15, 2021

Summer has turned to fall. The federal government did not relinquish jurisdiction to the army in the case of Sergeant First Class Donald Jenkins, the senior NCO assigned to my brigade. Considered a flight risk, he was kept in custody pending trial. Today he was found guilty on multiple charges for his actions on January 6 by a jury of his peers in a federal criminal court case convened in Washington, DC; one of the first offenders to have been tried and convicted by a team of Department of Justice lawyers. He is in a federal prison awaiting sentencing, which will not happen for a while.

In the meantime, the Judge Advocate General at Fort Campbell didn't have to wait on the sentence. Jenkins had been found guilty and that was grounds for administrative discharge from the army, and the JAG showed no mercy. Jenkins is given a bad conduct discharge. It's a triple whammy for him—jail, bad conduct discharge, felony conviction—all translating to "he is now officially screwed."

Jenkins's fate is well known around the military community at Fort Campbell, and along with it, the image of the Oath Keepers and Proud Boys has been tarnished. While they might have appeared to some to be patriotic, as the truth continues to emerge, so does their racist philosophy and their efforts to empower white authoritarianism. While I feel no sympathy for Jenkins, I do have some for his wife and two young children who have gone to live with her parents in Texas, the government offering no assistance, again, due to the conditions of his bad conduct discharge. They have lost all military privileges, including access to the post exchange, which is like a department store, and commissary, the military's equivalent of a grocery store. It is as if the Jenkins family has been banished. Several NCOs, apparently friends of his according to my sergeant major, helped her get packed and moved. My sympathy for the family, however, must be overshadowed by my responsibilities to my command and the army. I tell my sergeant major, "Top, I don't want to sound as if I don't care about the family, but I have to ask, what do you know about the NCOs who helped her move?"

He nods and saves me from further discomfort, "I'm ahead of you, sir. We know who they are. Good NCOs I think, but we know to keep an eye on them, just to be sure."

I do believe making an example of Jenkins is the right thing to do. On January 6, he abandoned his oath as a soldier to support and defend the Constitution.

2200 hours, November 15, 2021, the National Training Center (NTC), Fort Irwin, California

The kerfuffle over Jenkins has settled somewhat. It was distracting, but not sufficiently so as to curtail all the training necessary to keep this or any other army aviation unit prepared to accomplish its mission. My unit, the 101st Combat Aviation Brigade, has just closed on the NTC. We are scheduled for a thirty-day rotation that will train and then test all of the brigade's aviation assets. It's been a long day of briefings on everything from dining hall procedures, billeting arrangements, range procedures, even recreational opportunities here when we have downtime—which will be scarce. I am about to turn in, when my cell phone rings. It's Annie, and it's 1:00 a.m. in Empire. "Hey, honey, what are you doing up so late?"

"Jack," she pauses and then, "I wasn't going to bother you with this until I was sure."

Immediately I don't like where this is going. "What's wrong?"

"I got a call today from my OB-GYN. She wants me to come back in for another mammogram. She said I shouldn't be alarmed, but there is a suspicious spot they want to check out."

"It's OK, Annie. I'm glad you called. When do you go back in?"

"Tomorrow."

"That's quick."

"Yeah, I guess that's why I decided to call. I've never been called back before, much less had to go back so soon."

"Can you feel anything . . . a lump or something?"

"No, nothing."

I'm concerned. I'm fifteen hundred miles away from her and swamped with work. I desperately want to comfort her. But I don't know how. I'm not sure what to say. My instinct is to offer, *it'll be OK,* but I really don't know that do I? Neither does Annie. I ask, "Have you told the girls?"

"No! I'm not going to tell them anything."

In her voice, I detect a sense of near panic and that is unlike her. I'm scared. "Annie, I'm sorry. I didn't mean to upset you." This is so hard. I wish I could be there to hold her. Then I wouldn't need to say anything. I could just hold her.

"Jack," she pauses, "I wish you were . . ."

When she doesn't complete her thought, I complete it for her, "I know, Annie. I wish I was there too."

1700 hours, Pacific Standard Time, 17 November, 2021
I've closed the door to my tiny temporary office in the range control building at Fort Irwin as a signal to my staff that I desire some privacy. Annie was to get the results from her latest mammogram today. She doesn't answer my call and it goes to voicemail. My early warning radar is blaring as I leave a message for her to return my call as soon as she can. Fifteen minutes later, my cell phone rings and I reclose my office door. "Jack, sorry, I left my phone in the car. I'm at the stable with RJ. I just watched her and Rigley in the dressage ring."

"So, everything is OK, after the recheck, I mean?"

"Uh, listen, let me call you back. I can't talk right now OK?"

I don't like this, but I'm not there. I don't know what's going on. All I can do is say "Uh, well, OK. But call me as soon as you can."

1800 hours, Pacific Standard Time, 17 November, 2021
I close my office door for the third time in an hour as my cell phone rings. "Annie, is everything OK?"

She's crying. "I—I don't know, Jack. I couldn't talk before.

I thought I was alone, but RJ and one of her friends suddenly showed up. I'm home now. The girls and Dad are downstairs watching television. I don't want them to see me like this."

"It's OK, Annie. Tell me." I desperately wish I was there with her.

"The spot—the doctor says she wants me to come in for a biopsy. She says the mass is a large one, so she doesn't trust a needle biopsy. She wants to do a surgical breast biopsy and that will require a general anesthesia. It's outpatient, but I haven't told anyone about any of this, Jack. I don't want anyone to know, I didn't even want to have to tell you, but I had to talk to someone about . . ."

"Annie, it's OK. You've got to get this done. We've got to know what this is." As I am saying this, I have the thought, *Easy for you to say. You're not there for her—for them.*

"I know, but Dad's doing so well now that he's moved in with us. The girls—"

My mind is fully focused on Annie. I interrupt, "How about Marty? Could she go with you, bring you back home?"

1800 hours, Pacific Standard Time, 30 November, 2021, National Training Center, Fort Irwin, California
It has been nearly two weeks since Annie's outpatient surgery to remove and biopsy a lump on her right breast. We have spoken daily, but too briefly and that has contributed to making these two weeks among the longest of my life. Despite my distraction, our training has gone well, which says a lot for the excellence of the people assigned to my brigade. Tonight is the assault helicopter battalion's first crack at the night aerial gunnery ranges here at the NTC. I will be up all night monitoring the training from the large control room just down the hall from my temporary

office here in range control. My cell phone rings, and I answer it before it can ring a second time, "Annie."

She's crying as I hear faintly, "It's cancer, Jack. I've got breast cancer."

0900 hours, Pacific Standard Time, 1 December, 2021
I've called back to Fort Campbell and alerted the Assistant Division Commander for Maneuver, who I report directly to at division headquarters, that I'd like a few days leave. I tell him why. I've assured him I will not be gone for more than a week, less if possible. I've also alerted the commander and staff at Fort Irwin that my executive officer will assume command while I am gone. Everyone has been very understanding and wished us well.

December 2, 2021
I caught a red-eye out of San Francisco to Chicago and then a puddle jumper on to Manistee. I'm now back in Empire and Annie and I have decided to seek a second opinion. I have a doctor friend on the staff at Blanchfield Army Hospital who has recommended an oncologist in Clarksville, Tennessee. We contacted her office and we have an appointment tomorrow. All of Annie's medical test results have been digitally transferred from her OB-GYN in Traverse City to the oncologist's office in Clarksville.

December 3, 2021
Dr. Michelle Carole, Annie's Clarksville oncologist, carefully examines her after reviewing everything from her doctor in Traverse City. We are prepared for the worst, but still it stuns us when Dr. Carole confirms Annie's diagnosis and schedules surgery for the following day. I extend my absence from the NTC for

an additional four days with the permission of my boss at Fort Campbell. I've spoken to the operations officer at range control and he assures me my XO is handling things in my absence quite competently. Rita Rigley is on her way from Miami to Fort Campbell to help with Annie's post-surgical care as I will most certainly have to return to the NTC as soon as I know she is stable. She and Rita will stay in the house assigned to me at Fort Campbell for as long as is necessary. Danny Miller, much recovered from his debilitating grief, is not happy that Annie and I have decided to have this surgery performed here rather than at Munson Medical Center in Traverse City. Becca and RJ, of course, want to come to Fort Campbell to be with their mother. Annie, however, has been masterful in her handling of this. She's convinced her father he needs to stay in Empire and care for his granddaughters. Becca and RJ have been told they should stay in Empire and keep an eye on their grandfather. She should have been a psychologist!

December 5, 2021, the day of Annie's surgery
Dr. Carole approaches me in the hospital corridor. "The mass was quite large, but the surgery went well. She's in recovery now and you can see her as soon as she wakes up. We will keep her here tonight and barring something unexpected, she can go home tomorrow."

I thank her and ask, "Then you were able to remove all the cancer?"

She pauses and then, "We were able to remove all of the tumor, but I also removed several adjacent lymph nodes. We will have those tested . . ."

I think, *My God! She's still not out of the woods!*

Dr. Carole must be able to read the concern on my face. "Colonel Rigley, let's not get too far ahead of ourselves here."

I have to ask, "But if there is cancer in those lymph nodes . . ."

"If that's the case we will look at next steps."

Not the news I was looking for. There would be more waiting, more fretting. I tell her, "I'm split down the middle right now, Doc. My brigade is at the National Training Center in California. I have never been very good at being in two places."

She puts her hand on my shoulder. "I know. Your doctor friend from Blanchfield told me. He spoke very highly of you, said you were going to be the division commander someday at Fort Campbell. I've expedited the lab results on the lymph nodes. We should know something by tomorrow afternoon. Let's hope for the best."

I'm in no mood for flattery. All I care about now is Annie.

6 December, 2021

The news is not good. Both of the lymph nodes show the cancer has metastasized. Dr. Carole recommends aggressive chemotherapy to begin immediately and follow-on radiation if necessary. My heart aches for my sweet Annie. She, on the other hand, vows she will not let this be the end for her. She vows to get better. I must leave for the NTC tomorrow, leaving her and Rita to face the challenges ahead without me.

December 20, 2021

The rotation at the NTC is over. The brigade was awarded the certification of Highly Combat Proficient. I could not be prouder of these men, women, and the incredible machines they fly and maintain. Everyone will be home for the Christmas holiday. I cannot wait to get back to Campbell. My XO takes responsibility for closing everything out here at the NTC and I will take a commercial flight back to Clarksville, Annie, and Rita.

December 21, 2021
I am shocked when I see Annie, who is sitting in a chair next to a sun-splattered window in the living room of Quarters #4. She smiles at me but can't get up. Rita must see the desperate ache in my eyes seeing her like this. Standing next to Annie, she says, "She's been through a lot, Jack, but," she brushes back a lock of her hair which has already begun to thin from the chemo, "the doctor thinks she's responding well."

Responding well? I think, but force a smile as I bend down to kiss my girl on the cheek.

December 23, 2021
Danny Miller, Becca, and RJ will arrive this afternoon in Clarksville for the Christmas and New Year's holidays.

"Jack?"

"Yes, Annie." She's in a reclining chair across the bedroom from me. It's where she sleeps. She's not comfortable lying flat on her back and the recliner lets her adjust to many positions and to do that frequently. "I want to go home to Empire and finish this thing out." I am instantly against this and say so. She shakes her head and says, "Hear me out. None of us know how this is going to end. Not me, not you, not even Dr. Carole. If it ends badly, I want that to happen at home in Empire with Dad and the girls, you, and Rita."

I break in, "OK, then, but let's move everyone here to Fort Campbell. You see how much room there is in this big house."

She shakes her head, "No, Jack. I'm not going to do that to them—Dad and the girls, I mean. Dad's finally gone back to the store; something I never thought would happen. As to the girls, well, if you could see how happy they are, how busy they are . . . Becca's not going to want to abandon her teammates and RJ— she and that horse are attached at the hip."

I tell her, "There's a riding club here on post. We can board Rigley there. She can—"

Again, Annie shakes her head, "It wouldn't be the same for her, Jack. She's got a whole raft of friends in school and at the stable. No, I'm not going to pull her out of that. I'm not going to pull any of them up from where they are so happy. Their friends are all in Empire, the things they enjoy doing are all there as well. On the other hand, I can do the rest of my chemo and the radiation if necessary from anywhere, and I want that to be Empire."

"But, I can't be there!"

"I know that. That makes me sad. But you and I both know there's a star in your future. When I get over this maybe I can rejoin you on your journey." I want to protest but find myself at a loss for any words that wouldn't sound selfish. She smiles at me, "The girls are old enough now and Dad is so much better. We can't just pull up their—our—roots in Empire."

"Annie . . ."

She puts a finger to her lips, shushing me, then says, "For now we need to do what is right for the girls, for Dad. Don't you think so?" Inwardly, I know she's right. Our obligation—Annie's and mine—is to our family. But I'm unable for the moment to overcome my own selfishness. I turn my back to her and say nothing.

January 2, 2022
Everyone is flying home to Empire today aboard a NetJets charter. Rita insisted Annie was too weak to fly commercially. An

ambulance will transport her from Cherry Capital Airport in Traverse City to the Lake Michigan house. Rita will accompany her in the ambulance. Danny, Becca and RJ will take a limo Rita has arranged.

January 15, 2023
Six months from now—late next June or early July—I will relinquish command of the brigade. My boss, a brigadier general who is the assistant division commander for maneuver, has already asked me if I'd like to stay on as the division's chief of staff. It's a great job, a big one, but one I didn't think would be any more difficult than the job I did as the executive officer to the Director of Operations for the Joint Chiefs of Staff at the Pentagon. But, because of Annie's continuing struggle with cancer, I have not yet said yes or no.

I am sitting in my study in Quarters #4. It's been nearly two weeks since everyone left, and I am feeling utterly alone and lost. Work has become my salvation, so I grab a stack of folders on the desk in front of me and begin with the file on top of the stack. I am engrossed in writing an officer efficiency report for my superb executive officer when my cell phone rings. It's Rita, who has foregone her own life and has been a godsend throughout this terrible time. "Rita, how's everything in Empire?"

She doesn't answer my question, instead, she says, "Jack . . ." The pause tells me this isn't a just-checking-in type of phone call. "The doctor's here are telling us Annie needs radiation treatment to follow up the chemo."

No—no—no! After the shock, I stammer, "How can this be? They told us the chemo was working." I let my disgust become profane, "Dammit, Rita! Hasn't she been through enough?"

"I'm so sorry."

"How's Annie?"

"Down. How would you feel, if you've already been through what she has only to be told there's more to come?"

"Can I talk to her?"

"She's asleep. She will likely be a bit miffed at me for calling you, but I thought you should know now rather than later. She didn't want me to say anything. She's going to go ahead with it, even though it may make her sicker than the chemo she's already been through."

0900 hours, January 16, 2023, Quarters #4, Fort Campbell, Kentucky

After a sleepless twenty-four hours, I have made a decision. No, I haven't consulted with Annie on this. I know what she would say. But I've rationalized it's really my choice and mine alone to make, much like the decision not to attend West Point all those years ago.

I put a call into Ross Haverman's cell phone. He's now the executive officer to the vice chief of staff of the Army. I know if anyone could expedite what I want to do, it's him. After a few pleasantries, I go straight to the point, "Ross, I want to resign my commission."

TWENTY-THREE

Annie's Fury

Late afternoon, January 16, 2023, the Lake Michigan house on Storm Hill, Empire, Michigan

I have never hung up the phone on anyone, until just a few minutes ago. I am furious with Jack for the decision he's made without even the slightest consultation with me, the woman who's been through life with him since high school, the woman he married, the woman who bore his children, the woman who put up with the constant exigencies of military service. *How could you just give up like that?*

When he told me what he'd done, I ranted on and on. He never interrupted once. When I'd finished, he'd calmly asked, "So, if I had called and talked to you about this decision, would I have convinced you it was the right thing to do?"

It was the stupidest question Jack Rigley had ever asked me. I screamed at him, "Did you not hear a single word I just said? No, I never would have agreed to you resigning your commission! You can't do this, Jack! You can't let the world stop because I'm sick."

With an infuriating calmness he replied, "Well, now you know why I didn't call you first."

That's when I hung up the phone. It rings again. It's him. I don't answer. The doctors have all told me to avoid stress. A few have suggested it produces a chemical reaction in some people's body that can react negatively with the chemo cocktails I'd been taking. Right now, my body still holds some of those chemicals residually. A week or so ago, I started radiation treatments three times a week. I'm surprised I don't glow in the dark these days. I take a few deep breaths. My phone beeps that I have a voice mail. It's Jack. I listen to it.

> "Annie, it's me. I won't call back again until tomorrow because I want you to listen to what I have to say and then think about it. Being apart from one another is something we've always lived with. Remember when I was in college? Remember the tours of duty in Iraq and Afghanistan? Remember when we made the decision for you and the girls to return to Empire to help your dad? The difference between then and now is what's happened to you. Since your diagnosis, there's not a minute that goes by that I don't think of you, not a moment that I don't wish I was there in Empire with you. The two of us have sacrificed a lot. But your sacrifice over these last few years has been immense. I want our sacrifices to come to an end. I want us to be together. There's nothing more important in the world to me than you, Annie Rigley."

Cancer is a crappy card to be dealt. I don't know why Jack would even want to be with me. My breasts have been replaced with scar tissue. My hair is gone. I'm thin as a rail. Food has no taste, so I eat little, and only because I know I have to sustain this ravaged body someway. My mood swings are gigantic, so much so that I have no idea why Rita, Dad, and the girls will come near me, not knowing which Annie/Mom will pop up. I am so sick most days that I have no idea if I'm getting better or not. There are some days that I think the cure is worse than the natural course of the disease. But, of course, I know that is not the case. The natural course of cancer left untreated is death, and I will not give in to that—never. I'm too strong for that both mentally and physically.

5:00 p.m., January 17, 2023, the Lake Michigan house on Storm Hill, Empire, Michigan
My cell phone rings, and I can see on caller ID it's Jack. My mood over the last twenty-four hours has mellowed, as I hope his has. I'm sure I can convince him throwing away his career is not what he—nor I—want. "Hello."

"Annie? You OK?"

No, I'm not unless you've reconsidered. "Yes."

"So, can we talk about this rationally?"

Only if by "rational" you mean you've changed your mind and called Ross back. "Yes."

"Listen, Annie, I meant what I said yesterday in the message I left for you. Neither of us—" *Don't you dare go there, Jack Rigley!* "—can know how this is all going to turn out. What if. . . ." *No, seriously, you're really going to go there!* "What if it takes you away from me?"

That's it. I can't take this any longer. "Listen to me, Jack Rigley. I don't need your doubt. I don't need to think you think I can't survive this. I have to believe in myself and I can't do that if you don't believe in me." There comes an ominous silence that draws out so long I fear the call has been dropped. "Jack, are you still there?"

"I'm here, Annie. I'm sorry. You're right. I shouldn't think that way, but . . ."

In all our time together, I can't ever remember seeing or hearing him cry, but now he is. Insistently, I tell him, "You can't give up your life. If I hadn't been a part of it for all these years, I might just say come on home. But I've been there with you even during these past few years where we've had to be apart; when I've had to keep up with what you are doing by way of a telephone call from some faraway place, I've been there with you—the highs, the lows, all of it. I've always known how good you are at this, Jack, and so has the army. That first star is just right there in front of you, my love. It's yours for the taking. You are meant to be a general. You can't walk away from it like this." Another long pause, but I no longer hear him crying.

"Ross Haverman has told me the same thing, Annie. Would you like to know what I told him?"

I don't, but I answer, "Yes."

"I told him I didn't vow to love the army in sickness and in health like I did when I married you."

That pulls me up short. I can feel the lump in my throat, the one that comes just before I start to cry.

"Ross never found his *Annie* like I did all those years ago at that marina on Glen Lake. He hasn't ever had to try and go to sleep wondering how the only woman he has ever loved is doing after a chemo or radiation treatment. Ross is married to the army. I'm married to you, Annie."

Oh, God! I can't let him make me cry! I hold the phone out at arm's length for that reason until I hear him say, "Annie?"

I swallow hard; compose myself. "What about your

retirement, Jack? You're so close." A military pension from any of the US's armed services is one of the best in the world. At twenty years of service, he could retire at fifty percent of his base pay for the rest of his life. "You can't just give that up!"

"You know as well as I do that Rita has us in the trust. Then there's your dad's store. You know he expects us to take it over eventually."

"But you've worked so hard," I plead.

"I have and I don't regret a single day of it. But honestly, I'm ready for us to be together again. It's time for me to come home, Annie, to come home to Empire. Please let me do this . . . for you . . . for us . . . for our family."

I remember what I told him when we were struggling with the decision over his going to West Point. *It's your choice, Jack. No one can or should make that decision except you.* I'm suddenly so very tired. Some of it from the cancer treatments, some of it from the stress I'd felt after Jack told me what he was doing, much of it from just simply missing the man I love so very much. "I get it, Jack." Neither of us want to say goodbye, but after nearly an hour on the phone, it's time.

He says, "I love you, Annie." Then he asks me, "Remember the first time I said that to you?"

"I do."

"Just look at how far we've come!"

6:15 p.m., January 17, 2023, the Lake Michigan house on Storm Hill, Empire, Michigan
For the last few minutes, I've just sat here in the great room and stared out the window at the bluff and the big lake beyond it. My tears, which I let go after we'd hung up, have subsided now. Becca bounds into the great room and announces she's

home from basketball practice and she's going to get dinner going. Shortly after, RJ comes in. She's in her jodhpurs sans boots, which I'm grateful she's removed and hopefully left in the garage. I watch her head to the kitchen to help her big sister. Dad will be home soon, shortly after closing the store. *Just look at how far we've come!* I feel a calm like I haven't felt in some time now. *Jack will be home with us soon.* Tomorrow when we talk, I'll tell him just how much I'm looking forward to all of us being together once again.

POSTLUDE

What Might Have Been Pales in Comparison to What Is

5:00 p.m., June 29, 2023

It took much longer than I wanted it to, six months longer to be exact, but, after sixteen years in the army, I'm back home in Empire, for good, as a civilian. Annie sits in an Adirondack chair next to me, her bald head is wrapped in a colorful cotton scarf and laid back on a small pillow. She's asleep and snoring lightly. It makes me smile. I glance out over the vast expanse of Lake Michigan beyond the not-too-steep tree-covered bluff that stretches from our deck down to the shoreline. My eyes trace the two-hundred-yard-long path carved through the trees by our girls and their friends over the years as they've made their way down to the beach below. There's a light breeze blowing in off the lake. Summer is fully upon us, yet Annie complains of feeling cold much of the time. So, while I am in shorts and T-shirt, she wears a pair of long yoga pants and a heavy sweater pulled around her neck. She looks frail to me. I feel bad for not being here to help her through these last difficult six months, but her doctors are optimistic the surgery, the chemo, and the radiation have eradicated the cancer.

Behind me, I hear the slider from the family room open and our oldest daughter, Becca, warns, "Dinner's ready in fifteen." She asks, "What do you and Mom want to drink, Dad?" Annie continues to doze.

Meds prevent Annie from having alcohol, so I respond, "Water's fine, Bec. Thanks." Becca and her sister, RJ, are fixing our dinner. They say it's in honor of my homecoming. I say it's a Thanksgiving come early. They began their preparations mid-morning and I've watched them out of the corner of my eye. They both know their way around the kitchen thanks to their mom. She's taught them well, and much of it all by herself while I was either deployed or, as we have been for the last five years, voluntarily living apart; me wherever the army might want me, Annie here in Empire. The smile brought on by Annie's snoring disappears and I think, *You weren't here when you should have been.*

I reach over and gently wake her. "Hey, dinner's about ready."

Her eyes flutter open, she turns to face me and flashes the smile that's always dazzled me. I laugh and tell her she was snoring. Her simple reply warms my heart. "I am so glad you're home, Jack."

A lump forms in my throat. I want to cry, but I know that will only disturb her; there have been entirely too many tears in these last six months. Instead, I smile.

The slider opens and this time it's RJ. "Mom, Dad . . . dinner's ready."

I help Annie up from the low-slung Adirondack chair. She slips her arm around me, some of it for support, but I can tell, it's more than that; she's able to touch me, hold me. I put my arms around her and pull her close. I tell her, "It's good to be here." We walk in and the aroma of roast turkey with all the trimmings pervades.

My father-in-law, Danny Miller, has carved the bird. He lives here now not because he must, but because it's where he wants to be thanks to Annie's, Becca's, and RJ's presence in his life. I've only been home a little over thirty-six hours, yet it's easy for me to see who his universe revolves around. Then there is, of course, his store, Empire Feed and Grain, in which he has renewed interest after overcoming Rebecca Miller's death and his own grief. As we sit down at the table, he asks if he may say the blessing.

Becca answers, "Of course, Grampy."

We bow our heads and he begins, "Dear Lord, thanks for bringing Jack home to us—" I hear little else after this. It's as if the lump in my throat has moved to my ears. On Tuesday, July 5, I will start work at Empire Feed and Grain. Annie and I will be the heirs apparent to it. Annie knows it intimately. I know next to nothing about the feed and grain business, so there is much to learn. But for the next six days or so, I won't bother with business. There will be plenty of time for learning my new work responsibilities. For now, all I want to do is get to know my family again.

I hear Danny thank God for Annie's good doctor's report. He says, "Amen." He catches me looking at him, smiles and says, "Welcome home, Colonel. Glad you're here."

8:00 p.m., June 29, 2023
The Thanksgiving-dinner-come-early made by Becca and RJ was delightful. Danny, Rita, Annie, Becca, RJ, and I had crowded around the dining room table. Pete, Annie's brother, now an

assistant football coach for quarterbacks and running backs at Glen Lake High School, and his wife, Angela, a teacher as well, joined us for dessert. I am pleased, but not surprised to learn Lawrence Calderone is now the head coach at the high school. Pete and I swapped some stories about him before they had to leave. Angela is four months pregnant and was tired.

An hour or so ago, Rita and her two granddaughters left to attend a movie at the State Theater in downtown Traverse City. I think they said they were going to see one of the minion movies. Before I can ask what a *minion* is, they're out the door.

Annie has turned in for the night, her strength and stamina slowly returning after her final round of radiation completed a month ago. She has learned through all of this to trust her body to tell her when enough is enough.

It's just me and Danny Miller as we each settle into a seat on the deck overlooking Lake Michigan. This time of year, the days are long. Sunset won't be until sometime after 9 p.m., but there are just enough clouds on the horizon to offer the promise of a glorious one this evening. Danny has his ever-present mug of coffee with him. I have a bottle of water. For a long time neither of us says anything.

Ours is a complex relationship. From my perspective, he is one of the men I admire most in this world. A loving husband, a great father to his two kids, a wonderful grandfather, a true provider of all the important things in life to those he loves and who love him. But I can honestly say I don't love him like Annie, Pete, Becca, and RJ love him. Maybe it was because at the time of our first meeting, when Annie and I were dating, I was struggling with my own father. Maybe I had the feeling he thought I was an unwanted intruder into the family he and Rebecca had built together in Empire during those early days of Annie's and my relationship. I'm sure he's always blamed me for stealing his daughter away, taking her away from him and her mother, for taking her away from the tranquility of Empire and subjecting her to the vagaries of military life. Maybe it was all of the above. Yet in these past few years, when Annie and I had to exist apart, when others had to fill in the vital role of father that I could not perform in my absence, there is no one on this earth that I trusted more to be that person than Danny Miller.

"Jack," he says, breaking the silence around us, which is only disturbed by the muffled bumping of Lake Michigan's waves against the distant shoreline. "What took so long?"

He's always been blunt. It had never been hard for me to know when he was displeased, especially when I was the cause of his displeasure. I think I know what he's asking, but I try to blunt his bluntness with evasiveness, "What do you mean?"

"What took the army so long to get you back to us?"

My immediate urge was to apologize to him for not being here during this final trial of Annie's courage, but, instead, I stifle that. I tell him the reason as given to me by Ross Haverman. "I was in a critical command position—"

He interrupts. I can hear contempt in his voice, "C'mon, Jack. The army's a big operation. There must have been someone who—"

I resent his implication that I could have done something to speed up my return home. It pisses me off, so I tersely reply to his interruption, "Do you want to hear this or not?" He relents. "My replacement was in a critical position as well. He was one of a group of eight officers assigned to the White House. They carry the football for the President. That's what they call the briefcase containing the codes and equipment the President would need if he were ever to have to launch a nuclear strike."

I could tell from Danny's expression and his body language he wasn't buying it and that continued to fuel my anger. It would have been easy to just give in to the baser instinct, to simply lash out. Instead, I remember what has formed this man's thinking: a beloved brother lost in Vietnam, a hatred of war, especially the ones our politicians have most recently entangled us in. So, I offer the only defense I can mount, "I had an obligation to the men and women under my command, I had an obligation to the army, I had an obligation to the country. I couldn't be here, but I'm damned glad you were." I wait for a reaction, but there is none. He takes a drink of his coffee, heaves himself up from his chair and, without another word, leaves me sitting there.

In the fading light of my first full day back home, I push back on the opportunity to feel sorry for myself. He is who he is and I am who I am. I decide that, now that I am back home in Empire, I must start over again with him. I'm back to that high school senior who was falling in love with his daughter and having to deal with a protective father. I decide I can do this. I have to do this. I make another decision as well. I decide Annie doesn't need to know about this encounter with her father, not now, perhaps not ever. As I said, my relationship with him is complex, and in my estimation this little dustup tonight, while it certainly didn't make it any easier, in the overall scheme of things, it can only make things worse if I let it. And I don't intend to do that.

July 28, 2023
It's been a month now at home. I'm going to Empire Feed and Grain almost every day, but there doesn't seem to be a big push for me to "learn the business." Between Danny, Annie and Marty VanWert, things seem to be well under control. RJ has asked for someone to take her this weekend to the Great Lakes Equestrian

Festival. "Dad, these are some of the best hunter-jumpers in the world. Some of the riders are Olympic athletes. You don't have to go to any of the shows with me. It's free to just walk around the grounds. I've saved my money. I can pay to get into the competition arenas. You won't believe how beautiful Flintfields Horse Park is." Her profuse praise of this event is persistent, and she is elated when I tell her we will go together, just her and me.

I do, however, give her some chores to accomplish before we go on Saturday. By Friday afternoon there remains one she has not yet accomplished; Sophie, our dog, needs her bi-monthly bath. When she pushes back on that one, I kid her. "RJ, I don't get it. You give Rigley a bath all the time and never complain a bit. Sophie, on the other hand, who's one-twentieth the size of your horse, only has to be bathed every two months, and you would think I've asked you to alter everything in your life, forever."

She says, "Rigley just stands there and lets me turn the hose on him, clean him and brush him out." I just continue to go about what I'm doing. She pleads, "Dad, you know how Sophie is." When I offer no response, RJ correctly assumes I'm not going to give in. She shrugs, grabs the leash, and calls for Sophie to come. Seeing the leash, Sophie rushes to her thinking a walk is in order. Little does she know what RJ's up to. We've all learned to disguise our purpose carefully from Sophie on bath day, otherwise it's a game of hide-and-go-seek. I know it's really a two-person job giving her a bath—one to hold her, the other to wash her. But, well, RJ's a resourceful kid. She'll figure out a way to get it done by herself or con her big sister into helping her.

2:00 p.m., July 30, 2023, Flintfields Horse Park, Williamsburg, Michigan
I'm standing next to a corral looking over the fence at six of the

most beautiful horses I've ever seen in my life. The man standing next to me says, "They are magnificent, aren't they?" I tell him I agree but then add, "And I know next to nothing about horseflesh."

He chuckles and asks, "Then what the heck are you doin' here?"

"My daughter." I turn and point to a building housing an arena and add, "She's in there . . . a horsewoman already at the tender age of ten."

"Is she competing?"

This time it's my turn to chuckle, "Naw. Her horse isn't a thoroughbred, but she loves it just the same. She rides almost every day, but Rigley's not a jumper. She's studied hunter-jumpers though—European warmbloods, I think she calls 'em. Is that what these are?"

He points a finger toward a beautiful black horse, "See that all-black mare standing there?" I nod. He continues, "She's the reigning world hunter-jumper champion. Crowned right here last year. This is her last year in competition. Next year her foal will be worth about a million dollars." I whistle through my teeth. He turns, points his finger in the air and then moves it around as if tracing the panorama that is Flintfields Horse Park. "None of this was here ten years ago. Wanna take a guess how much the GLEF brings into this area every year?" I've heard that acronym so much this past week from RJ that I don't have to ask what GLEF stands for—Great Lakes Equestrian Festival—not to mention the fact, I've gotten pretty good at acronyms over the years!

He must know by now, I am clueless as to horses and even more so about the horse business, but I venture a guess, "I dunno, fifteen, maybe twenty million dollars. I know horses are expensive to keep up."

Again, he chuckles and then says, "How 'bout three hundred to three hundred and fifty million dollars a year and increasing all the time."

I laugh at my own naiveté and then ask, "Are you an owner?"

He turns, offers his hand and says, "No, just a vet." Then he gives me a wink and points again to the black mare in the center of the corral. "But when she's here in Traverse City, I'm *her* vet. John Crystal's my name." We shake hands.

"Jack . . . Jack Rigley. Pleased to meet you, Doctor?"

"John, Jack . . . call me John. You live around here?"

I tell him I'm from Empire. He asks what I do there and I tell him, "My family owns Empire Feed and Grain." We talk some more until his cell phone rings, he answers it and then apologizes for having to tend to a client's horse.

I ask, "So, you have other owners who have you on retainer while their horses are here?"

He says, "'Bout twenty-five or so, last count." He needs to go, I can tell, but before he leaves, he asks, "Listen, Jack, OK if I give you a call at the store sometime . . . better yet give you a call and we meet for lunch? I've got an idea I'd like to talk over with you since your family is in the feed and grain business." I nod and offer him one of our business cards, a supply of which I've started to carry in my wallet. As he strides off, he says, "Good. I'll be in touch."

September 16, 2023
I had lunch today with Dr. John Crystal. We discussed the possibility of Empire Feed and Grain becoming a supplier of specialty feeds to the horses he cares for. What he proposed seemed like a good growth opportunity for the store.

8:00 p.m., Saturday, September 17, 2023

In the three months or so since I'd returned home a new tradition had been born. The Lake Michigan house was the gathering point for Sunday afternoon dinner, a kind of family potluck. Tonight, Annie and I barbecued a batch of baby back ribs, Pete and Angela brought a tossed salad and baked beans, Rita, Becca, and RJ did a great job with a key lime pie and Danny—well, Danny ate sumptuously. After cleanup was complete and it was just Danny, Rita, Annie, and me remaining, Annie suggested, "Hey, Dad, fill your coffee mug and let's go out on the deck."

Once we are all outside, I begin, "Danny, what do you know about the Great Lakes Equestrian Festival and what's going on in the horse business around Traverse City?"

He harrumphs . . . never a good sign. "What's to know? A bunch of rich people showing off their thoroughbreds."

Annie had prepared us for this not to go well, but I forge ahead, "I've been talking with a veterinarian who has quite a few clients whose horses are competing in the GLEF."

"What's that?" he asks, his tone dripping disdain.

"It's the Great Lakes Equestrian Festival . . . just one of a series of horse shows and competitions held at Flintfields Horse Park." He harrumphs again, a sign it's only getting tougher.

"A friend of mine, a vet, Doctor John Crystal, has asked me if we would consider getting into the business of specialty feeds for the horses under his care."

Danny Miller just stares at me, that same stare he gave me that night he caught Annie and I innocently holding hands while seated on the floor of her bedroom as we studied together; the stare that implies I'm interfering in the normal ebb and flow of his life and he wishes I would just go away. When he finally does say something, he surprises me with his question. "Do you have any idea how many customers Empire Feed and Grain has?"

Danny Miller can be quite cagey and I sensed he was trying to set me up. The truth is, I didn't know the exact number. I could have ventured a guess and probably been within fifty to a hundred of the number. But, I suspected he knew the exact number and guessing wrong, I thought, would play right into the point he was about to make. So, I shake my head, "No, not the exact number."

"Last I checked, which was just about a week ago, four hundred nineteen active accounts with us—most of 'em small farms—a few head of cattle, some sheep, goats and the like. They all try to be as self-sufficient as they can . . . none of 'em wealthy and well-heeled like that bunch up in Traverse City. What they can't raise on their farms, they come to us for. Forty years . . . that's how long Empire Feed and Grain has helped them get along and Rebecca and me, we made a pretty good living helping them. Whose gonna take care of them when we start chasin' after these rich folks?" There's a long pause. I look to Annie for an answer, but before she can say anything, Danny continues, "Besides, it's too expensive. We don't have the ability to mix feeds. That takes space, a big network of suppliers . . . a helluva lot bigger than we got now. Special equipment, transportation to move it once it's mixed . . . where the hell we gonna get the money for all of that?"

Out of the corner of my eye, I see Rita, who's been sitting and listening. She gets up, walks over to him, puts a hand on his shoulder and calmly asks, "Mind if I join in the conversation?"

Without looking at her he snorts, "Don't matter to me . . . free country . . . do what you want."

Annie pipes up, "Dad, there's no need for you to—"

Rita holds up her hand in Annie's direction. "It's OK, Anne."

Then turning back to Danny, she says, "You're a good man, Danny Miller. These folks around here have been good customers and you owe them your loyalty. But what if I were to tell you, you could take advantage of this business opportunity in Traverse City and at the same time help out all of your customers around these parts."

Firmly he asks, "How we gonna do that?" Before anyone can answer he skeptically adds, "Not possible? Where's all the money gonna come from? I've seen it before with other businesses . . . they get too big for their britches and before you know it, they're out of business. Then who's gonna help our customers?" He slaps his hand down on the tabletop. "No, I am not gonna let that happen to Empire Feed and Grain."

"Neither am I, Danny," she snaps back. "Are you willing to hear me out?" He gives that a moment, and rather rudely waves his hand as if to say *go ahead, but I ain't gonna listen*. Rita continues, "What if we move Empire Feed and Grain under my holding company? You'd still be the man-in-charge of that operation. But we can leverage the profits coming from Icon Realty and International Yacht Brokers to the advantage of your feed and grain business. That's where the money will come from to acquire the space, the equipment and transportation to expand into the Traverse City market."

He harrumphs, again. "Who's gonna run that operation? Jack? Annie needs him here, dammit!"

Annie jumps in. "Dad, you just stop right there! I don't need you feeling sorry for me. I don't need you to protect me. I'm over this. The doctor says so. You will not use me as some cockamamie way of missing out on something that could make things better for the people you say you are trying to help."

Rita says, "Well, I wasn't going to recommend Jack. I was

thinking that Marty VanWert could be the one to run the Traverse City end of Empire Feed and Grain. I've watched her. She's got a good head for business and God knows she's a hard worker." Rita was countering his every effort to withhold his consent and she was saving her best for last. "Let's talk about those small farmers around here . . . your loyal customers. Some of them are just squeaking by I'm guessing?" He nods. "So, how would you like to plow some of the profits from all those rich folks with their thoroughbreds up there in Traverse City into subsidies for your loyal customers who could use the help? I know, Danny, you are already giving any kid who's raising an animal for a 4-H project their specialty feed at your cost. How'd you like to be able to just give them the feed for free?"

Danny ponders that for a second, "First off, how can you be so sure we'll be that profitable in Traverse City?"

Rita shrugs, "There's a risk in any business venture. I don't have to tell you that. Just remember those first few years you started Empire Feed and Grain, you and Rebecca. Didn't you worry then? What if you and her would have just given up when the customers and the money were scarce?" She gave him just a moment to reflect on that and then asks, "Have you been up there to see what's happening around Flintfields Horse Park?" He shakes his head. "RJ took me up there a couple of weeks ago. It's amazing what's happening."

It gets very quiet until the silence is broken by the sound of the slider screen door opening. Becca sticks her head out and says, "Good night, everyone. Mom, Grandma, don't forget my volleyball game tomorrow afternoon after school. RJ's already asleep. I turned off her radio, she'd left it blaring." I smile and think, *Big sisters . . . what would the world do without them?* Annie and Rita tell her they wouldn't miss her game for the world.

Annie looks tired, so I suggest we follow Becca's example. Danny still hasn't said anything.

Rita says, "You don't have to give me an answer tonight. Think about it, though. I'm going to bed." Suddenly, it's like I was that first night I was back home for good, only this time it's Danny who's left on the deck by himself to contemplate things.

6:00 p.m., September 26, 2026, the Lake Michigan house, Storm Hill, Empire, Michigan

It's been an incredible three years of growth for Empire Feed and Grain. The table in the dining room is crowded tonight for this expanded Sunday night dinner. The whole family is here, but also included are Dr. John Crystal, his wife, and Marty VanWert. We are celebrating the end of the horse show season at Flintfields and the anticipated end of Empire Feed and Grain's first profitable year since it opened its Traverse City operation.

We did, in fact, require the financial backing of Rita's holding company during our first two years of operation. We were able to purchase existing warehouse space, rather than have to lease it, but this was just the tip of the iceberg. Equipping them to store, mix, package, and ship specialty horse feeds was where the real expense lay. That first year we supplied feed to fifty clients, all of them with thoroughbreds competing in various events as part of the Great Lakes Equestrian Festival. The second year that number rose to one hundred and fifty, with fifty of those clients permanently based in Traverse City. This past year, our client base was over five hundred horse owners served out of the Traverse City facility . . . an unbelievable increase which put a huge burden on Marty VanWert, Empire Feed and Grain's Vice President for Traverse City Operations, but she was more than up to the task. Our network of bulk feed suppliers has grown to over a thousand. We've added bulk grain holding bins in our warehouse so we can stock larger amounts of various feeds and supplements and added additional mixers, conveyors, and bagging machines. Dr. Crystal's practice has hired a full-time vet. She's a recent graduate of Michigan State University's vet school, young, energetic and has done some post-grad work in equine science. Based at our warehouse, her primary responsibility is to verify each client's order is properly mixed. This year, instead of using our own trucks to transport the mixed feeds to our clients, we have contracted with a trucking company. And, because some of our shipments are to Europe, Asia, and the Middle East, we have a full-time freight forwarder on site to manage all international shipments. There is every expectation that our spectacular growth will continue as Traverse City's reputation as a center of everything equestrian continues to grow.

Annie and I enjoy a rich life together. Her cancer is in complete remission. Two years ago, she completed the last of several reconstructive surgeries. Neither of us have a regular work schedule at either the store in Empire or in Traverse City. Instead, we fill in when asked as long as it doesn't interfere with our priorities. We've taken up golf and we play at least once a week together. Then, Annie plays once a week with a group of women she's friends with here in Empire, but only after she asked me to reassure her she wasn't becoming a Liz Haverman. I play with a group of shysters who like to take a fiver or two from me in our regular weekly 5-5-5 Nassau.

A year ago, we created The Rigley Foundation. We target grants to riding stables around the country, providing funds for them to offer free riding opportunities for any veteran of military service. So far, we have grants to over one hundred such stables in over twenty-nine states. Our goal is to have at least one stable in every state.

1500 hours, October 16, 2026, the Lake Michigan house, Storm Hill, Empire, Michigan

The fall color season has enveloped us. Through the window on the back side of the house, I see a car pull into the driveway. I call to Annie in the kitchen, "He's here." Becca and RJ are shooting some hoops in the driveway as Major General Ross Haverman gets out and greets them both. He's in uniform, having driven over from a conference he was attending at Fort McCoy, Wisconsin. While it's been a while since the girls have seen him, they remember him from our time at the Command and General Staff College at Fort Leavenworth, Kansas. They are the first to greet him. Ross is our house guest overnight and we have planned a dinner for this evening. Becca and RJ have their own plans. Becca is taking her sister out to the movies, then the two of them are spending the night at a friend's house.

Ross apologizes for the uniform. I tell him, "No apologies necessary, General. Would you like to change into something more casual though?"

After he's changed, Annie and I spend the remainder of the afternoon catching up with one of the army's newest two-star generals, who has just been named the Commander of the US Army Personnel Center at, of all places, Fort Knox, Kentucky. All of us realize how much water has spilled over the dam since that summer of our first meeting.

We've invited two couples, friends of ours, and Marty VanWert to the dinner party this evening just to keep the numbers even. Marty divorced her high school sweetheart five years after they'd married. Never remarried, she now lives in Traverse City to be close to the work she does for Empire Feed and Grain there.

Likewise, Ross never remarried after his divorce from Liz. I remember he told me once, "She could never come to grips with the fact I had a mistress—her name is The Army." He wasn't kidding. I know for a fact that during those arduous Pentagon tours, Ross kept a cot folded up in the corner of his office and a fresh uniform hanging nearby. Using the Pentagon Officers' Athletic Club as a shower point, he was known to make use of the cot and the fresh clothes on an all-too-regular basis. Annie and I'd decided it was probably in the best interest of everyone that he realized his intense focus on his work could be problematic in a relationship.

Before the meal, Ross and Marty seemed to hit it off rather well. There was no prearranged seating plan for dinner, but both Annie and I take note as the two of them settle in next to one another. Their casual conversation continues through dinner, into dessert, and then spills out on the deck afterwards where we enjoy an after-dinner drink.

While the two tried to be discreet, Annie and I both notice as they exchange numbers before Marty departs for the forty-minute trip back to her home in Traverse City. Ross has excused himself after getting the WiFi password, and has retired to the guest room to look through the emails he's accumulated since he'd last checked them just before arriving. As Annie and I are just finishing up clearing the dishes, she looks at me and asks, "Did you notice Ross and Marty?"

"Pretty hard not to," was my response.

Annie's comedic timing is perfect as she asks, "So, do you think we should warn Ross?" I explode in laughter.

It's after 1:00 a.m. as Annie snuggles close to me in bed.

"Can I ask you a question and do you promise to give me your honest answer?"

"Sounds ominous," I reply, then add, "what's on your mind?"

"That could have been you getting out of that car this afternoon. You would have been at least a two-star general by now—maybe three-stars. Any regrets?"

I put my arm around her and pull her closer to me, "Annie, if I think back on everything that could have been, it makes me realize the *what is* is all that matters. No regrets. Not a single one." A few minutes later, I realize she is asleep in my arms.

CATEGORY	Insignia of the United States Army						

	E-1	E-2	E-3	E-4		E-5	E-6
ENLISTED (Green and Gold)	no insignia Private	Private	Private 1st Class	Corporal	Specialist	Sergeant	Staff Sergeant

	E-7	E-8		E-9		
	Sergeant 1st Class	Master Sergeant	1st Sergeant	Sergeant Major	Command Sergeant Major	Sergeant Major of the Army

	W-1	W-2	W-3	W-4	W-5
WARRANT OFFICER (Silver and Black)	Warrant Officer	Chief Warrant Officer	Chief Warrant Officer	Chief Warrant Officer	Master Warrant Officer

	0-1	0-2	0-3	0-4	0-5	0-6
COMPANY AND FIELD GRADE OFFICER (Gold and Silver)	(gold) 2nd Lieutenant	(silver) 1st Lieutenant	(silver) Captain	(gold) Major	(silver) Lieutenant Colonel	(silver) Colonel

	0-7	0-8	0-9	0-10	0-11
GENERAL OFFICER (Silver)	Brigadier General	Major General	Lieutenant General	General	General of the Army

UH-60, Blackhawk Helicopter

The Blackhawk is a utility helicopter serving a variety of needs. It can transport both troops and equipment internally and external loads of equipment and supplies. It is the prevalent helicopter in the army's inventory and is built by Sikorsky Helicopter.

AH-64 Apache, Assault Helicopter

The Apache is an aerial weapons platform with a wide variety of interchangeable guns and missiles. It can be used for close-in combat support, but with improved missile technology, the platform can also be used to fire missiles at great stand-off distances. It is manufactured by Boeing and its purpose as an aerial weapons platform is specific. The aircraft has no other uses within the army.

OH-58 Kiowa Scout Helicopter

The OH-58 Kiowa is a light helicopter used for observation, utility, and direct fire support. Tactics first developed during the Vietnam War used the Kiowa as a "low bird" to detect enemy emplacements by receiving fire. Once the enemy gave away its location through weapons fire, a "high bird," normally an assault helicopter, would descend to deliver high volumes of fire on the enemy position. Later models of the Kiowa are equipped with more sophisticated sensors able to detect enemy positions from greater distances and with greater precision. The aircraft is manufactured by Bell Helicopter.

A version of this helicopter, the TH-67, is used as the training helicopter for pilots attending initial entry rotary wing flight training at Fort Rucker, Alabama.

When paired together with the AH-64 they are referred to as a "Hunter-Killer Team."

CH-47, Chinook Helicopter

The CH-47 Chinook is a combat-hardened veteran of the Vietnam War, incursions into Panama and Grenada, the First Gulf War, and the Global War on Terrorism. Built by Boeing, it is capable of hauling troops and equipment internally as well as sling-loading supplies and equipment.

MALTESE CROSS

A Maltese cross similar to this is often used to designate a helicopter take off or landing spot on an airport. Because of the helicopter's ability to takeoff and land nearly vertically, they may or may not be located at either end of an established runway, and could be located anywhere on airport grounds it has been deemed safe for a helicopter to approach or take off from.

ACKNOWLEDGMENTS

I have been asked if I thought writing was a lonely enterprise best suited for introverts. My rather noncommittal answer to this is, "it depends upon why one writes." I write because I truly enjoy my time behind the computer crafting a good story. I write because I am aware of issues impacting our military to which I'd like to expose the reading public. To help me ensure my work is as interesting as it is insightful, I am surrounded by a great team whose contributions to this book have been invaluable. So, I want to give them my thanks.

First, I must thank my publisher, Mission Point Press. Anne Stanton, Doug Weaver, Heather Shaw, and I found one another almost a decade and six books ago. In that time, they've taught me about this competitive industry of publishing, connected me with the best editors, project managers, graphic designers, and promoted me. Where would I be without them? The answer: likely unpublished.

Second, I owe another deep debt of gratitude to Susanne Dunlap, my line editor now for the last three books. This book covers a lot of time—over two decades—and I needed her to keep me on the straight and narrow. Hart Cauchy is the copy editor and made a bunch of corrections that are by no means minor. Finally, Darlene Short gets the last look as the proofreader, doing the difficult job of crossing all the t's and dotting all the i's.

Tanya Muzumdar has worked with me on some of my other books, but on the last two, she's been the project manager. She pulls all the details together and gets my book out on time, every time.

If the old saying, "You can't judge a book by its cover," were true, people like Sarah Meiers would be out of a job. But the truth is, we all judge books by their covers every time we walk into a bookstore looking for our next read. A delight to work with, Sarah did a great job with this book's cover.

I also have a wonderful group of beta-readers—friends of mine who likely cringe when they see an email from me, because they know I might be asking them to take a lot of their valuable time to read and comment on my manuscripts. They never fail to make the book better. For *The Road to Empire*, I want to thank Tom and Cathy Johnson, Dr. Rolla Baumgartner, Marie Showers, Jan Creamer, Fred Meyer, Mike Gravlin, and Mark Benjamin. I also owe a debt of gratitude to US Coast Guard Commander Andy Schanno for teaching me up on the flight characteristics of a Blackhawk, a helicopter I have never flown.

I owe a real thanks to Chuck and Carol Walters, whose farm is just across the street from Flintfields Horse Park. I had heard of the Great Lakes Equestrian Festival, but these two wonderful people gave me a true insight into just how big Flintfields and GLEF are.

Finally, I must thank my wife, Diane, whose boundless patience, critical eye for detail, and unfailing help when it comes to speaking engagements or book signings makes my work as an author possible. I couldn't/wouldn't want to do any of this without you.

ABOUT THE AUTHOR

John Wemlinger is a retired US Army colonel with 27 years of military service. He is a veteran of the Vietnam War, where he was a helicopter maintenance officer and pilot. *The Road to Empire* is his sixth novel. He writes about what he knows: the military culture, service, and its importance to national security. He speaks often at libraries, service clubs, churches, and book clubs about his books and his writing methods. In his spare time, he serves as a member of the Onekama Village Council. He lives for most of the year in northern Michigan, close to the Lake Michigan shoreline, with his wife, Diane, and their border collie, Sydney, who is happiest when chasing a stick on the beach or swimming after a ball tossed into the waves.

He can be contacted at his website, www.johnwemlinger.com, or you are invited to follow him on Facebook.

OTHER BOOKS BY JOHN WEMLINGER

WINTER'S BLOOM // A powerful novel about a veteran suffering from PTSD, and the unlikely path that leads to his salvation. *Winter's Bloom* is a poignant tale of loss, love, and redemption that will keep you turning the pages.

OPERATION LIGHT SWITCH // Cleveland Spires was a highly decorated and respected soldier until he was wrongfully convicted of a crime he did not commit. After a decade in prison, now he's out, trying to pick up the pieces of a shattered life, until he returns to his hometown and stumbles onto a clue that might prove his innocence. What he discovers will thrust him into an international conspiracy, and what he does next will take all of his courage—and an unflinching faith in a system that has already failed him once.

BEFORE THE SNOW FLIES // Major David Keller is on his way to becoming a general until a roadside bomb in Afghanistan takes his legs. Angry, grieving, and carrying a loaded gun, he returns home to mend a few fences before using that gun to end his life. But before the snow flies, his family, his community, and Maggie McCall, someone he's tried to forget, will prove to him that life in the small town of Onekama, Michigan, can be great once again—if he will only let it . . . and if murder doesn't get in the way.

THE WIDOW AND THE WARRIOR // Intense, raw and timely, *The Widow and the Warrior* is set in Frankfort, Michigan, along the shores of Lake Michigan. It tells the story of one wealthy family's tragic 130-year history. Anna Shane, national political editor for The Washington Post, is poised on the brink of turning her family's tragedies into triumph until a secret society and a greedy relative conspire to have her murdered.

THE CUT // Alvin Price and Lydia Cockrum literally bump into one another in the summer of 1870 and fall in love. But love is seldom without its struggles. Alvin is a farmer, and Lydia is the privileged daughter of an engineer aligned with northern Michigan's powerful lumber industry. *The Cut* tells the story of the two interests at odds over a dam powering a sawmill.

All books are available at your local bookstore or at Amazon.com.

Printed in the USA
CPSIA information can be obtained
at www.ICGtesting.com
LVHW041645250823
754881LV00021B/99